IN THE PINK
A Rural Odyssey

MOLLY WATSON

HUTCHINSON
LONDON

First published in 2004 by Hutchinson

1 3 5 7 9 10 8 6 4 2

Copyright © Molly Watson 2004

Molly Watson has asserted her right under the Copyright, Designs and Patents Act,
1988, to be identified as the author of this work

This book is sold subject to the condition that it shall not,
by way of trade or otherwise, be lent, resold, hired out, or otherwise
circulated without the publisher's prior consent in any form of
binding or cover other than that in which it is published and
without a similar condition including this condition being imposed on
the subsequent purchaser

Hutchinson
The Random House Group Limited
20 Vauxhall Bridge Road, London SW1V 2SA

Random House Australia (Pty) Limited
20 Alfred Street, Milsons Point, Sydney
New South Wales 2061, Australia

Random House New Zealand Limited
18 Poland Road, Glenfield
Auckland 10, New Zealand

Random House (Pty) Limited
Endulini, 5a Jubilee Road
Parktown 2193, South Africa

The Random House Group Limited Reg. No. 954009

www.randomhouse.co.uk

A CIP catalogue record for this book is available
from the British Library

Papers used by Random House are natural, recyclable products made from
wood grown in sustainable forests. The manufacturing processes conform to
the environmental regulations of the country of origin

Typeset in Goudy Old Style by Palimpsest Book Production Limited,
Polmont, Stirlingshire
Printed and bound in Great Britain by
Clays Ltd, St Ives plc

ISBN 0 09 179526 5

For the Jams and their Jar.

Written with enormous affection and gratitude to the members and supporters of the Ledbury Hunt and all the stories they told me about each other that were too hot to print.

1

April

My sister Bee has always been a practical joker. When we were children, April Fool's Day never passed without her leaving an effigy of my favourite pet lying stricken in the lane that ran in front of our house, or scratching 'Bee is a Pig' deep into the mahogany sideboard in the hall and then sticking around to watch when my mother, her purple flogging espadrille already in her hand, came to collar me for it. But a decade has passed since then. Woodworm has done for the sideboard, and now that she no longer has the time nor the handicraft skills to knock up a convincing tabby cat carcass, the best Bee could manage this year was to ring up and pretend that her boyfriend had given her the elbow instead.

I returned from scavenging for cut-price Easter eggs at the petrol station at the end of our street to find an Oscar-winningly bleak message from her on the answering machine. Snivelling from a fug of tear-soaked paper hankies in a voice faltering with hurt and

1

exhausted rage, she told me it was all over between her and Daniel. He didn't love her. Maybe he had never loved her. Would anyone ever really love her again?

As jokes go it was pretty lame, mainly because it would never happen. Annabel Vivienne Watson, blonde, twenty-three years, 34-22-32 inches, is not the type of girl to get dumped. Ever since she was old enough to understand the rules of kiss-chase she's been besieged by men frantically reciting their best comic material at her in the hope that she'll stay still and in view for just a little while longer. These boys have a point. Bee's charms don't stop at her face and figure. She's extremely good company and blessed with an almost French capacity for pouty sulking. Even her own sisters, usually relegated to crowd control roles when she attends parties, have occasionally been struck by how beautiful she looks when she's angry.

Like I said before, the whole point of Bee is that she's never going to get ditched.

WEDNESDAY 3 APRIL
EARLS COURT

Or is she . . .

She's certainly behaving very oddly. Today she took her first ever sickie from the head-hunting firm for whom she works with ruthless efficiency. I know this because she tipped up at our basement flat, a venue she usually avoids on health and safety grounds, soon after breakfast. This time she came in and went to lie face down on my flatmate Christy's bed.

Christy and I immediately abandoned the grubby corner of

the sitting room where we languish in front of our laptops reading the newspapers so slowly that we never get any of our own writing done, and beetled through to hear the details. But alas, Bee refused to be squeezed for juice or even to turn over.

It appears she may have actually walked here. Only a five-minute stroll through the canoodling rent boys of the Brompton Cemetery separates this flat from Bee's, but her decision not to take a taxi even for a piddling distance like that shows she really isn't herself at all.

She seems to be in a bad way – something a tiny, horrible, sisterly part of me can't help feeling slightly cheered by.

THURSDAY 4 APRIL
EARLS COURT

She's sunny side up today but still not speaking. Conversely we've had much chatter from the couple of dozen boys who rang to check if she was okay about the break-up and feeling up to letting them buy her dinner yet.

I made an executive decision not to relay this rash of condolences. Bee needs her rest, and after a lifetime of watching her glide along in a golden shimmer of male admiration that has always been tantalisingly out of my older, uglier grasp, I find I need to prolong the tonic of seeing her lovely face swollen from crying for as long as I can.

Christy and I have been admirably quick off the mark with the unsolicited advice though. As a veteran of Manhattan, the most inhospitable dating climate on earth and a place where rejection is analysed with scientific rigour, I told Bee that she had simply fallen victim to a recognised seasonal phenomenon. The theory goes that all over the world men made dizzy by the first days of spring sunshine offload their girlfriends in the hope of acquiring a better model for the bikini season. Yet as summer passes and the warm weather wanes, their feelings of regret increase. By September Daniel would be apologetic; by Harvest Festival he'd be begging for reinstatement.

Christy told Bee that what she needed was a few glasses of Campari and then maybe some wine.

Bee told us to please draw the curtains and go away.

FRIDAY 5 APRIL
EARLS COURT

I spent most of the afternoon in a spa being rubbed with mushed-up ginger in the hope that my skin will be so tingly and fired up with pheromones that Rob, a gorgeous young management consultant and one of Bee's most persistent callers, won't be able to keep his hands off it at dinner tonight.

Unfortunately this meant I left for the restaurant smelling like an undercooked biscuit, but all went well over dinner. According to Rob, Bee has 'gone to the mattresses' – a classic mafia crisis tactic. Ideally one should get one's men and their mattresses round to a deserted warehouse and then spend a few days lying around on said mattresses arguing about the Sicilian way to make a rigatoni sauce until someone with a name like Clemenza gets word that it's time to make a hit on the rest of the Five Families. When she'd stewed long enough on her mattress Bee would be ready to take revenge.

It soon emerged that Rob for one wanted a ringside seat when she did. As we sat close in a taxi on the way home he leaned in towards me so tantalisingly slowly we could have been in a movie. But the big screen kiss never came. When I opened my eyes to find out what was causing the hold-up he whipped out his Palm Pilot and asked me for the best address to send her flowers to.

SUNDAY 7 APRIL
EARLS COURT

Morale's still low but she's recovered enough to be calling out for magazines. All I could find was an ancient copy of *Vogue* and the latest issue of *Horse & Hound*, purchased yesterday in the vain hope it might have had hot Grand National tips. To commemorate the Queen Mother's death, this week's cover bears an archive photograph of her cowering beside and partially obscured by an elated-looking racehorse.

MONDAY 8 APRIL
EARLS COURT

Bee is up, dressed, and demanding to buy a horse. I fear this is retail therapy of the most dangerous sort.

Due to a lack of transport from our neck of the Brecon Beacons to amusements like the Pontypool roller-disco and Cwmbran hydraslides we spent most of our childhoods messing around with ponies. But, fearful of developing the bristly chin, spreading bottom and braying bossiness that my father warned was the eventual fate of all horsey women, I made my exit to London aged eighteen. I still have a nagging fear, fed by the kindlier of my male friends, that I did not get out soon enough.

Thanks to a tendency to fall off so strong that the St John's Ambulance first-aid team used to go to battle stations whenever she rode into the ring at local gymkhanas, Bee was even quicker to convert her interest in horses from life in the saddle to life on the sofa with a Dick Francis and a packet of chocolate biscuits.

While our four younger siblings joined the Pony Club (one of them was actually presented with a horsemanship trophy by a lady called Mrs Trot), she and I set about transforming ourselves into glossy urban creatures. I was posted to New York to work as the *Evening Standard*'s correspondent there and prided myself on coming home for Christmas kitted out in shoes designed to totter only the few metres from yellow cab to nightclub entrance and cashmere barely able to cope with the damp seeping up the walls of the sitting room, let alone helping with the mucking out. Bee burned her wellies, grew her fingernails and e-mailed me in triumph when she heard the others had started calling us the Dry Clean Onlys.

Yet today as she read aloud from the Horses for Sale section filling the back pages of *Horse & Hound* all the attempts I'd made at sophistication over the last decade seemed to crumble away. Suddenly I was fourteen again and fantasising about riding at the Horse of the Year Show, the equine equivalent of playing live to a packed-out Wembley Stadium; transported back to the heady days when boys were beginning to be boys but a girl's love was still reserved for her pony.

However, if the runners and riders in this week's issue are anything to go by, a lot has changed in the decade since I stopped fiddling about in the tack room. The first thing that struck me was the prices. While the best pony I ever had cost £600, in this week's magazine there was a little 'rosette machine' retailing at an astonishing £18,000. You can buy yourself a couple of houses for less than that in the Welsh valleys. Then there was the fact that many sellers have gone metric. I can still remember that a horse standing 17 hands high can carry a huge fat cavalry bandsman and his drum kit around a military tattoo, while an 11-hand pony is not much taller than a half-decent dog. But being informed that a steed measures 147 cm means nothing to me.

Another problem is that today's horse experts have developed jargon to rival the geeks of Silicon Valley. We could just about work out the age, colour and sex of the horses advertised but totally failed to make sense of phrases like 'Now JA, potential 148/P. Fabs, FEI' and 'Scope BN, Discovery, BSJA £157, 12 BD points'. Worse still, to make up for all the techno-speak about their nags' competition successes, the sellers had really reached for the syrup when choosing their names. Among the worst offenders were animals christened Broadstone Cassanova, Comberton Crème Brulée and Brookwater Titania.

Expensive, unintelligible and strewn with the bile-churningly twee, yet somehow the small ads made for absolutely compulsive reading.

TUESDAY 9 APRIL
EARLS COURT

We have spent the day hurtling across the Midlands in a small red car and the grip of some kind of revolution.

As we drove westwards out of London along roads cleared in

readiness for the Queen Mother's funeral cortège Bee declared that she was hell bent on going to look at a mare near Ludlow that was allegedly both 'bold and careful' but had inexplicably managed to break her rider's back. I was busy saying what a bad idea that sounded and flicking through *Horse & Hound* when this caught my eye:

EVENT POTENTIAL

6-year-old TB grey gelding, 16 hands 3 ins. Very talented young horse, ready to event this season. Very good XC, excellent showjumper. Lightly hunted this spring. Also 16-hand bay gelding similar.

We deduced the horse in question was a thoroughbred bachelor who excelled at cross-country (courses of big natural jumps like hedges and ditches with lots of galloping between them). But being able to understand the advert didn't alter the fact that my idea of an event had become a champagne reception celebrating the opening of a new Prada boutique, or that Bee planned to spend every season for the foreseeable future firmly within the confines of the M25.

Never mind, she reasoned as we found ourselves bouncing along the Worcestershire hedgerows to make a detour through Tewkesbury, we simply were becoming the time-wasters we noticed were occasionally mentioned with disgust in *Horse & Hound* when an animal was being re-advertised. People idly looked at houses and tried on shoes all the time, she pointed out, it was just that to soothe her broken heart it was going to take inspecting horses. Understood. As we pulled into a haphazard but well-kept yard surrounded by paddocks dotted with decrepit jumps we agreed this was just a bizarre but innocent form of window-shopping.

Hearing our engine, Barry Joyce, a horse dealer of massive charm dwarfed only by his reserves of cunning, stepped out of his farmhouse into the mild spring breeze to greet us. A brass fanfare should have heralded his entrance, for it was at this point that all hope of good sense prevailing was extinguished.

The first thing the spider said to the flies was in such a strong Irish accent lisped out past a lone, jaundiced tooth that we didn't understand it. Then he started laughing at how tall the flies were and at their silly city clothes and how slowly they drove considering he reckoned he could do Tewkesbury to Windsor in less than two hours in his wagon. Next, having expertly appraised our riding skills without us putting so much as a foot in a stirrup, he informed us that there was no way we would manage the horse he'd devoted the advert to but we could try out the 'bay gelding similar' if we liked.

I was so transfixed by Barry's appearance that most of these exchanges passed in a blur. As the result of a riding accident in which a horse actually trod on his face, followed by a pretty agricultural attempt at reconstructive surgery, his nostrils had the cavernous look of railway tunnels and were skewed in an east-south-easterly direction underneath eyebrows that had been botched into a permanent quizzical arch. The ensemble was held together by an archipelago of giant blackheads tracing where his jaws had been stitched back on in front of his ears and topped off with a thatch of hair that he had started to dye a rich chocolate-brown colour but seemed to have downed tools on halfway through.

After eyeing Bee's pinstripe suit and my sandals with scorn he invited us up to his farmhouse to see if he could find us some boots to borrow. Stepping through his back door we entered an equine Hall of Fame which made it clear that the obstacle had not yet been devised that was too big or too frightening for this family and their mounts. In the dusty kitchen alone there were close to a hundred photographs of assorted Joyces riding over vast jumps or holding ropes attached to ponies festooned in rosettes. In the filthy downstairs loo the bath and most of the floor space was stacked to the ceiling with tattered old board games, dusty LPs, kites, fishing rods, cookery books and motorbike magazines – a testament to the hobbies and interests sacrificed to Team Joyce's quest for horsey glory.

But there was one weak link in this equestrian powerhouse, and I found him slumped in a sagging armchair in front of the telly wearing full football kit to watch Manchester United take a penalty against some team in blue. When I told Michael Joyce, Barry's teenage son, that I was there to look at a horse he just shrugged despairingly in his seat and shoved a framed snapshot of a whippet-thin black gelding surging past a winning post out of his line of vision. Crushed, I rushed back to the loo and checked myself out thoroughly for the first signs of bristles and immense buttocks. Couldn't detect anything sinister, but it is early days.

Back in the kitchen Bee was staring at a photograph of Barry riding a bright chestnut gelding over an enormous hedge with all the intensity of an art historian examining a newly discovered Florentine fresco. I hadn't realised that the breakneck scenes in those fox-hunting prints that publicans and pensioners like to hang on their walls are still happening. But here was a sporting pastiche straight from the world of Jorrocks re-created in celluloid.

The scene captured in the photo is of rolling fields dominated by a fat, brown, unlaid hedge at least five feet high and just as wide. It seems to be raining. To one side of Barry a horse and rider are toppling headfirst into the yawning mesh of hawthorn. Beyond him the rest of the mud-splattered mounted followers are queuing ignominiously to walk through a gateway rather than attempt the hedge. But Barry is sitting bolt upright as his horse leaps over with room to spare. The way his feet are jutted forward and the devil-may-care tilt of his bowler hat give him the air of a redneck riding a stolen Harley Davidson. Apart from some riderless horses and a couple of crumpled bodies lying squirming in the mud, the only rider ahead of him is a rather shaken-looking huntsman in a pink coat. Okay, so it wasn't the Horse of the Year Show, but Barry looked pretty cool. No, he looked more than cool. When we arrived in his kitchen he was nothing more than a squat little middle-aged man with bandy legs who was unwittingly going to sacrifice the best part of his afternoon to taking Bee's mind off Daniel. Ten minutes later he had become our pocket-sized demigod.

After gulping down an oily brew that was presented to us as coffee but prepared on a draining board between a sack of slug pellets and the innards of a chainsaw, we went out to inspect the something similar. I liked him immediately. He was huge and he had the kind of lavish figure that the word horseflesh truly conjures up – a juicy brown backside and a well-sprung barrel of a body set on rather elegant legs. Anyone French would have been hard pressed not to start at him with a steak knife then and there.

While Bee messed about feeling his ankles in a faux-knowledgeable way I stood and faced him, dimly remembering that a kind eye is one of the most important features of a good horse. As I stared into his giant black pupils he rolled his eyes to the heavens and let out a long, bored, 'not that old chestnut' sort of sigh. There was more huffing and puffing when Sandra, Barry's groom, tried to lead him away from his hay net and trot him down the lane so we could see how he moved. They should have put something about a GSOH in the advert.

As Sandra tacked him up Barry started his patter in earnest. He told us how this horse was wasted on us, how his parents were famous Irish show-jumpers, how he'd jump anything, do anything, yet was so relaxed we'd need an alarm clock to wake him up. He had apparently been destined for a high-level competition yard in Kentucky, but the orthodontic-obsessed American buyers had rejected him when they discovered that he had an overbite. A victim myself of the efforts of several dentists to winch my English smile into some kind of order, I immediately warmed to an animal whose teeth had lost him his chance of a Green Card.

Barry's sales pitch was a masterly display of extreme confidence combined with a carefully ambiguous choice of words. My attempts to pursue a businesslike question-and-answer session with him never stood a chance.

'So does this horse jump hedges?' I asked as Sandra put the bay into a long-striding trot.

'Ah now, ladies,' Barry began, rocking back on his heels and smiling indulgently at the preposterousness of my enquiry. 'A good hedge is meat and drink to him.'

'Is that a yes then, Mr Joyce?'

'Ah come on, girls,' he responded, leaning in now as if he were pressing a pair of humourless teetotallers to a glass of wine at a cocktail party. 'Sure you've nothing to fret over. He's a lovely animal.'

'But would he jump a big mean hedge like the one in the photo?' I persisted. 'A hedge in the rain with a ditch in front of it, and barbed wire across it, and no other horses in front to encourage him?'

Back came the genial grin, accompanied this time by a small flutter of his left wrist that sought to brush away my trifling enquiry. 'Meat and drink I'm telling you, ladies,' Barry cajoled. 'Meat and drink.'

'And what about water? Does he jump water and cross streams okay?'

In trying to pass myself off as an expert I think I might have gone too far. Twitching with irritation, Barry lurched upright and declared more forcefully, 'Really now, girls! 'Twould be but food and wine to him. He'd suit the pair of you a treat. Sure he's a quality animal and he knows his job.'

I wanted to ask about the horse's competition record and how much it really had hunted, but didn't dare try Barry's patience any further. It says something for his skills as a salesman that he managed to make me feel that by questioning him any more I would be looking a gift horse in the mouth, regardless of the fact that he was a dealer trying to sell me a mount with unusually dicey teeth.

Suspecting that I had inadvertently dented Barry's honour, Bee stepped in to smooth the situation. Widening her china-blue eyes to maximum capacity and twirling a lock of blonde hair through her fingers, she cooed, 'Well he looks absolutely lovely to me, Mr Joyce. What did you say his name was again?'

At this Barry paused and fixed his gaze on some far-off point on the Malvern Hills. I readied my stomach for some moniker like Candyfloss ClipClop, but instead he coughed shiftily and admitted that despite allegedly owning the horse for over a year he wasn't sure of his name.

'Could be Northern something,' he eventually volunteered.

'Norman?' said Bee brightly. 'Like the conquerors? Ooh yes! He looks like a Norman.'

The more I saw of Norman the more I liked him. When Sandra rode him at a fence two feet high he jumped two feet and one inch. When she pointed him at a jump four feet high he jumped four feet and one inch. He never knocked any poles down, he never even rapped them with his hooves, but he certainly didn't strain himself unduly. This horse was clearly a thinker. Whether that was a good thing or not, I couldn't tell.

Bee had at least found a crash hat to fit her, but when Sandra dismounted she stepped back and became engrossed in a patch of stinging nettles, leaving me to get on Norman first. After years of not riding it was like clambering on to an oversized conker, but I soon discovered that this conker came with power-assisted steering, fuel-injected acceleration and excellent brakes. Norman's best asset was his suspension though. He glided around the rutted paddock popping over the jumps however inaccurate the instructions from his rider.

After only ten minutes aboard, the skin on the inside of my knees was rubbed raw, my right shoulder ached, I was drenched in sweat and an itchy rash was spreading across my neck. I was also spent from a peculiar kind of anxiety that I hadn't felt in years – the nervous tension of jumping a strange horse under the silent but critical eye of people who could ride it far better than me. It was definitely time for Bee to try Norman out. She looked like a doll perched on a grand piano but he was equally saintly to her. There was something so considerate about his manner I could almost imagine him clumping upstairs to bring her a cup of tea in bed each morning.

It was clear as we stood about in the mild spring afternoon, Norman nosing around our pockets for mints and blowing his warm meadow-fresh breath on the nape of my neck, that we were at the beginning of the relationship. In my experience with men this kind of attentive treatment wears off after a fortnight or so. But given that he would have about twenty-two hours of down time each day lounging about in a field and depend on us for food, water and shelter, I was hopeful that Norman might sustain bouts of best behaviour for years.

Seeing us both flushed with pleasure, Barry told us that by purchasing Norman we could 'live the dream'. Then he named his price for the dream: £4,500. Gulp. Not that we were actually going to buy him or anything, but shelling out the equivalent of a round-the-world airline ticket for a horse did seem steep. Feeling that we might as well enter into the spirit of the thing I told Barry that £3,000 might be a more reasonable price tag. If he heard my suggestion he certainly didn't show it. In any case, whatever thin vestige of bargaining power we might have had disappeared when we returned to the yard and had to don smocks made out of dustbin bags in order to protect the owner of the Nissan Micra we'd borrowed for the trip, a friend with a severe allergy to animal hair and dust, from our now contaminated clothes.

We were absolute beginners at this game and Barry knew it. When we told him we were en route to see a rival mount he grinned and assured us good-naturedly that it would be a 'guaranteed suicide vehicle'. (The hex worked. Bee sat on the back-breaking mare for about a minute before it gave an exhausted sigh and toppled over sideways like a domino.) It couldn't matter less that we hadn't sought an expert or even a second opinion on Norman, the first horse either of us had ridden in years. If we let Norman go, he warned us beadily, we'd be looking for one like him for ages.

His final masterstroke was to mention, in a storyline that lost none of its power for its similarity to *Black Beauty*, that tomorrow other people were coming to look at Norman who probably wouldn't be a kind home but that he'd be forced to take the first offer he got for the asking price. The flies had not even driven out of the spider's sight before earnest discussions began about how they could find the money to 'save' Norman.

WEDNESDAY 10 APRIL
EARLS COURT

I woke up with my legs jammed into a worrying croquet hoop configuration from yesterday's spell in the saddle and exhausted from a night of alternating dreams.

One featured me sailing effortlessly over massive hedges on Norman to gasps of admiration from watching crowds and the massed ranks of the world's media. In the other an abused and emaciated Norman had become a poster child for an RSPCA campaign against cruelty to horses.

I managed to hold out for exactly eighty-nine minutes before ringing Barry Joyce and telling him we'd take Norman at the asking price.

THURSDAY 11 APRIL
EARLS COURT

Bee appeared at dawn brandishing the latest issue of *Horse & Hound* and saying she'd found us another nag. When I asked why we needed any more given that an afternoon's idle window-shopping had already committed us to £4,500 of excess horseflesh we had no conceivable use for, she presented The Plan For A Happier Life. It went something like this:

1. She resigns from her job. (Actually it turns out that she already did that bit last night. Excellent. So far, so insane.)
2. We move to a corner of the countryside as far away from loathsome Daniel as possible.
3. We go fox-hunting before it gets abolished.
4. I take out a hefty overdraft in order to finance stages 1, 2 and 3 of the operation until, with the help of our sexy fox-hunting outfits, one or other of us successfully seduces some inbred local squire who can pick up the tab.
5. Free of charge Bee will take on the role of glamorous accomplice, claim eighteen per cent of any profits but accept no part in any losses.

Then she left to sink the best part of £40 into a jar of Clinique's Weather Everything environmental face cream to see her through steps 2 and 3 still able to meet the job description for steps 4 and 5. Presumably she'll invoice me for it later.

I can only remember going hunting twice. What sticks in my mind most is getting up in the dark and spending about four hours tarting first my pony and then myself up to the nines. The other highlight was the meet. This involved spending a stressful half-hour outside a pub in a mêlée of horses and hounds trying to eat a mince pie and hold a plastic cup of sherry at the same time as stopping my overexcited pony from trampling on groups of bystanders who had gathered to admire the Olde Worlde spectacle. Soon after that something would happen that was so unpleasant that I had to go home.

When I was twelve the unpleasant thing that happened was my pony throwing itself on to the bonnet of a car with such violence that I still have a small scar where the windscreen wiper jabbed into my spine. The moment we had resumed an upright position I was told to go home. Five years later, when I had paid off the final instalment of the bill to repair the car's suspension, I felt ripe for another go. Apart from being asked for £30 before I had got anywhere near the mince pies, it was pretty much the same drill. After about an hour of trotting very fast up and down the same stretch of road while the hounds nosed about out of sight in a wood, my horse reared up on his hind legs and conducted an extravagant orchestral piece with his front feet. I was told to take him home.

But, try as I might, I couldn't write off Bee's plan altogether. Hunting did not have to be this way, and Barry Joyce had the photographic evidence to prove it. I kicked around the flat for a few hours before resorting to what hacks generally do when trying to decide if a story is a goer or not – asking the internet and, failing that, asking their mates.

Internet upbeat. Jodhpurs remain a winter staple on the Paris catwalks and, according to the *Daily Telegraph*'s online archives, the fate of fox-hunting became a white-hot political potato last month when the government sounded its death knell by promising to use the Parliament Act to overcome opposition to an outright ban in the House of Lords and push through anti-hunting legislation before the next election.

If we do chuck in London and take up hunting, at least in the brief minutes before we are sent home, I'm hopeful that there may be more to it than having our bottoms pinched an awful lot. We could become part of history in the making. Or should that be its undoing? The accounts book of Edward I's Comptroller of the Royal Wardrobe for 1299 details the Crown paying sixpence a day for the services of 'twelve foxdogs with one man and two boys' who were grudgingly given thirty-four pennies each year to buy new suits as well as tuppence for the keep of their horses. But barring a surprise reprieve, next winter will be one of the last ever seasons that the 700-year-old sport is allowed to take place in the country of its birth. It has already been banned in Scotland.

Mates relentlessly downbeat. My friend Luke, a banker who now lives in Mexico City, didn't even hear out my pitch before branding The Plan 'a cliché of a bad idea'. The countryside and accounts of unspeakables and uneatables scrambling across it had, he said heavily, 'been done to death'. I certainly found that the foam-flecked parliamentary furore over whether hunting is a cruel, class-ridden abomination or the exact opposite had failed to raise the blood pressure of the average man in the street, or at least the average man in my address book.

My former colleagues in the newsroom of the *Evening Standard* laughed themselves sick at the idea of Bee and me moving to the country to follow hounds and sent an e-card of commiseration to the Two Thin Ladies. The couple of people I spoke to in New York couldn't really see past stage 2 of The Plan. When I said I might move to the country they asked what I was going to do for food. When I explained that the arrival of Tesco in the shires meant life there wasn't an epic Swiss Family Robinson-style struggle for survival they asked me what I was going to do for opera. My London friends told me I was deranged, then immediately asked what or whom I'd done recently to make me want to run to the sticks in shame and suggested dissecting my latest crimes in depth over a few drinks.

FRIDAY 12 APRIL
EARLS COURT

It's the sort of really lovely spring day that's not best enjoyed morbidly hungover in a London flat, the contents of which are beginning to curdle in the heat. But I can't find a place outside where dozens of other people aren't already sunning themselves or driving past very loudly.

I've lolled in bed for much of the day buffeted by waves of nausea and an unsettling bout of introspective thinking that Manhattan coffee-shop types call an ILA (Involuntary Life Analysis). I've concluded that a major part of what's wrong with my world is that I no longer am a Manhattan coffee-shop type. By moving back to London in August I may have ingeniously given Osama bin Laden the slip but I also exchanged a life of *Sex and the City* for an existence of Occasional Nocturnal Scuffles in Fulham. A year ago I was living off the fat of an expense account, jetting across the States to report on everything from the Oscars to each hanging chad of the Bush/Gore election débâcle. In my spare time I went on dates to *Vanity Fair* parties with men who had voices like Cary Grant and names like Bartle Brock III Jnr embroidered on the inside of their hand-crafted shoes.

If that sounds like a dream, it certainly feels like one now. On my return, spoilt by two years of independence in America, I ditched the office grind and joined the overcrowded tide of only quite bright, quite young things floating around the periphery of the London media world and calling themselves freelance writers. Six months on I'm living off my US tax rebate haunted by the notion that I'm gradually turning into little more than a vagrant with a laptop.

And that's not the worst of it. The main reason I came back from America was to rekindle things with the love of my life. He knows who he is but we'll call him Mr Smith. Suffice to say that on my return the fire between us was slow to ignite, rallied for a few glorious months and then blazed into an inferno of regret and recrimination leaving all concerned in a charred, miserable mess.

Bee's plan is madness but I think I could do worse than to put some clear blue sky between myself and my problems – and it might as well be the kind of sky that has a patchwork of fields beneath it rather than the polluted grey tumour of pavements and concrete that houses the bright lights I used to love so much. It would also be a relief to find a far-off place where I didn't lie awake at night fighting unclean thoughts and the urge to bung on some flame-retardant gloves, hop in a black cab and head off in search of Mr Smith.

Norman has become a talisman for a fresh start. In a single afternoon our expensive expedition to Tewkesbury has scuppered my decade-long endeavour to escape my muddy Welsh roots and pass for a genuine townie. I keep catching myself day-dreaming about making a life in the country. I suspect it's probably all pretty standard 'Somewhere over the Green Belt' stuff – picturing myself skipping about dizzy with fresh air outside a tumbledown yet extremely comfortable farmhouse, knowing the difference between a mushroom and a toadstool and brainstorming with Beatrix Potter at Neighbourhood Watch meetings, etc.

Christy, hardened by nearly five years of freelancing from the filthy clutter of occasional tables and empty sherry bottles that fill our flat beneath her great-aunt's house, takes a dim view of all this. She says my symptoms are nothing another night of heavy drinking and high jinks won't cure.

IN THE PINK

SATURDAY 13 APRIL
EARLS COURT

Equilibrium was temporarily restored by a prolonged session on the dance floor. We arrived home at eight o'clock this morning minus my handbag and the bottom section of Christy's dress. Limping over to the scaffolding across the street, we bribed the only builders in the metropolis who persist in working on Saturdays to take a two-hour tea break while we sank into a coma zone where no drills would wake us.

But my yearning to move to the sticks wasn't quashed for long. While we were sleeping, Bee dropped by and wedged a copy of Siegfried Sassoon's *Memoirs of a Fox-Hunting Man* into our letterbox along with a detailed but incomprehensible set of sums allegedly showing why her mortgage payments prevent her from taking out a loan to bankroll The Plan herself. She had underlined in red those of Sassoon's passages that she felt best made the case for the fallback scenario of a rustic wedding should my overdraft facilities fail us before the end of the hunting season.

Well forget fallback scenario. If we run across anyone like fast-living Jack and Charlie Peppermore – described by Sassoon on pages 234 and 235 as 'desperately fine specimens of a genuine English traditional type which has become innocuous since the abolition of duelling' and who were 'reckless, insolent, unprincipled; but never dull, frequently amusing, and, when they chose, had charming manners' – all resources will be channelled into enticing them to kiss us all over at their earliest convenience.

April

Another day, another audition. My pride has recovered sufficiently from my disastrous dinner with Bee's admirer Rob to allow her to persuade him to drive us to Oxfordshire to look at a twelve-year-old hunter described as 'a bargain for an experienced rider'. I'm still not convinced that twenty minutes of bouncing around on Norman qualifies us as experienced riders, but its £1,500 price tag made this horse required viewing.

The seller this time was a venerable egghead called Professor White. In fact, as eggheads go, the gentle, skeletally thin boffin who met us at his garden gate was something of a double-yolker. Not only was the Professor an Oxford biochemistry don, but his bald skull had a speckled shell so papery that his immense brain looked as though it would burst through the parchment of skin at the slightest tap. He told us he was flogging his bay mare, Buttons, because his wife had been run over but not killed by a passing car in Ross-on-Wye and now they were in their seventies they couldn't risk having two fallers in the household.

A glance at the horse as she barged in from her field, tail swishing crossly and hind legs jabbing out at anyone who strayed too close to her, was all one needed to sympathise with his problem. As we say in Wales, Buttons had it on her. Anyone who has escorted a noisy and overtired toddler around a supermarket will be familiar with the public torment of someone who has it on them. 'It' is a deliberate and wildly obstructive stroppiness worn very much on the sleeve. Although Buttons had hunted nearby with the smart Heythrop pack and so was probably capable of some pretty big jumps, I didn't fancy our chances. When I

23

attempted to take her rug off she sank her teeth heavily into my arm, and Professor White admitted that the last person to take a second look at her had been scared enough to bring a National Hunt jockey along to ride the beast for them.

He certainly looked green with fear when the time came for him to get on her, and as he wobbled around the stable yard on the snorting mare it soon became clear that we were witnessing the mastery of horse over owner. Buttons had a long My Little Pony-style mane because she wouldn't let him neaten it up, and she was missing a couple of shoes, presumably because she didn't enjoy the attentions of the blacksmith either. Bee soon suggested we move off to the softer landing of a nearby meadow. The Professor reluctantly agreed, but warned that Buttons might play up in a more open space and adopted a petrified pose in the saddle reminiscent of the brace position recommended to airline passengers in the event of a crash landing. He managed a few hurried circuits amongst the dandelions before Bee mounted Buttons.

To fully comprehend the irritation of the next fifteen minutes it is important to take into account what everyone was wearing.

Professor White: old cords, plastic riding boots and an ancient jersey.

Bee: skin-tight designer jeans, a clinging T-shirt, trainers, lipstick and industrial-strength mascara.

Rob: a variation of binoculars, reading glasses and driving glasses depending on how far away he was stationed from Bee's stretch-denim-coated backside.

Me: a long face thanks to an outfit that Bee (clearly taking precautions for the possibility that the Professor might have been made of the kind of Peppermore material that we would go head to head over) had thrown into the car for me. It comprised an orange road-mender's jacket and trousers made for someone half my height and double my circumference that once I was in the saddle made me look like an ice-hockey player with bum cleavage.

Buttons went like a dream for Bee. She stopped messing about and pranced around the paddock. I'm fairly sure though that I was the only person admiring the horse rather than Bee's pert bottom moving in perfect time to its rhythm. By the time I got aboard the mare a few dozen children from the housing estate that stretched along one side of the field had come out to watch the equestrian display. They were not to be disappointed. Buttons trotted a couple of slightly bolshie figures of eight before launching into a series of bucks that had me flailing around and clutching at the reins like washing clinging to a line on a blustery day. As I struggled not to fall off, or let my trousers fall off without me, I could hear ecstatic squeals of delight from the assembled kids, the dry scratch of Professor White suppressing his giggles, and soaring over them all like the song of the first cuckoo of the season, came the jubilant crescendo of my sister laughing properly for the first time since she got dumped.

Over tea in the Whites' kitchen, surrounded by photographs of the Professor as a young oarsman standing on the riverbank with his sepia-ed friends and looking about a foot taller than his current five feet nine inches, Mrs White gave us a blow-by-blow of her accident and asked us beseechingly if we would buy Buttons. If it hadn't been for the fact that her grandchildren were among the little brutes who'd howled with laughter at my exposed buttocks during the bronco episode I would have crumbled.

Bee gave it chapter and verse all the way back up to London

about how we should definitely buy Buttons. She takes some riding of course, but she's only £1,500 and, I suspect the real clincher this, she hates me. Thankfully Rob stalled things by offering to assess our acquisition opportunity in a strategic consultancy capacity.

MONDAY 15 APRIL
EARLS COURT

Norman has passed his medical. Well I say passed. The vet's report made his legs sound as though they belonged to Nora Batty rather than a sprightly six-year-old. Apart from sporting assorted lumps and bumps called splints and curbs, the descriptions of which ran to several pages, he has a swollen knee and scars all over his ankles. He also has misshapen feet, a suspected sore back and his overbitten teeth are hellishly sharp.

When I rang the vet to find exactly how bad all this was, he sucked his teeth and said his fee would be £156.07. To pay for it I cancelled my latest order at Amazon.com and walked from Fulham to Soho to take a lovely Diane von Furstenberg wrap dress I'd just bought back to the shop.

WEDNESDAY 17 APRIL
EARLS COURT

Woke with a start. It was Barry calling to ask when I would be collecting my horse. He normally charges £100 a week in livery fees for horses that stay in his yard once they've been sold, and he said getting Norman fitted with new shoes would cost £48.

April

My horse. The words echoed around my head. Like someone expecting a baby who realises with a thud that parenthood is as much about providing pushchairs and nappies as it is about getting gooey over children's names, I was suddenly hit by the recognition that all this horse-owning business is for real. For the first time in my life I have a dependant, one who despite his dental problems seems to eat money, and who at the rate Bee's going won't be my last. The idea that our financial futures and Norman's winter fodder supply rests on us hustling some mythical barley baron up the aisle before our cash runs out has stopped sounding adventurous and become plain silly.

Sobered by the weight of responsibility I had taken on in buying Norman I went for a long think, leaving Christy watching *Rocky II* on video in an effort to get herself sufficiently pumped up to brave the hordes at the Paul Smith sample sale. As she remarked when she returned home bruised from a bare-knuckle brawl over a cost-price chiffon shirt, people who claim hunting is dangerous can't ever have endured the sort of aggression that is unleashed when you grab hold of the last pair of size 10 hipsters at the same time as a rabid fellow shopper who thinks she saw them first.

One thing I do know is that there won't be any chiffon shirts or Paul Smith hipsters for me for a long stretch. The only way I can see us bankrolling The Plan is to go on an immediate economy drive, pray that with her feminine charms back at full throttle Bee will indeed nail the heir to the manor of whatever village we settle in, and in the meantime try to raise the money to keep us in straw bales and girth straps the only way I know how – by writing about it all.

THURSDAY 18 APRIL
CATHEDINE

I set off very early for Wales to break The Plan to my mother and persuade her to come and collect Norman with me.

Best suited for a career as the highly charismatic dictatrice of a rogue South American country, Mum somehow got diverted away from her natural calling and ended up marrying a Welsh Omar Sharif lookalike and having six children. Although she tends to think of Stalin as a bit of a drip, she doesn't let the fact that her zone of terror ends at the Radnor Hills instead of the Urals get her down. Forced to pursue the finer points of Realpolitik in a Taffy backwater rather than on the international stage she deserves, she has by turns established hegemony among local wheeler-dealers in the market for English lessons, holiday cottages, second-hand school uniforms, hand-painted clocks, meadow hay, horses and even cervical smear tests. She is the strongest, warmest and most indefatigable person I know. Yet it is not the immense force of her character that is terrifying so much as the inconsistency with which it is deployed. Mum saying she liked something this morning, or last Thursday, or every week for years is no indication that she won't violently disapprove when you mention it next.

This time I got lucky. I put my success down to her being slightly unsettled by having all but one of her children at home at the same time. I am the eldest, and after Bee follow Flora, Nell and Cleo. Apart from Bee the rest of us are all around six feet tall, look very similar and to complicate things further often wear one another's clothes. At the end of this set of Russian dolls is the treasured tsarevich, the youngest child and only son, my twelve-year-old brother

Archie. Mum is normally pretty clear about who he is but she can have problems identifying her brood of daughters.

I sensed the Easter holidays were taking their toll when, as I arrived, she heard the sound of a television on in the sitting room and broke off from kissing me hello to investigate. Next door we discovered the curtains drawn to blot out any stray shafts of daylight and the furniture dragged into three rows of cinema-like seating. In the middle of the room Cleo, thirteen, was stretched across a sofa watching *The Shining* over the heads of our three lurchers who were following the action from the edge of their front-row seats.

'Nell!' my mother bellowed at her. 'The only person in this house allowed to watch telly during the day is me. Turn it off and go outside and get some fresh air.'

Even before Mum started yelling the three dogs who had been watching engrossed from their separate armchairs made a bolt for the door. But the long, jeans-clad figure on a mound of sofa cushions didn't stir. From behind a mane of tangled blonde hair a bored voice said, 'I'm Cleo actually, Mum.'

When Cleo held her ground on the sofa Mum made a bid to bring the fresh air to her, and, yanking back the curtains, began to heave the sash window open. There was a terrible splintering of wood and a cloud of dust and flies billowed out from the window casing as bits of the rotten frame fell to pieces in her hands. Realising the confrontation was about to turn nuclear, Cleo slunk off the sofa and out of the front door while I ushered Mum into the kitchen to explain The Plan over a cup of tea.

Her reaction to the news that her eldest daughters were jettisoning their careers on a whim in order to take up hunting was to recommend in the event of an accident that we get ourselves killed outright.

'I don't want to have a couple of cabbages on my hands if you get bashed up,' were, I think, her exact words.

Looking around at the piles of school uniforms yet to be name-taped and the latest batch of solicitor's letters from a learner driver she had rammed on a roundabout outside Brecon muddled in with the airline tickets for a business trip to Japan, I could see there was no way she could add nursing to her already hectic existence. But this does not mean Bee and I are going to be allowed to fend for ourselves. The kettle had scarcely boiled before she was trying to flog me a horse. Norman was clearly very overpriced but naturally she had just the mount for us, who, as luck would have it, lived en route to Tewkesbury.

Clarence sounded like an underage blind date. Twelve years old and extremely handsome and athletic with excellent manners, he had been hunted at Christmas by Flora and had flown over everything in his path. Better still, his owner, a gentrified version of Clint Eastwood called Brigadier Cartwright, had slipped a disc and so was considering lending the horse out for nothing if a buyer didn't materialise soon.

Having fired me up with dreams of a free horse that behaved immaculately out hunting with a slip of a girl on his back, my mother led the way to a paddock outside Abergavenny. In it we found a thin grey gelding looking appalled to find himself inexplicably living outdoors when he was so clearly cut out for metropolitan life and a job at a glossy magazine. Clarence actually had high-heeled horseshoes on. He refused to come to the gate because the ground around it was muddy and studiously ignored his stable mates with the attitude of someone used to dividing their time between Harvey Nicks and the Met Bar who finds themselves travelling coach class to Welwyn Garden City. When we rattled a bucket of pony nuts his companions cheerfully galloped up hoping for a mouthful but Clarence gave an anorexic sniff and tottered off to stand under a tree, batting his white eyelashes and finding it all so crashingly provincial.

Feeling certain that I'd never want to ride an animal that was going to complain about my dress sense, I said I'd have to come back and try Clarence out properly with Bee and steered us back to the A40, the road that led to Norman. We're not out of the woods yet though; Mum has gone into a bulldozing charm mode that normally signals that the first skirmishes in a battle of wits in which she controls all the big guns are not far off.

I'd been longing to see how she made out against Barry Joyce; half hoping, half dreading that she'd give him one of her notorious horse-buying spiels – a speech which begins as a vote of thanks but ends up insinuating with maximum bonhomie that if she's being sold a dud she'll send someone muscular round to torch the place. Sadly our entrance at the Joyces', which I had imagined kicking off with my mother declaring that if her little princesses were being ripped off there'd be hell to pay, fell rather flat. Barry was in the tack room having a heated argument with someone about the ownership of a hoop of leather he called a martingale that we listened to bashfully before he came out wreathed in smiles to load Norman into the trailer.

When art and antique dealers move pricey *objets* around they wrap them up in as much protective padding as they can lay their hands on. Much to his chagrin I took a similar policy with Norman, bandaging foam around his legs and tail in the hope that he wouldn't get damaged in transit. I think mainly to avoid the smirks of the other horses in the yard he marched straight up the ramp of the trailer and just managed to squeeze his well-covered hips inside. Once installed he looked like a ship in a bottle – the sort that might try to set sail down the front ramp at any moment. Every time he shifted his weight the trailer lurched so alarmingly that we were forced to start the car, throw the largest cheque I have written in my life at Barry and drive off before the whole convoy capsized in his yard.

Nearly three hours later we uncorked Norman in Wales. It was a great moment. In order to bankroll half a dozen children with all the trimmings my parents turned the most comfortable parts of our house into an enterprise that is supposed to be a state-of-the-art international conference centre but has never entirely shaken off the overtones of Cold Comfort Farm. On the outside of the Georgian façade buttermilk-coloured paint fights a losing battle with mildew, and the house doesn't nestle against the hills so much as stand backed up against them, looking like a giant slice of malignant wedding cake already braced for the day the decree nisi officially ending the marriage is announced.

But as Norman emerged from the trailer into the dappled evening sunshine the whole scene softened. The gaggle of Italian pharmaceutical executives who had been picking their way through the molehills and dog turds on the lawn like chickens scratching for grain broke off their mobile phone conversations and followed Flora, Nell and Cleo to form a nervous guard of honour down each side of the ramp. The dogs stopped belting round the lawn after young swallows, Archie took thirty seconds off from *The Simpsons* and even my father looked up from whatever he was prodding at in the bottom of a trench that had been dug out under the dining room windows. With a regal turn of the head to his welcoming committee Norman pushed out a huge pile of dung smack outside the front door and strolled off amiably to meet my siblings' ponies.

FRIDAY 19 APRIL
CATHEDINE

A sleepless night c/o Cleo. Just as I was dropping off in the top bunk she idly observed that in a couple of days' time I would be twenty-seven, which meant that in a mere thirteen years' time I would turn forty, while ironically she would not be forty for another twenty-seven years.

I lay floundering under that devastating piece of arithmetic until dawn when I decided to take Norman for an inaugural ride before breakfast. Alas, he is not such an early riser. I found him lying in the dewy grass with his legs tucked under him and his head curled in so neatly that from behind he looked like a Cornish pasty awaiting the oven. He was completely out for the count and snoring so deeply I couldn't even lever his face off the ground, let alone wrestle him to his feet. Maybe Barry Joyce was serious about that alarm clock.

The only bonus of getting up so early was that I was able to spend some time with my father. Brought up in a naval family, he tends to treat Cathedine as a ship rather than a house. We minor members of the crew steer her through the day, but when the last of his children go to bed in the early hours of the morning their captain takes over the graveyard watch. Today I found him in the kitchen, his moustache dripping with seriously strong coffee brewed to ease the effects of another long night of shuffling around the house in his dressing gown.

Exhausted by these nocturnal perambulations and his daytime duties of amusing monosyllabic foreigners with ultra-English activities like croquet and charades, by the time he retreats behind the green baize door to face his progeny Dad doesn't usually have much fight left in him. Long before reinforcements arrived in the form of my brother, he learnt to cope with being constantly outnumbered by six women by adopting a modus operandi close to that of a deaf mute. Having given up trying to make himself heard over our incessant chatter, he shows scant signs of listening to us either and gets through mealtimes by silently mulling over any niggling clues from the day's *Times* crossword and mentally reliving his top fifty Welsh rugby tries.

Pouring myself a cup of coffee, I went and sat down next to him.

'Good morning, Dad.'

Silence. I waited for my words to penetrate the golden commentary of Gareth Edwards passing the ball to JJ Williams. Behind my father's dark bloodshot eyes, JJ sprinted, dummied past the flanker and whipped through three other lumbering white English shirts before being brought down. Then out of the scrummage it was a Welsh ball again. Evans to Edwards . . . the Cardiff crowd are on their feet now . . . JJ . . . Edwards again . . . the five-yard line in sight . . . on to JPR . . . he runs . . . he's past the last defender . . . and it's a try!

Sunrise spread over Dad's face. 'Morning, honey. Very exciting news about this hunting idea.'

I was dumbfounded. My father's dislike of horses and horsey people is so intense that it is rumoured he tried to have Archie and Cleo's ponies included in a livestock cull when the foot-and-mouth epidemic threatened this area last year. Yet here he was, greeting the prospect of Bee and me immersing ourselves in a world of fetlocks and feed buckets that he always claimed would make all sane men allergic to us with his version of unbridled enthusiasm.

It was only when he assured me of the wisdom of our decision to move far away from Daniel and Mr Smith that I remembered I was talking to a man who lives with the dreadful prospect of paying for five weddings. While my mother is keen to offload her daughters as quickly as possible, Dad can't meet a new boyfriend without being tormented by the thought of pink and white striped marquees and champagne toasts. The way he would look at it, his two eldest daughters being administered with a strong dose of horse in the middle of nowhere was likely to secure him a few more years agreeably free of father-of-the-bride duties.

Bee arrived at teatime, just in time to join a compulsory session of Scottish dancing with the conference guests. An hour later, when we had finished spinning Alfredo and Giuseppe around the drawing room to a cassette of the eightsome reel, we went down to the meadow and had a good gush over Norm. After agreeing to a revised version of The Plan in which as glamorous sidekick she's obliged to pose on the cover of this book naked except for peek-a-boo leather chaps if that's what it takes for me to secure a publishing deal, she produced a copy of Rob's Buttons presentation.

He'd sent a covering letter urging us to 'impact all Corporate Social Responsibility spectrums' and offering to diarise a series of events that he would resource. Thanks to a Power Point decision tree strategy to analyse our SWOT (Strength, Weakness,

Opportunities and Threat) factors everything is so much clearer. He even speculated that Mrs White's injuries might somehow not be the work of a careless Herefordshire motorist but were more than likely suffered at the hooves of her husband's vicious horse. Buttons is a liability and, while not entirely worthless, her potential re-sale margins are worryingly volatile. If we still want to buy her we should only pay danger money for her.

We got hugely overexcited at the idea of paying danger money for anything but managed to calm down and play hard to get to the Professor's call minder.

SATURDAY 20 APRIL

CATHEDINE

It took Bee in her pointy suede kitten-heels delivering blows to his soft underbelly to rouse him but we finally got Norman upright today. We towed him up to the stables mewling for his new pony friends back at the field only to find that none of our saddles fitted him at all. It's as though we've bought a farmyard animal from the wrong set, a pig that stands taller than a combine harvester or something. Norm is Duplo when most other horses are Lego.

Anxious for some kind of horsey fix and mindful of Rob's suggestion that we formulate an Efficient Consumer Response rather than always buying the first nags we see, Bee booked us in to try Arian, a Welsh mare for sale just outside Camarthen. Arian's advert in *Horse & Hound* included a picture of her waiting patiently at a meet while from her saddle a huntsman who looked like the jolliest of Santa's elves delivered what seemed to be a classic anecdote to an unseen crowd of admirers. Even more encouragingly, a lady holding a tray of mince pies right next to Arian had not come to any visible harm. The mare was also a fantastic colour; her face and spine were a snowy white that gradually dappled with iron grey and then deepened to black at her knees.

Arriving at his farm, we discovered the jolly elf was Owain Llewellyn, master of a local farmers' pack who had been loaned Arian last winter. Owain looked as though he had accidentally dressed in the mufti of one of the other, slightly slimmer elves, but it could have been his constant giggling that put his buttons and zips under such pressure. Between chortles he explained in his wonderful singsong accent that he was Arian's biggest fan but that he wanted a horse younger than her eight years and cheaper than the £2,750 her owner was asking for her.

After a tour of his dairy cows Owain teamed up his John Wayne chaps with a flat cap and clattered off down the lane on Arian roaring with laughter. Initially I thought he was being run away with, but no, it was just that he and Arian, used to being at the front of the hunting field, liked to operate at speed. As he charged through a stream and into thick brambles still cackling at full throttle my mother muttered darkly that Arian trotted with one of her toes pointed out like a duck. In her view we'd be better off buying Starry, a new horse of hers that currently had a gash in its stomach but was coming on a treat.

By the time Bee swapped on to Arian Mum had identified a host of other hideous defects in the mare but her best effort was to screech 'Gerrrt on!' as Bee approached a tiny jump made of milk crates. Startled by the bloodcurdling howl, the horse swerved violently to the left, dodged the jump altogether and Bee very nearly fell off. When I got on, my mother changed tactics and started giving a loud critique of my riding, pleading for me to sit up and stop hauling at her mouth. Smaller than Norman but seemingly powered by rocket fuel, Arian bustled around the field as if she were an ambitious PR girl running late for an important presentation. With her little legs going like pistons she was tricky to steer and unwilling to stop but she had a huge wild jump and seemed full of pluck.

As I motored past trying to get to grips with a mount that trotted like a kamikaze sewing machine, I overheard Mum telling Owain that Arian deserved a decent buyer who could really do her justice. In response he let slip that Arian's owner, a mysterious woman called Hayley who we never met because she was too busy running her fridge magnet business, was desperate to sell to anybody after a fortnight in which absolutely nobody had expressed an interest in the horse at all. Hearing this, we sprinted home to consult Rob's presentation for tips on how best to SWOT jolly Owain Llewellyn.

SUNDAY 21 APRIL
CATHEDINE

It doesn't look like it'll take much. Owain rang up as soon as he'd finished the milking at 6.25 a.m. to ask whether we'd made a decision yet. In the sleepy silence that followed he apologised for ringing so early but said Hayley would kill him if he didn't make a sale this time.

Typically Mum interpreted this keenness as conclusive proof that there's something very wrong with Arian and devoted most of my birthday breakfast to pitching Starry, her famous new horse who by this morning had developed a gross skin condition called

Sweet Itch to go with her punctured stomach. She wound up by saying that if we wouldn't take Starry then we should really think hard about borrowing Clarence.

At the mention of Clarence, Flora, down from Newcastle University to recuperate from a term studying archaeology and nightclub interiors, began to choke so violently that she catapulted great chunks of Weetabix from her epiglottis on to everyone else's plates. As she struggled for breath, Mum pushed her cereal bowl aside and made a snap decision to go to church. We heard her departing wheels skidding on the gravel as Flora held out her hands to us.

'Look what he did to me,' she wheezed bitterly. 'It's taken four months for them to heal.'

There were long dark welts across each palm and sore, flaky places along the inside of her little fingers.

'I expect Mum told you that when I hunted Clarence he jumped everything brilliantly. Well we're talking literally everything.'

Shuddering at the memory, she elaborated, 'That bugger wouldn't stop for any money. When everyone else was standing waiting he went bonkers galloping around the place. He jumped into the back of children on little ponies if they got in his way. He even barged over a fence on to the main road. When I got home my hands were bleeding from yanking on the reins to get him to slow down. Mum just told me to brace up and remember to wear gloves next time. Like there's going to be a next time. Honestly, he's mental,' Flora concluded. 'I blame the drugs.'

Drugs? Yes, drugs. The reason Clarence wears horse-sized Jimmy Choos is that he has navicular syndrome, an incurable inflammation of the bones in his front feet, which means he goes lame unless given orthopaedic platform shoes, medicine that starts at around £50 a week and daily snorts of bute, a painkilling equine version of cocaine that is only available without prescription at chemists in the Republic of Ireland.

After a last coo at Norman we fled to London before my mother returned from church, her soul cleansed, to bait another trap for us. But our getaway was delayed when, at the first bend in the lane, we met Nell coming towards us on a bicycle. As she flashed past our front bumper and into a deep drainage channel, I noticed she was wearing a high-necked frilly white shirt from the dressing-up box, her hair in plaits and the impossibly pious expression of a young nun. For some time after we'd got her bike out of the gully she stayed grubbing around in there on her hands and knees, ignoring our enquiries about why she was a) up before noon and b) wearing fancy dress. When she finally emerged she was holding a battered old RNLI collecting box with the catchy new slogan of SAVE THE LIFEBOATS written across it in fluorescent magic marker. Plaits and piety somewhat askew by now, she prised the lid off the tin, counted out five pounds in small change and, pushing it across the bonnet of the car, wished me a very happy birthday. I don't even want to think about which good folk of this parish I should be thanking for her generosity.

MONDAY 22 APRIL
EARLS COURT

An encouraging day. My agent thinks I may be in with a shout of getting some sort of book advance. I was slightly concerned when she suggested getting my life insured in readiness for a *Lord of the Flies* denouement to our rural adventure, but not so concerned that I didn't go back to the shop and re-purchase the Diane von Furstenberg dress without a word yet written or a penny yet paid.

Christy gamely came out to give the dress a spin at some new members' club that's opening in Soho, but when we got back to the flat she loaded up the dishwasher for the first time in living memory. I think all this book talk must have got her rattled. She's the first to admit that her career prospects have been stunted by her inability to play office politics or accept any kind of instruction. Her usual reaction to queries from any employer about her performance is to clear her desk and never return. Yet since my return from America she's always rebelled safe in the knowledge that her best friend was making even less progress in the world of work. It's understandable that the idea of her backstop unexpectedly making good was worrying. It's no fun being Butch if Sundance gets on the straight and narrow. Still, it's fine by me if the possibility of me getting a jammy break drives her to finally do some clearing up around here.

TUESDAY 23 APRIL
EARLS COURT

I think Professor White may be cracking. He left a weary message admitting that he still hasn't managed to shift Buttons and wants to talk terms. About ten minutes later there was a follow-up call from Mrs White, who pleaded for us to 'come and take it away soon'.

WEDNESDAY 24 APRIL
EARLS COURT

Bee and I had lunch to discuss some cost-cutting measures. She claimed to have done good work on this front. Not only had she persuaded Owain to let us have Arian for the knock-down price of £2,400, but last night she'd also submitted to a bout of light petting from a new admirer in order to get her dinner paid for.

'He was grim news, Mol,' she told me. 'But I notched up a glass of champagne, a foie gras starter, the rack of lamb, half a bottle of red and a chocolate soufflé all for free.'

A noble effort in the name of efficiency but I can't see how we can convert such rich pickings into the sixty-odd quid Norman has just run up at the vet's getting his teeth filed.

FRIDAY 26 APRIL
EARLS COURT

I have told a focus group of two of what I used to think of as my most reasonable friends that I am serious about going through with The Plan. But as we ordered the most achingly cool pad thai in London I had a hard time making the case for my new life of endless rounds of cheese ploughmans to Katie, a high-flying commodities trader, and her architect brother Toby. When I finally admitted that I had wiped out most of my savings to buy Norman they were aghast.

'You've bought a horse?' Katie shrieked, slopping noodles all over her silk combat trousers. 'You impulse-bought a whole live horse?

42

'Jesus. I can't believe it. Do I know you at all? Do you have a secret life where you go home and wear Alice bands in your hair and read gardening books under cover of darkness? What are you going to do stuck out there all day? Have you any idea how long it takes for decent films to reach provincial cinemas? And what about all those horrible little towns crammed with people buying the same horrible clothes from the same horrible shops. Ugh. What you're proposing is lifestyle suicide.'

Toby castigated me for abandoning the London singles scene, claiming that just because I hadn't got my oats lately there was no need to run off after 'some ruddy-faced tractor driver' and absolutely no reason to deprive the capital's men of Bee's magical presence. When I retorted with a description of the Peppermore brothers Toby told me to wake up and accept they were fictional pre-war characters, but Katie looked shaken.

SATURDAY 27 APRIL
EARLS COURT

I knew it. Katie's game face has slipped right off. She e-mailed me this morning during a lull in the crude oil market saying that if by any chance I did meet a rural hunk and he had a friend to please let her know. She'd always liked the sound of John Archer, a young farmer on the radio soap who was crushed to death by a pig or a similar agricultural tragedy a few years ago.

I was still making a giant mistake and would be bored witless before I knew it but might there ever be a bed in the cottage for her at weekends?

TUESDAY 30 APRIL
EARLS COURT

Vive les giant American publishing conglomerates!

In what was easily one of the top five most enjoyable days of my life, I spent yesterday going from one publisher to another talking about myself in an extremely loud voice. Would you believe it, and personally I'm still half waiting to be rung up and told there has been a hideous mistake, but after a brief exchange of telephone calls that fell squashingly short of a bidding war, Random House today offered to pay me for my story. As a result I am singing about my chores, buoyed up with surprise, jubilation and utter relief while Christy manhandles the Hoover around me.

2

May

Typical. The publisher's cheque hasn't even cleared my account yet but with the exception of Archie, who has started work on a novel of his own, the rest of my family are already shoving their snouts into my newly enriched trough. I spent yesterday batting away requests from each of my sisters for sponsorship for their holidays, clothes and CD collections, only to have my cash card swallowed up by a hole-in-the-wall machine this morning before I even had a chance to punch in my PIN number.

After many hours investigating claim and counterclaim from those charlatans at Cathedine I learnt that the best part of £2,000 had been transferred overnight from my account to a Brecon builders' merchant. The money has bought a shipment of a special tar-based quick-drying cement that Dad is at this very moment smearing over the leakiest sections of the roof of our house. My parents allegedly happened upon my bank details cluttering up the back of a drawer in my old bedroom, and, after setting my recent windfall against the hundreds of thousands of pounds they've squandered over the years feeding, schooling and entertaining me, had assumed that I'd be more than happy to loan them the piffling sum we were now quarrelling over.

THURSDAY 2 MAY
CATHEDINE

In retaliation for my being 'boring' about the cement, Mum refused to lend me the horsebox, so I enticed a naughty young farmer from across the valley, known locally as No Good Boyo, to come and collect Arian with me. As we trundled along the lanes with his sheep trailer No Good threw some local lore at our situation. Apparently Arian means money in Welsh, but less auspiciously Annabel means disabled, and if I knew what was good for me I'd bin The Plan and beetle off on a Club 18–30 holiday while I still could.

When we arrived at Owain's farm, an idyllic jumble of stone buildings with a name pronounced like a dog throwing up, No Good showed off by reversing the trailer around the yard at top speed while I followed Owain into the farmhouse so he could count the £2,400 he'd insisted I bring in cash. To the right of the hallway an open door led into a gloomy room in which two stout, beleaguered figures were wedged into armchairs placed at point-blank range in front of a giant telly. Owain glanced in, shouted, 'Rrrright you are then!' over the din of a talk show and shut the door. I later learnt that the occupants of the dark room were his parents. They lived in the ground floor of the house while Owain shared the second storey with his wife. We reached his quarters by stomping, still in our filthy wellies, along a narrow path of rubber mats that led through a series of immaculate rooms and up the stairs.

As Owain, rocking with characteristic hysterics, counted the loot I had a chance to enjoy the hunting memorabilia in his sitting room. He didn't have quite the same quantity of stuff as Barry Joyce but there was more of an obsessive, arts and crafts element to it. Owain is in the habit of painting little pewter horses so that they resemble his various mounts. In one case he had even tried to file a bit of mane off one of the ornaments to make it look more like one of his old hunters.

The only time I saw him manage a minute without a chuckle was when we loaded Arian into No Good's trailer. As the mare skipped gamely up the ramp he wiped away a tear and said he'd be in touch to see how she settled in.

SATURDAY 4 MAY
CATHEDINE

He rang at a record-breaking 6.02 a.m. this morning to do just that. Mind you, I'm almost grateful for the attention. Owain is the only person I've encountered who can raise you from a deep sleep to a roaring good mood in under ten seconds, and after only a couple of days away from London the missed-call tally on my mobile has fallen to an abysmal 2.5 per day with most of those made up of Christy ringing to ask how to retrieve work from her computer now that she's spilt Campari/Guinness/red wine over its keyboard.

Worried that as far as my friends are concerned I really am out of town, out of mind, I caught the train service from Newport to Paddington. One of the main attractions of rail travel is that I can indulge my new hobby: train hunting. From the comfort of my Inter City seat I visualise me and Norman zooming over some of England's best hunting country as the Great Western line swings through Gloucestershire and Wiltshire.

After a happy half-hour scanning fences for barbed wire and hidden ditches before picturing myself sailing over them, a man with a bleating mobile clipped to his tracksuit joined the train at Bristol and sat down beside me. As we chugged through the suburbs he busied himself letting his wife and the rest of the carriage know that he had just managed to catch the train by the skin of his teeth. But when we reached what I think must be the edge of the Badminton Estate and the heart of the Beaufort Hunt's territory he began to pay close attention to the scene outside our window. After tensing in synchrony over a series of whopping hedges and inhaling sharply together as the train passed an iron six-bar gate he introduced himself as Roy Abbot and asked who I hunted with. It sounds as though we should join his local pack, the Radnor and West Hereford, which he described as 'a great gang to crash and burn with while you get your eye in'.

Roy makes his living as a washing-machine repairman in Swindon. But he funds his lottery habit, an annual week in Spain and half a season's hunting on a cob called Bandit that he shares with his brother by moonlighting in Kensington three nights a week as a plumber. Hopefully we'll be able to make a trip to join him out with the Radnors sometime.

May

Owain allowed me his version of a Sunday morning lie-in and rang at seven o'clock this morning. When I said I was in London he responded in awed tones as though I were speaking from a moon crater before asking how I was fixed for the Royal Welsh Show. He'd be stewarding the cob classes if his silage making went smoothly and he hoped to see me there.

Christy has snatched back the crown of being this flat's highest achiever in audacious style. I noticed she was very much restored to her old self when she arrived back last night and started absent-mindedly using a wine glass I was still drinking from as an ashtray while she geared up to tell me her big news.

Big news? It's massive. My book deal has been trumped by an engagement ring clustered so profusely with diamonds that she can hardly lift her left hand under their weight. Never again will she have to stay up half the night writing a theatre review on one of this flat's seven reproduction Victorian side-tables. She's escaping the basement and her laptop to marry her doctor boyfriend and embark on what she describes as the leisure-heavy, low-skill, no-wage non-career of being a GP's wife.

It's always encouraging when someone one really likes gets swept off the shelf in a tornado of confetti but this is excellent. The flat and my sorties beyond it won't be much fun without her, but the irony of a hard-drinking chain-smoker of Christy's calibre becoming the wife of a healthcare professional is delicious. There is also the possibility that, if he's not too busy treating her for bronchitis and liver failure to tend to his surgery, her husband's salary might stretch to letting her join us for a couple of days' hunting every fortnight. Her involvement should hopefully see off quite a lot of the saddo Watson sister comments from the rest of our friends. Here is someone that someone else wants, legally, for life and she wants to be part of The Plan.

TUESDAY 7 MAY
EARLS COURT

News of the engagement has somehow leaked across the Severn Bridge into Wales, prompting my mother to ring up Christy on the sly and attempt to sell her Clarence for £3,000.

THURSDAY 9 MAY
EARLS COURT

A really terrifying book arrived in the post today. The weight of an encyclopaedia and with the demeanour of the Bible, it's called *Baily's Hunting Directory* and every year since 1897 it has published details of every hunt from America to Africa, ranging from foxhounds to bassets and even mink- and coyote-chasing packs.

The manual, which may never be published again if the future of fox hunting still looks dicey by the autumn, contains gems like accounts of the Perth Hunt Club galloping around the outskirts of Sydney and admiring the city's skyline. It pays tribute to a lone Italian contessa who has acted as master and huntsman to the Caccia a Cavallo Hunt near Milan since 1969 and describes the antics of the New Zealand Mangonui pack where children allegedly ride up front and tackle eight-strand electric fences in pursuit of hares 'with the greatest of ease'.

Yet it is in the British Isles, where hunting began, that the most spine-chilling riding still seems to be on offer. My blood ran cold just reading about the action-packed North Galway, whose Irish followers are routinely confronted with 'ditches, gates, hedges, banks and walls; but undoubtedly the most common are walls, ranging in height from four to five feet and a rider can expect to meet at least thirty of these per mile'.

And no way do I fancy spending much time with the Holderness Hunt in Yorkshire. Their blurb boasts that 'the best-bred horse and the boldest of riders is required' to cross their country and stay in one piece. In some areas even the quarry sounded daunting. The Irfon and Towy Hunt in Mid-Wales report that in their neck of the woods 'foxes are stout, good runners, and take a lot of killing'.

The whole book, from the way the obituaries of great huntsmen past were interspersed with adverts for carcass incinerators to endless descriptions of the 'going' and 'barnburningly' good chases over icy ground undertaken by riders already injured from previous falls, was disturbingly hearty. Part of me wanted never to pick it up again but a bigger part wondered whether Bee and I, and more importantly Norman and Arian, would ever hold our own in the kind of situations that filled its pages. To date I had witnessed Arian jump a milk crate at the third attempt. Would she one day be the kind of 'strong, robust horse able to gallop and really jump' recommended by the Blackmore and Sparkford Vale Hunt in Dorset to take on their big fences and treacherously deep mud?

FRIDAY 10 MAY
EARLS COURT

I've turned to the heartiest person I know to navigate me through the pages of *Baily's*.

My abiding memory of my cousin Lucy's mother Victoria is that she often turned up to collect us from teenage parties in robust good cheer in spite of having bits of her thumb missing or a leg in tatters from her latest riding accident. She also presided over the kind of kitchen where there was a fighting chance that the meat-covered spoon she was busy dishing up your supper with had just come out of a tin of cat food.

In my limited experience Victoria stands out as the ultimate hard woman to hounds. Although she has got a minute bottom and to the naked eye is bristle-free, she would think nothing of self-medicating with a nip of horse tranquilliser to take the edge off the pain of a broken collarbone. In short she's middle-aged and female but Peppermore material through and through.

As luck would have it she's currently chairman of the Belvoir Hunt based around Melton Mowbray. Its write-up in *Baily's* made no mention of any kind of stiff jumps, and imagining a set-up where people cantered gently from covert to covert, snacking on the occasional pork pie, I suggested we might set up camp near her. In the nicest possible way Victoria hinted that any attempt by amateurs like us to start our hunting careers in Leicestershire on inexperienced horses would lead to us getting hospitalised pretty much immediately. The reason that the authorities at the Belvoir and its neighbours the Quorn and the Cottesmore don't scaremonger about the enormity of their hedges is that they don't have to. That would be like the International Olympic Committee putting the word out that athletes might want to put in a bit of practice before the games commence. Situated in the cradle of English fox-hunting, theirs is still the most impressive and expensive hedge country in the land.

While advising us to set our sights somewhere easier and cheaper than the crème de la crème of fox-hunting, Victoria did give us some invaluable advice about selecting horses for our venture. We should avoid animals with odd feet, and rather than take anyone's word that a horse behaves well out hunting we must insist on having a trial day on it before parting with our cash.

Oops.

She also mentioned in passing that the hunting season was now over until September so if we wanted to save money we shouldn't start looking for nags until August.

Double oops.

MONDAY 13 MAY
EARLS COURT

Bee is in decisive mode. She has finally told the Whites that Buttons is not for us and insists that we pursue our hunting careers with a pack where she can jump the exact same hedge we saw Barry Joyce zooming over in the photograph.

'When I'm old and grey in fifty years' time or young but

paraplegic in six months' time, I want to look at a photo like that of me and know that I did that kind of stuff,' she argued.

'More importantly I want to be able to bandy it around and show other people that I did it.'

According to *Baily's*, Barry Joyce is based with the Ledbury, a hunt whose country straddles the intersection of the borders of Herefordshire, Gloucestershire and Worcestershire. Sandwiched between the Malvern Hills and the River Severn with the M50 meandering across its territory, the Ledbury's write-up in the directory sounds ideal. Life with the pack is illustrated by a photograph not of the hounds at full cry but of a cocktail party. The hounds live at an idyllic-sounding place called Eggs Tump and they only hunt on Mondays and Fridays, meaning that the number of followers stays quite low. We may not even have that much to fear from most of the riding either. *Baily's* says of it: 'The Monday country is mixed farms and woodland; the Friday country is dominated by vale hedges, hunt rails and natural country divided by the Malvern Hills.'

WEDNESDAY 15 MAY
CATHEDINE

A man from a rather bijou tack shop outside Leominster came to measure Norman for an extra-large saddle today. However, in the month or so since he came into our ownership Norman has swelled to such an immense size that there isn't a saddle in production that will fit him. The trouble is that he's now so fat that he can't even fit through the door to his stable to begin his diet and so stays out at grass piling on the pounds.

The boutiquer, perhaps used to catering for customers longing to squeeze into a smaller size, had a cunning plan. From the back of his van he produced a horse muzzle, a sieve-like contraption that attaches to Norman's headcollar and should reduce his calorie intake as he grazes by about fifty per cent. Next week when he would have some idea of the shape of Norman's back underneath the rolls of flab he'll return and sort him out with a saddle.

THURSDAY 16 MAY
CATHEDINE

Norm has eaten through the muzzle during the night. It's like that scene in *Jaws* when they finally think they've got the shark beaten and it munches through an underwater iron girder.

FRIDAY 17 MAY
EARLS COURT

I've made a special pilgrimage to town to see Gwyneth Paltrow in *Proof* with my friend Orlando Fraser, a boy with a knack of getting into VIP events by representing his famous friends and relations. We watched the play, Orlando creaking and straining with desire like a galleon at full sail beside me every time Gwyneth appeared on stage, in seats intended for Taki and Lady Antonia Fraser. It was a blow to be denied entry to the after party on the grounds that the real Taki was already in attendance but the mood picked up once we were installed at a table at The Ivy reserved for Orlando's supermodel cousin, Honor Fraser.

Noticing me sitting agog at the sight of a paunchy breakfast television presenter digging into a goat's cheese salad, Orlando told me that he thought my time in the countryside was already taking its toll. Not only had I lost the metropolitan knack of being studiously unimpressed by anyone remotely famous, but before the play he had spotted me halfway up St Martin's Lane consulting an *A to Z* to find my way to the theatre.

It is astonishing how quickly I've begun to fall out of the swing of things. Glamorous outings like this evening's have dried up to the extent that even my clothes are starting to smell like they don't get out much. Yet I feel surprisingly unbothered by my gentle fall into disrepair. Just so long as I don't end up cutting my own hair, making my own shoes and setting out with a 12 bore instead of a shopping trolley every time I want something to eat.

SUNDAY 19 MAY
CATHEDINE

Today we lanced the boil and took Norm out bareback.

Bee found a book in the attic called *Getting Horses Fit* by a Sarah Pilliner that instructs you to walk them for the first few weeks of exercise, so I didn't think it would be too risky to volunteer to ride him while Bee gave Arian her first spin. We soon discovered that neither Norman nor Arian seem to subscribe to Ms Pilliner's theories. Arian cantered off down the road sideways while Norman refused to budge at all until Archie started taking pot shots over his flanks with an air rifle.

TUESDAY 21 MAY
CATHEDINE

After three outings in which Norman wouldn't start and Arian wouldn't stop it's clear we need help. The time has come to send for William Black, the chap who used to give us riding lessons years ago. However, a few telephone calls quickly established that nobody sends for William any more. He is now a Fellow of the British Horse Society, an actual professor of riding with a catch-him-if-you-can reputation that reminds me of the A-Team. If you've got a horse, if it's got a problem and if you can find him, maybe you can hire The Black Man.

TUESDAY 28 MAY
CATHEDINE

After only a week of campaigning we've managed to wangle a lesson with William but we've had to buy a lorry to do it.

Norm can just about squeeze into his new saddle but his mighty circumference means he can't travel in the trailer and William no longer makes house calls. The answer is a twenty-year-old Ford TK cattle wagon that the mechanic who strengthened the floor to carry Norm's weight claims has a bus engine inside it. I paid £1,750 for it to a delightful couple who I failed to spot both had arms like Popeye. Power steering the lorry doesn't have. In fact, even without the horses on board the only time it feels power anything is when you try and brake. After about thirty seconds of slamming your right foot to the floor there is a wheezing noise and very gradually your speed drops in a series of bone-crunching jolts. My first go at manoeuvring it to a petrol pump involved a gruelling seventeen-point turn and I still ended up smashing one of the brake lights.

WEDNESDAY 29 MAY
CATHEDINE

We arrived at a local livery stables for our lesson with William fraught from the constant noise of kicking coming from the back of the lorry and a seriously near miss at a mini-roundabout outside Llangattock. I really enjoyed the camaraderie between lorry drivers though; nearly every oncoming truck waved or flashed us and not because we had a flat tyre.

William had not changed at all since we had last seen him. A slight, wiry figure, gladiator-style leather shin guards and boots moderating the campness of his jodhpurs, he came slouching over and immediately started taking the piss out of us and asking if it was even worth unloading the donkeys we'd bought. As we rode out to the dressage arena (a shallow sandpit with a fence around it), I remembered why it was that William had cornered the market in riding lessons for most of Herefordshire and the Welsh Marches. It boils down to the fact that scores of women are regularly prepared to pay £30 for an hour of mild flirting with him.

I can't say I blame them. William is the only man on the circuit and he looks like a ruggedly handsome young buck rather than his actual sun-dried forty-plus years. He also never shouts but has the gift of all truly talented teachers of making his pupils desperate to please him. In part this is because he never really praises them, so behind his jokes there is an undercurrent of someone playing hard to get. 'That's a little better' is by far and away the biggest compliment he has ever paid me.

Most importantly every lesson ends on a feelgood note. If your horse has shown sufficient improvement, William will smile his Paul Newman, twinkly toothed, even twinklier-eyed grin at you, which makes you feel as though you'll swoon out of the saddle and lie prostrate on the ground gurgling with pleasure for about a week. Better still, if you don't seem to be making any progress he'll ride your horse himself for ten minutes. If that doesn't sound like much of a treat I should explain that watching William Black ride round a paddock is like seeing John Travolta work his moves across a dance floor. There's some magic ingredient at work that makes them look better and effortlessly sexier at it than anyone else.

Today William's task was to get us going. Given that the bristly faced authors of *The Manual of Horsemanship* decree that 'When a horse is going correctly he should present a picture of perfect harmony and grace that accepts the bit', is perfectly balanced, rhythmic and moves with just the right amount of energy, and we were still struggling with basic speed control, I felt he had his work cut out. Yet after half an hour of William reminding me to keep still, look up and not fiddle around with his mouth Norman was bounding elegantly around the arena, barely recognisable as the lazy brown slug that had waddled out of the lorry. According to William, Norm had obviously been taught all about dressage and just needed someone to send him the right signals in order to respond properly – even with a muppet like me on board he moved beautifully.

Despite jumping with characteristic fizz Arian was less impressive. Her habit of leaning inwards like a motorbike on corners and speeding up when Bee used her legs to steer her gave her away to William as being completely uneducated. When he rode her at the end of the lesson he declared that she was willing to learn but, the lucky dog, she would need to come to his yard for a week of intensive education.

3

June

My eyes are practically cuboid after I heeded Katie's warning about all the new releases I'll miss in the sticks and went to the cinema five times in twenty-four hours. Stumbling out of a matinée I bumped into Damian, an old friend from Oxford. Since we graduated he has got himself on the long list to be the King of Lombardy, married a construction-industry heiress, bred himself some heirs of his own and was fresh off the plane from delivering a lecture on advanced physics at Harvard.

I never expected my news to hold up to that kind of competition but when I told him I was chucking in journalism for a better life and taking Bee with me he promised he'd call me if I made it back. He's not the first person to treat our move like an intrepid, if foolish, journey into the dark heart of England. It makes me wonder whether we should be getting ourselves inoculated against potato blight and rain scald.

MONDAY 3 JUNE
EARLS COURT

Goodbye Piccadilly, farewell Leicester Square. We slunk away from London in the very early morning unable to face a leaving party that would feature toasts to a new life that will begin with us living back at home with our parents.

As we hurtled along the M4 in a knackered Renault 5 Bee has bought to prevent us having to undertake every journey in a five-ton lorry with a top speed of forty-five miles an hour, London-bound traffic was already angrily swarming to a standstill near Heathrow. It seemed like an ideal opportunity to christen the moment we opted for a road less commuted by tuning into *Farming Today*, but when we got Radio 4 going we discovered the programme had already finished. The message was clear – Bee's hay-feverish nostrils might be itching with the first hint of pollen in the air but we are not country mice yet.

THURSDAY 6 JUNE
CATHEDINE

We had another lesson with William today. Arian still has a tendency to tank round the ring like the Duracell bunny but she's much improved after her week with the maestro. Norman jumped so well that William even declared he might be 'too good' for hunting and possibly jeopardise his potential career as a competition horse by getting injured charging after the hounds at breakneck speeds through deep plough.

At the end of the session William took us aside. We were

hopelessly out of practice but by complete fluke he thought we'd bought a pair of green but extremely genuine and talented young horses. In his opinion the worst thing we could do now was 'prat about like part-timers', letting them slop around semi-fit and riding only occasionally.

This left us with two choices. We could really get to grips with Norman and Ari over the summer by riding every day, having regular lessons and giving the horses and ourselves vital experience by entering events and competitions every week. William was confident that if we stuck faithfully to a sensible schedule of disciplined work then come September our whole cavalry would arrive at the Ledbury on top form and with a reasonable chance of coping with whatever hunting might throw at us. Alternatively, we could turn the horses out to grass and give all concerned the summer off – hoping against hope that when we came to ride them again Norman and Arian would be refreshed but not too silly to forget all that he and Barry Joyce had taught them and far too kind to remember the dirty tricks they had learnt all by themselves.

It sounded like an absolute no-brainer. Never expert horse-women, in recent years Bee and I had spent barely more than a couple of hours in the saddle between us. Now we were about to move far away from home to enter the alien world of fox-hunting armed with horses who seemed willing but were scarcely more knowledgeable than their riders. The way William put it, for us to doss about in the sun for the next three months while Norman and Arian went to seed would be tantamount to signing our own death warrants.

MONDAY 10 JUNE
A CROSS-CHANNEL FERRY HEADING FOR CALAIS

The ink is still wet. But don't sweat – it'll soon dry when we finish loading up with factor 15 and sauvignon blanc and get ourselves out on deck.

4

July

Intermission for the bikini season.

5

August

SATURDAY 24 AUGUST
ITHACA, GREECE

An enormous white plastic boat, allegedly chartered by that
chubby tycoon who started up Easyjet, is parked in the bay beneath
the villa. This means that the boys in our party are busy water-
skiing around it far too fast and the girls are lolling topless on the
jetty concentrating feverishly on their holiday reading. I should
be down at the beach looking for shells myself but finding the
house unexpectedly deserted for the first time all week is too great
a temptation. For seven blistering days my willpower has held out
but now I'm beaten – I've simply got to try on the new pair of
jodhpurs that are lurking like contraband in the bottom of my
suitcase.

Oh dear. Oh dammit. The Peppermore brothers would be quietly
sick if they could see what's staring back at me from the mirror.
My designated outfit for the next seven months is an absolute
disgrace. In fairness, acres of creamy, Lycra-injected cotton

probably aren't best accessorised with flip-flops and moderate sunburn but the results are still pretty punishing. My legs look passable, but the svelte yet peachy effect I had hoped for across my bottom isn't happening at all. An untoned shambles currently fills up the rear of my jodhpurs. Every unkind contour and swag of flab between my waist and my knees is accentuated by the clinging material, and my bum has contrived to look both huge and yet also somehow deflated – each buttock a slack sack hanging down from the immense girth of my hips.

TUESDAY 27 AUGUST
CATHEDINE

Curses. I arrived home to find Bee recently returned from a trip to Thailand and striding about in the same pair of breeches she wore as a snake-hipped fourteen-year-old. But after trudging behind her up the hill beyond the house to check on the horses I have to report that even her arse isn't looking an absolute gem. There's not much of it, but what there is wobbles at the sides.

Morale in the ranks is not at all good. Because they kept frightening the German students who had to walk through their field to reach the tennis court, Norman and Arian have spent the last couple of months banished to a little sheep paddock steep enough to qualify as a red skiing piste. Ari passed the time endlessly pacing round the perimeter wall maddened by flies and boredom, while Norm sulked in a disused pigsty. On the flight back to Heathrow I had envisaged a tearful reunion between horse and owner in which I would whistle like the boy in *Lassie* and they would come galloping joyfully to my feet. Instead, I was confronted with a case of the strops so serious that it bordered on mutiny. The horses, furious at being neglected in the heat of the summer, scuffed about rubbing their grimy flyblown faces and burr-tangled tails on the gatepost and pointedly failing to recognise us. Even a long shampoo and soak under the hosepipe couldn't clean the cross expressions off their faces.

The rest of the family didn't produce much in the way of home-coming celebrations either. I expected Archie, who is still of an age where the prospect of eating anything other than Coco Pops fills him with profound gloom, to eye tonight's barbecue supper like a panda deprived of bamboo shoots. But the others weren't any better. Cleo was in heavy mourning for the pair of 'totally pants' new school shoes that had been foisted on her and Nell was exhausted from a day of trying to sell Pimm's at a local agricul-tural show to farmers who refused to even try a beverage that was cluttered up with fruit and ice. Even my jolly descriptions of my Greek holiday fell flat once Mum ascertained that I hadn't thought to swim over to Stelios with one of her brochures between my teeth and pitch an Easyconference venture to him.

We ate in depressed silence. The occasions when quiet falls over the Cathedine dinner table long enough to give my father a chance to speak are like domestic versions of a solar eclipse; incred-ibly rare and filled with a sense of wonder and foreboding. I chewed on a lamb chop expecting God to smite me down at any moment, but Dad was too preoccupied with the injury problems of the Welsh rugby touring squad to notice the hush. He only came to when the telephone rang. It was Flora, calling to say she's got a cool new boyfriend called Chutney.

August

WEDNESDAY 28 AUGUST
CATHEDINE

Their months of leisure have left Ari and Norm out of shape as
well as out of sorts. Walking them over the Black Mountains today
was like hauling a couple of asthmatic sumo wrestlers up a mile-
high fire escape. When Norm finally waddled his way to the
summit of the hill cocooning Llangorse Lake he let his legs collapse
under him like a pantomime mule and lay groaning in the bracken
until Bee got off him and loosened his girths.

As we waited for him to get his breath back Bee related the
trouble she's had finding us somewhere to live in Gloucestershire.
Despite buying the horses and lorry, weathering the bikini season
and enduring ongoing attempts by the management at home to
levy a tithe on my book advance, we still have enough of it left
to play with and had been confident that we'd have our pick of
Cotswold rentals. How wrong we were. Not being prepared to
take a maisonette in central Cheltenham and install Norm and
Ari in the double garage beneath it, the only cottage she'd found
in more than seven weeks of searching that was vaguely within
our price range was whisked off the market when a pair of week-
ending advertising executives gazumped her by offering to pay fifty
per cent extra for the place once they noticed there was a view
of an ornamental dovecote from the bathroom window.

Quickly learning that every last cowshed within two hours' drive
of London was now fully renovated, manicured to within an inch
of its life and fetching rents not far off Kensington prices, Bee
moved her search westwards to the Malvern Hills and into
Herefordshire only to discover that property prices are almost as
dizzying there. In desperation she'd turned to our old friend and

taken out an advertisement in tomorrow's *Horse & Hound* pleading for anyone in the Midlands with temporary accommodation for two reforming townies with a pair of horses in tow to please come forward.

THURSDAY 29 AUGUST
CATHEDINE

A man in Bromsgrove called up with two mobile homes for sale. We'll have to join a local swimming club to be sure of getting regular showers but he insists that if we park the caravans in the lay-by of our choosing with enough determination it could be January before the council evicts us.

SATURDAY 31 AUGUST
CATHEDINE

We're getting the hell out of here.

Apart from a nasty incident a couple of days ago when she fractured a friend of Nell's wrist during a game of Racing Demon, Bee and I were beginning to think Mum was turning into a mellowed, more docile version of herself. Since we've been back at home we haven't once been told to tidy up – a battle cry that traditionally heralded her doing a sweep of our bedrooms in which she picked up any stray clothes she found on the floor and threw them out of the window, giving us twenty minutes to retrieve them before she set a man with a lawnmower on them. Nor has she ejected any of her children from a car mid-journey and left them to find their own way home as punishment for irritating her. But today we discovered we had been lulled into a false sense of security.

Returning from a slightly faster-paced ride on the bloaters, Bee took a disturbing phone call from a lady from the Berkeley Pony Club ringing to fix up a time to bring her son to try out the eight-year-old grey jumping pony she'd heard was for sale. It soon became chillingly obvious that Mum had not been idle in our absence. Ari is on the market for £2,850. Norm should count himself lucky he's not in tins.

When Bee explained that Ari was not for sale because she was about to begin her career as a hunter if only we could find somewhere to live, she was surprised to find the lady sympathised entirely with our situation. Not only was she herself plagued by a husband who kept trying to sell her horses in order to fund his tropical fish collection, but to our eternal gratitude she gave us the number of a man who knew a man she thought she'd heard had a cottage with stabling to rent near Upton-on-Severn. She said we'd been wasting our time searching through newspapers and estate agents as nobody she knew around there with a half-decent place would dream of advertising it – you never knew what muck you'd pick up that way.

Armed with this local knowledge, we tracked down the owner of the cottage and, hearing it was a converted cider house, took it sight unseen. Hasty I know, but with our charges in danger even the unplumbed caravans were sounding increasingly appealing. Our safe passage secured, we resolved to evacuate at dawn and spent the rest of the night arguing about which of us could lay claim to be Moses in the current escape scenario and which one had to play his lone Israelite.

6

September

With Mum safely distracted by an offer that she couldn't refuse from some Korean clients to go ten-pin bowling in Aberdare, we packed up and trundled to safety and our new home in the nether regions of Gloucestershire.

Scorned by some for being the wrong side of the River Severn, the Leadon valley is a heavenly stretch of country. The land is arranged in ripples of low round hills and ridges so that one only has to stroll up a few fields to see for miles across Gloucester and its river meadows to Birdlip Hill in the east or swivel round to gaze across the hop gardens and church spires that dot the undulating westerly view over to the obelisk in the Eastnor Castle Deer Park. And the whole place smells so pungently ripe it nearly gives you a headache. The heavy scent of darkening blackberries and newly shorn stubble wafted into the cab of the lorry as we chugged along past villages set in the shadows of ancient tithe barns. Beehives clustered in the leafy corners of many fields and every few miles or so someone was selling home-grown rhubarb or duck eggs from their back garden. I don't want to oversell the rustic charm bit here but even the occasional hideous new bungaloid or mock-thatched roof sticking out like pimples from amongst the pink-brick Chartist cottages couldn't break the sleepy spell we fell under just driving along the A417.

Our particular corner of the Ledbury country is one of those rural addresses that computers programmed for house numbers and street names can't understand and our friends will only be able to reach via a vortex of tangled lanes. The word cottage is actually rather too expansive for it. We're paying £550 a month for a two-up, one-down squeezed into part of an old apple store. Estate agents would call it petite, but given that the ceilings are so low that I can't stand upright in my bedroom or most of the bathroom, I call it midget. The Cot's only downstairs room doesn't have an Aga or an open fire. The bath is little more than a bidet, the plank beds are crippling and the interior is painted a vexing shade of pistachio. I fell in love with it immediately.

The moment you look out of the Velux windows all is forgiven. To one side are arable fields lined with avenues of teenage lime trees that lead down to a willow-fringed curl of the River Leadon. On the other is an immaculate old-fashioned barnyard where Norman and Ari are standing in their palatial stables, rooted to the spot in astonishment at their good fortune. Their looseboxes have enviably high ceilings, more generous floor space than our bedrooms and their own dual-aspect views over towards the Forest of Dean. Like out-of-towners staying at the Four Seasons the horses seem to be finding the deluxe accommodation slightly too sophisticated for their tastes. They haven't yet figured out how the automatic water troughs work and found the fresh sawdust bedding so clean they were nervous about treading on it.

With Ari and Norm settled in we had planned to spend our first evening outside admiring the sunset. But alas, once we emptied the lorry and the Renault 5 of our luggage, both doors out of the Cot became blocked by a barrage of suitcases and boxes. In our haste to escape the enemy lines at Cathedine, Bee and I had packed anything that looked either useful or sufficiently fashionable that it would be pilfered by our younger sisters if left unattended at home. The result is that on top of the mountain of horse kit and saddlery that now occupies the whole of the shed at the back of the Cot, we must find space for fifty-seven pairs of shoes, nineteen evening dresses, eleven packing cases of what Bee calls her 'daywear' and a solitary mink coat in a residence with one wardrobe and a chest of drawers the Lilliputians must have thrown out.

By midnight the problem had become quite literally overwhelming. The last thing I heard before dropping off to sleep should have been the replete thump of an apple falling from a tree in the quiet outside my window. What I actually heard was the crash of a pillar of cardboard boxes marked 'Belts and Trousers' clattering down on top of Bee as she dozed the other side of the paper-thin wall dividing our bedrooms.

September

MONDAY 2 SEPTEMBER
THE COT

The daywear had hardly settled down for the night before I was shaken awake in the small hours by some inconsiderate fiend driving round and round the cottage in a low gear. I instinctively suspected joy riders but when I poked my head out of the skylight I was blinded by a giant tractor wearing a tiara of powerful lights stuck on its roof carefully traversing a nearby field. Very puzzling. Was the driver trying to steal whatever was growing there, brushing up his crop circle technique or committing a clumsy and extremely noisy act of agricultural sabotage?

Eventually I gave up on getting any sleep and, leaving Bee soundproofed by boxes, set out on foot through the luminous chill of the early morning for the village post office. I'd barely pottered half a mile along the lane breathing in the combined scent of cow parsley and cow pat before it became clear that I was completely giving myself away as an interloper. Virtually every passing car stopped to find out what my trouble was, assuming I must be lost, broken down or worse. Proper country people, I soon learnt, never walk for walking's sake. Bicycling is just about acceptable so long as you're wearing farm overalls and resolutely pedalling towards the nearest silage pit, but a recreational stroll is considered a colossal waste of time.

I had a rather desultory chat with the postmaster who sold me a couple of stale doughnuts and said he bitterly regretted moving to the country. But I did spare myself further blushes by accepting a lift most of the way home from a hawk-nosed old chap in a Land-Rover who explained what all the ruckus with the tractor was about. Apparently contract farmers are so hi-tech these days that in clear weather it is normal for them to cut wheat and maize right through the night and drive it to silos the other side of the country before it rains. The roar of machinery that punctured my dreams was actually the sound of the harvest getting underway. So much for a rural idyll. Where did all the corn dollies go?

I returned too psyched up for what I now know to be one of the biggest challenges of country life to eat my doughnut. Unlike the amorphous cast of strangers I occasionally passed wading through junk mail in the stairwells of everywhere I've lived in cities, neighbours really matter out here. My friend with the Land-Rover says we've been lamentably slow to introduce ourselves to the people we'll be relying on to break down our door when the blizzards come and join in the search if our horses get out. Given that Timothy and Susan Yarwood, our only neighbours for miles, live in the farmhouse across the yard from the Cot and are also our landlords, making them like us will be a high stakes operation. But it has to start sometime. Smiling like maniacs we went out and presented ourselves at their back door.

Early signs of compatibility were scarce. Mrs Yarwood, a beautiful woman in her sixties with the lithe figure and dress sense of the tomboy in the *Famous Five* stories, has the most immaculately neat house I have ever seen. When we sat down for a cup of coffee there were even pre-peeled KitKats waiting on our saucers. And when they aren't tidying up the Yarwoods spend their time performing dressage tests on stallions they trained themselves. So important is equestrianism to them that they are in the process of wallpapering their tack room, a vestibule arranged like a long gallery in which, instead of oil paintings, visitors admire rows of glistening saddles and rosettes with heads the size of cauliflowers.

But there were encouraging signs of life beyond horses in the

Yarwoods' conversation. Timothy farmed in Uganda for many years and he and his wife are regular theatregoers who read, paint and speak fluent Spanish. As hopeless housekeepers and pretty mediocre horsewomen, I can see that Bee's and my only hope of impressing them will be through the exchange of cultured bon mots when our paths cross at the muckheap each day. Keen to make a start on this tactic we drove to The Boat, a pub teetering on the banks of the Severn, to decide what we really thought of Proust over a few pints of Speckled Hen and home-produced pork scratchings.

WEDNESDAY 4 SEPTEMBER
THE COT

My hands are still bleeding from what was billed as a leisurely hack round the farm with Mrs Yarwood. It started off pleasantly enough when she saddled up a rather odd-looking brown brood mare called Georgina with a long back and a low saggy tummy. Feeling rather well mounted by comparison we fell in meekly behind her along the track past more arable fields and plantations of young oak trees and were just beginning to relax and enjoy the sunshine when she suggested a gentle pipe-opener around an oval-shaped meadow next to the river.

As Georgina glided into a fantastically slow and controlled canter Ari forgot how unfit she was and began to accelerate reck-lessly. Norman, egged on by the dappled-grey hornet buzzing at his heels, was soon overtaken by an irresistible urge to show off. He bucked fifty-three times during our first circuit of the river meadow. On the second circuit he lowered the frequency but put more topspin on the flips. By the third circuit my knuckles and the delicate veins across the backs of my hands had been rubbed raw against the front of the saddle and I was looking for soft stretches of pasture to bale out over. Thankfully the fourth circuit ended prematurely when Bee had to steer Ari into a tree at point-blank range to prevent her belting off back to the stables.

We rested up, riders and wicked horses panting in the shade, while Mrs Yarwood did ten minutes of something she called 'schooling' on Georgina. The gymnastic display that followed would have made the people at *The Manual of Horsemanship* weep for joy. It was horse ballet. Georgina, the damage pregnancy had wreaked on her figure a distant memory, nonchalantly pirouetted, reversed, trotted with baby strides and then giant ones, skipped, cantered sideways from a standstill and spun round on her hind legs while Mrs Yarwood sat astride her not appearing to be doing anything at all. I felt like throwing carnations at Georgina's hooves in appreciation. Alas, Bee threw herself on to the back foot and spent the ride home trying unsuccessfully to toady up by relating the most turgid parts of her thesis on Alexander the Great. Every time Mrs Yarwood was about to make an interesting remark, she interjected another tedious mot about evaluating imperialism into the conversation. Pretty soon even Norm was bored into submission.

To make up for such an inauspicious start we spent the afternoon on a confidence-boosting tour of the oral ironmongery for sale at a saddler's outside Newent. Perusing the fearsome array of bits on display had exactly the desired effect of convincing us that if Norm and Ari's behaviour doesn't improve dramatically we can take the fight right to them. Unfortunately a horse can buck to its heart's content whatever apparatus you put in its mouth, but the man behind the counter promised that his arsenal of steel gadgetry guaranteed every rider better brakes and more respect from their steed. Each bit had a title and its own particular brutal action that could have given the Gestapo a few pointers.

A single tweak on the Pelham, a contraption with a barbarous-looking curb chain and lip strap, will put instant pressure on a horse's tongue, lips, chin and even the soft insides of its mouth. The innocuous-looking gag exerts a fiendish force on the top of its head, and my personal favourite, the Dr Bristol, has a cunning central iron lozenge set at an angle that whips down on the tongue at the slightest touch. It was heartening stuff and we turned for home reassured that our getting bashed into a permanent vege-tative state might still be some way off.

Parking the car on a ridge above Upleadon on the way home we checked our mobiles for messages and immediately gave ourselves something else to worry about. Despite leaving her our new address and phone number, my mother has made no effort to contact us at all since we left Cathedine. We had expected our abrupt departure to infuriate her for a couple of days, but this is more ominous. Prolonged silence usually means she is marshalling her forces. All we can do is sit and wait for her to strike.

THURSDAY 5 SEPTEMBER
THE COT

More shopping – this time at the agricultural merchant's in Gloucester. After much silly giggling at the udder cream shelf and a Mr H.J. Biggins, whose card in the window offered customers the chance to enjoy a day with him and his rather sadomasochistic-sounding Bobcat Skidster complete with grab fork and rotary brushes, the lady in charge lost patience with us. Straining to see out from behind the vast crest of her crochet-covered bosom she declared that she didn't have any time for browsers. Within minutes I was writing a cheque for eighty-odd quid and Bee was taking two boilersuits and a dainty piece of kit called a Poop Scoop out to the car.

A Poop Scoop is a small black plastic pyramid with one of its sides cut out and a handle attached to its tip. Using the miniature fork provided with each scoop one is supposed to artfully flick bits of horseshit into the pyramid. The overalls are a great deal cooler. Purchased to protect our daywear from the grime of the horses, they are matching royal blue all-in-ones with red piping and water-resistant strips sewn down the front of the legs. Even though the crotch on mine skims my kneecaps I'm fairly sure I've got a hip astronaut-meets-*Italian-Job*-getaway-driver look about me.

Back at the ranch all that talk about gags and Dr Bristols seemed to have done the trick with Norm and Ari. Despite being frightened by the rustling of the astrosuits when we went to catch them, they trotted very contritely around some apple orchards. Mr Yarwood doesn't think we should leave it there though. There is a hunter trial being held on Saturday near Leominster, a sort of obstacle course of natural jumps designed to help horses and riders prepare for the hunting season, which he thinks we should enter. Waving casually to a straggly blackthorn hedge patched with high rails that forms the boundary between his furthest fields, he said it had produced a couple of broken arms and a dislocated shoulder the last time the hunt had crossed the farm but that we were welcome to practise our horses over it whenever we felt like it.

Once he had retreated inside for a sundowner, we crept out for a closer look at the hedge. I think it's safe to say that we're never going to feel like it. The main bulk of the branches were chest height with longer spikes growing up over our heads, and although the rails were lower they exposed a dyke on the landing side that was otherwise camouflaged by undergrowth. Standing either side of the hedge we couldn't even touch fingers across the thinner sections of greenery. Jeepers. And this was only the warm-up.

We just stood there, faith in The Plan dribbling away into the ditch at our feet, shivering in spite of the balmy summer evening. What would be the point in dressing up in seductive hunting clothes only to be laid out for our wakes in them? Bee kept repeating over and over again, 'But Ari's only jumped a milk crate. She can't manage more than a milk crate. She'll never get over that even with a Pelham in her mouth. She's only jumped a milk crate . . .'

Then she went inside and did something really drastic. She rang up odious Daniel.

The news that he is alive and well and showing no obvious signs of remorse was not well received. Such a deep sulk settled over the Cot we didn't even have the energy to change channels when *I'm A Celebrity . . . Get Me Out Of Here* came on the telly. Bee was beginning to make a number of dejected parallels with her own situation of the 'I'm An Attractive Amusing Young Woman Who Made a Grievous Mistake . . . Get Me Out Of Here' variety when a coffee-coloured Rolls-Royce drew up outside. It was my great friend Antonia, who had driven over from Stroud to see how we were settling in.

There are a number of remarkable things about Antonia. First, she is the only person I can think of who doesn't look a prat at the wheel of a Rolls-Royce. Second, her bosoms are so big and her legs so thin it defies the laws of physics that she can stand upright unaided rather than reclining on a billboard in the Hollywood Hills *circa* 1932 like every other dream girl of her dimensions. Third, she knows us and she knows foxhounds. This girl's grandmother died on the hunting field so it was not surprising that she spotted our mistake immediately.

According to Antonia, the best way to feel brave about jumping hedges is never to approach them on foot or in cold blood. She assured us that everything looks much smaller from the top of a horse that is galloping flat out. Generous helpings of drink heat the blood but, she said, nothing gives courage like the cry of the hounds, the wind whipping in your face and the knowledge that if the dozen other riders going full tilt at whatever you're frightened of clear it and you don't, you won't be able to sleep at night for rage.

Hmmm. Personally I can't imagine feeling anything at the end of a day's hunting except relief at still being able to breathe without assistance.

FRIDAY 6 SEPTEMBER
THE COT

Horrific visions of what could befall us when we have to put our riding skills to the test over hedges may punctuate our dreams at night, but the pace of our days is dipping into a deep lethargy that I've only previously experienced after four helpings of Christmas turkey.

On Mr Yarwood's advice we're keeping the horses in their stables at night to stop them eating so much grass and giving them a portion of something called coarse mix for breakfast that looks like muesli and is meant to help turn their flab into muscle. The down side of this new regime is that we can no longer lounge in bed summoning up the strength to go shopping on their behalf but instead must heave ourselves into the yard by eight o'clock each morning to feed the horses and muck them out.

Hunched over our shit-filled Poop Scoop, trying to distract ourselves from the stomach-turning thought that Mr Yarwood does this bit with his bare hands, we ruminate all the while about the injustice of there not being a cellulite-busting breakfast cereal on the market for humans. We then trot Norm and Ari round the local lanes and orchards, shielding our eyes from any particularly enormous hedges we come across and poking our noses up driveways that look as though they might lead to a neighbouring barley barony.

All our chores for the day thus achieved by ten o'clock, we retreat inside to inspect our bottoms for signs of subsidence. Hanging up the tape measure, relieved that so far there hasn't been a change for the worse, we have breakfast. Then, moving on to the sofas to speculate about the day we'll get around to emptying the stack of twenty-two cardboard boxes that lines two walls of the Cot and blots out one of its downstairs windows, we make a start on the serious business of doing nothing very much. Not that we're bored. Plotting yet another grisly demise for Odious Daniel forms a daily digestif for the first half an hour after our bacon and eggs before we set the world, or at least those bits of it that pertain to all the boys we ever kissed and the majority of our blood relatives, to rights.

All this idle talk is a high-risk strategy. For as long as we've busied ourselves exchanging gobbets of gossip and making pronouncements about everyone we know we've got on brilliantly. But we're only seven days into a long winter and I'm already running short on ticklish material to feed Bee. My worry is that before long we're going to find ourselves with no one else left to chew over and each begin concentrating our mind on the other's hundreds of irritating habits and opinions. That alone would probably be fairly explosive in a place as small and remote as this. But now that we've swapped so many secrets and unkind words, if we do fall out and start repeating what we've heard to other interested parties, our mutual destruction is assured.

Anxious to conserve the amicable man-hours we have left, I ducked out of our daily grocery run to the garage on the main road and ended up wandering about outside wondering what a proper country person would do to pass the time on a Friday morning in September. There are no cows to milk or orphaned lambs to feed around here. The corn has been gathered in and I don't have a tractor to help with the ploughing. I was just debating whether to join the local branch of the WI when I noticed the brambles growing alongside the muckheap. They were festooned in blackberries. Perfect. I would pick the berries in the name of self-sufficiency and pickle them ready for the rainy season.

By the time Bee returned with some elderly sausage rolls for lunch, I was truffling about like a pro – decked out in what I hoped was a timelessly elegant blackberrying outfit of dungarees accessorised with a spotted handkerchief tied round my neck. She got out of the car and stood watching me from a safe distance.

'Gross,' she said after about five minutes. 'They're growing in horseshit, Mol.'

'It's only fertiliser,' I replied heartily. 'Honestly, they're delicious,' I added, popping a blackberry into my mouth and crunching on something that felt ominously like a maggot.

Looking at me as though I had just butchered my own pet pig

for breakfast, Bee said, 'They're bound to have bugs in them. Why don't you leave it at that and come inside for a glass of Ribena instead?'

She eventually agreed to help with the blackberry harvest on condition that she didn't have to touch any actual blackberries. Reading from *One is Fun,* a cookbook geared at lonely spinsters that my mother picked out for my last birthday, we discovered that blackberry jam is an absolute cinch to make. Apparently all we needed to do was boil the berries up for hours, scoop off any debris floating on top of the mixture and add sugar to taste. We duly filled up every saucepan in the place with blackberries, and, as the room filled with a delicious smell of stewing fruit, sat back and imagined ourselves sweeping to jam-making victory at every village fête for miles around.

By bedtime the entire Cot smelled like a fruit pastille factory but Bee, worried that six hours on the boil wasn't enough to kill off listeria and the host of other bacteria she is convinced riddle all foodstuffs that don't come swaddled in supermarket cellophane, suggested we let two of the biggest vats simmer through the night.

SATURDAY 7 SEPTEMBER
UPPER WALL END FARM, MONKLAND

She is now lying on her back outside the refreshments tent making an odd fizzing noise, the result of a marathon of heavy drinking. My guess is that she's trying to forget the horrible state she has got our kitchen into.

The good news is that while it won't be winning any prizes this year, we can rest easy that our jam is free of bacteria. Thanks to

Bee's cooking recommendations it has reached temperatures at which no organisms can survive. The bad news is that we came downstairs this morning to a scene out of a science-fiction movie in which blackberries achieve nuclear fusion. Either that or during the night a few pints of toxic black gloop somehow spurted out of the earth's molten core, coating the cooker, singeing patches of the carpet and melting the plastic kitchen worktops with a mixture that would have damp-proofed the roof at Cathedine brilliantly. The two simmering saucepans of blackberry jam had burnt away to nothing, leaving only a sticky black coating on the ceiling and thick sugary fumes in the air.

Deciding that the blackberry lava and our tempers needed time to cool, we drew the curtains to shield our culinary efforts from the Yarwoods and set off for the hunter trial. By the time we arrived there Bee had already drunk so much of a local brew called Black Fox in preparation for tackling the course that her blood began to overheat while we were still walking around the fields memorising which jumps we had to do.

I put her falling off Arian when she faltered at the fourth fence, a small row of tyres with a plank on top of them, down to too much cider, but she insisted the problem was that she hadn't had quite enough and set off on foot for the black-and-white timbered village a few fields away in search of a top-up. When she started her second attempt at the novice course her courage was at an all-time high but her ability to steer seemed impaired. They got over the tyres this time but after taking the wrong route over some straw bales Bee came what the commentator gleefully called 'out of the side door' on top of a wide log when Ari refused to jump over it into a stream and she catapulted drunkenly over the mare's left shoulder. Unable to remount for laughing, she was told to clear the course and retire from the competition.

Having to untack Ari and attempt to sober up Bee meant that I missed my chance to try the novice course and had to take Norman in the open class instead. The open course was made up of twenty fences set over three miles of galloping. Among its horrors was a stiff brush steeplechase fence, a pen which you jumped into and could only get out of by leaping over a full-sized picnic table, a pair of rails with a ditch between them called a Coffin and, most terrifying of all, a high black telegraph pole set diagonally across a gaping ditch.

My terror increased considerably when I bumped into William Black by the practice jump. As Norman frolicked about, sauntering sideways and bounding forward every time another horse cantered past him William smiled grimly and asked how much disciplined work he had been getting recently. Another intimidating factor was my fellow competitors. The novice class had been dominated by nervous-looking middle-aged ladies all on enormous horses. Yet now the jumps had reached a size where one could really do oneself a damage on them the only riders I could see warming up for the course were plucky twelve- and thirteen-year-old kids on nippy little ponies. Each child was wearing a foam back protector under-neath a brightly coloured rugby shirt coordinated to match the bandages on its pony's legs and was trailed by an extensive entourage. Ordinarily the support team comprised a mother wearing waterproof trousers and a harassed expression born of already worrying about how on earth she was going to reverse the Discovery and trailer out of the car park, a bevy of whingeing younger siblings, a sweaty picnic and a Labrador on a lead.

Waiting at the start I could well have wet my knickers and not known it. Every bone in my body ached in anticipation of the crashing fall that was coming. Eyes tight shut I somehow made it over the first fence. As I tried to steer him away from the other horses Norm shook his head crossly and cantered crabwise but hopped over the second happily enough. Then as we left the first field behind us he clicked on to autopilot. With the exception of an alarming habit of twisting his neck round to look at me every minute or so and neighing loudly to Arian waiting back at the lorry, he took over entirely. He never rushed but he never faltered, bunching up carefully so as not to fall into the Coffin, giving a mighty bound over the big ditch and all with no help from me. By the time I was coming up to the picnic table I could hear the commentator congratulating me on how balanced he was, despite the fact I hadn't done anything to assist him at all except keep still and steer as the broad brown shoulders beneath me lolloped along gliding over the jumps and furlongs. It was meat and drink to him – just as Barry Joyce had promised.

I've tried to explain to Bee the feelings of elation and gratitude to Norm that my clear round inspired but she and Black Fox are still in a euphoric stupor all their own. Lying prone in her black body protector and crash hat she looks like an upturned and increasingly drowsy beetle.

SUNDAY 8 SEPTEMBER
THE COT

Feeling like Shackleton giving the *Endurance* a final lick of paint before setting out across the pack ice, I'm sitting in the non-blackberried end of the Cot cleaning my tack and feeling like Shackleton giving the *Endurance* a final lick of paint before setting out towards the pack ice. Tomorrow we are going to make our hunting debuts at Eggs Tump. The fact that we won't actually be hunting proper yet but autumn hunting or cubbing, which I read is a slower version of the real thing done to teach young hounds what to do and disperse any fox cubs that are still living in litters with their families, hasn't pacified the increasing turmoil in my bowels. Why on earth should it? When you've got the South Pole in your sights not having to wear your extra-pointy hard-core crampons for a month or so doesn't do much to dissipate your fears.

One comfort is that we'll be able to wear part of our sexy hunting outfits. After many hours in front of the mirror I've settled on some mushroom-coloured poplin breeches, a blue-spotted stock (an elaborate scarf held in place with a pin and supposed to stop your neck snapping when you fall on it) and a lovely pair of long black leather riding boots I was given as an eighteenth birthday present. Miraculously all concerns over the texture of my bottom were eased the moment I put my boots on. Somehow they make my legs look very long and slender and even the width of my hips no longer seems quite so gross. I practically want to pinch my own bum in appreciation when I see myself in them. Better still, Nell nicked Bee's boots long ago and her replacement pair are still being made so she's having to wear some less flattering suede gaiters over her jodhpurs.

Alas, she does have the advantage over me in the hacking jacket department though. For cubbing everyone but the pink-coated huntsman and his team in charge of the hounds wears tweed jackets. Bee cleverly managed to unearth a lovely old one with a minute tailored waist from the dressing-up box at home, leaving me to send off my vital statistics to an equestrian mail order company. The made-to-measure jacket that subsequently arrived in the post couldn't have looked less like the garments in the brochure modelled by doe-eyed blondes leaning over stable doors. It would fit John Prescott a treat. The arms are curiously short but the worryingly shiny torso is a perfect square. It's at least five inches too wide across the shoulders and it doesn't have even the whiff of a waist. With the buttons done up I look like I'm wearing a wattle-and-daub sandwich board.

I was busy trying to ease myself into Bee's corset-like coat when she returned from grooming the horses and sent me outside in mine claiming that if I scoured it against the stable wall it would scuff up nicely. I reappeared a few minutes later with my jacket unscathed but my face crimson after being caught rubbing myself up against the back of the hay barn by a man delivering sawdust.

MONDAY 9 SEPTEMBER
THE COT

It's called the crack of dawn for a reason. The alarm went off at 5.20 this morning just as a single chink of light spilt out from a gap in the doors to the heavens, sounding an end to a sleepless seven hours. I had whiled away much of the night studying a book by Anne Holland written specifically to help and encourage newcomers to hunting. The early chapters, given over to describing how all across Britain complete strangers arrive at meets and are quickly enveloped by the warm social atmosphere, were very comforting. But it soon degenerated into pages of action photographs of riders 'making mistakes', i.e. smashing themselves up at jumps, and tales of her father clouting his nose when he fell off at a gate only to be asked by a concerned field master if he'd broken it – the gate that was.

I lay in bed feeling sick from nerves listening to Bee in the bathroom actually being sick from nerves and then hurried out to wake up Norm. He was lying down sound asleep but I shone a torch into his eyes until he got up and I was able to bags him. My thinking was that if things go pear-shaped today my only solace might be looking less foolish than Bee, and given his hunter-trialling performance Norman probably holds out the best hope of preserving my dignity. Unfortunately Bee had the same instinct and when she arrived at the stables an ugly row ensued over whether by tacking him up I had legally reserved Norm. I won it.

Soon after six o'clock we arrived at Eggs Tump, which turned out to be a run-down semi-detached brick house flanked by a pristine yard of stables and outhouses set in gently rolling grassland that abruptly shelves away to accommodate the M50. Sitting in the cab of the lorry listening to the howling from the hunt kennels pierce the chilly morning air and watching as a handful of efficient-looking riders unloaded their horses we admitted to each other that we wanted to go home. It all looked very different from the drinks party we'd seen in *Baily's* – the same people sipping shandy in floral dresses then were now geared up to slaughter things before they'd even had breakfast.

Over the summer I had rung the Hunt Secretary, a very friendly sounding lady called Sally Evans, and asked whether her organisation tolerated cretins. She had assured me that no matter how cretinous we proved on the hunting field, if we became full subscribers to the Ledbury at a cost of a little over £730 each for the season we would be welcomed with open arms. We had bought the horses, rented the cottage, paid up and made loud noises about a fresh start; but the sense of acute but unfathomable danger that clung to the still dawn mist around us was so strong that we fell into what Somerville and Ross describe in their Irish hunting tales as 'a blue funk'. Cowards that we are, we climbed into the back of the lorry, emptied our bladders noisily on its aluminium floor and made a pact that at the first sign of trouble we would forget living the dream, run away from Eggs Tump and never come back.

Shaking with nerves we unloaded the horses and swung into our saddles. When we joined the other riders I was conscious only of the fact that Norman's heart was beating so wildly his whole body was rocking back and forth as he stood goggling at the hounds. He felt as though at any minute he would explode with excitement. Arian, dammit, was a picture of calm and Bee was soon flicking her head towards a debonair man with touches of grey at his temples sitting completely relaxed aboard an ugly bay and mouthing, 'Borderline Peppermore?' at me. Not one to waste any time, when the whole cavalcade trotted along behind the hounds to a nearby coppice, she drew alongside him and, I kid you not, asked him if he came out often. Grinning, he introduced himself as Thomas Harvey and explained that yes, as a joint master of the Ledbury Hunt he did come out fairly often.

For the first hour or so we footled around some dairy farms, relieved that although Norman was putting in the odd buck his heart rate was declining and trying to work out what precisely we were supposed to do when Thomas told us to ride ahead or keep an eye on a particular hedgerow. Before we knew it he was asking us to 'stand point' at the edge of woods and we were nodding sagely and bluffing off in the general direction that he had indicated. The idea that we didn't look as totally clueless as we were, and that Norm and Ari were happy to copy what the other horses were doing made us feel much less feeble. Albeit we didn't have the faintest idea what was going on, but the sense of imminent danger I'd felt at the meet gradually faded away as we cantered about through the dewy grass of a landscape so neat and quiet it reminded me of the undulating green surround of a tabletop railway set when nobody is playing with the trains.

The biggest hazard we came across for hours was a flawlessly turned-out young woman who arrived late and furious after ordering somebody on a horse that was rearing and going crackers to take it home. She cantered along, a picture of elegance in long brown boots and a beautiful hacking jacket that fitted her perfectly, chuntering venomously about something or other being 'bloody ridiculous'. All of the other half-dozen riders out with us kept a respectful distance from her and when Bee and I bobbed alongside her grinning like Cheshire cats to try and introduce ourselves she curled her lip and rode off officiously to the far end of the stubble field we were crossing. Our subsequent attempts at conversation withered as she shrugged off each question with what seemed to us like a sneer or a scowl. We had just had our first encounter with Laura Wallace, head prefect meets Crown Princess of the Ledbury Hunt.

Cub hunting seemed pretty innocuous by comparison. The general drill was that the hounds were sent into a thicket, often followed by a pink-coater or two, while the rest of us formed a circle round it and shouted, 'Aye, aye, Charlie' like a team of lecherous builders eyeing up a particularly buxom piece of totty from their scaffolding. After twenty minutes or so the hounds would return into view and loll about panting in the long grass until we moved on to try our luck at the next covert. I stopped shouting once Bee had confirmed my fears that I was yelling 'Aigh, aigh, Charleigh' in such a high-pitched cut-glass accent that aigh maight have been the Queen. Bee refused to shout at Charlie at all until someone explained to her who he was.

We eventually worked it out when a large dog fox slunk out of a drainage pipe and a chatty radiologist standing alongside us on a grey horse raised the alarm. My first impression is that Charlie is as cunning as they say. Much smaller and slighter than I'd expected, with a lovely face but a coat less luxuriant than the fox furs one sees slung around women's shoulders in old movies, he looked more like a ginger cat than a dog. He moved surprisingly slowly and thoughtfully and rarely seemed in danger of getting caught. The pair of young foxes that later broke from a patch of brambles further down the hill exhibited faultless strategic thinking – seeming to know exactly who to run at, they scampered off to freedom right past Bee and me, who, in our surprise and excitement, could only manage a bit of waving and inarticulate squealing that nobody heard.

Luckily Mary Clarke, a kindly bespectacled milkmaid with a voice like Clarrie Grundy came galloping to the rescue. We were, she explained, trying to 'hold up' the various woods we visited, which meant trying to stop whatever foxes were inside from getting out. Later on in the season we'd let them run out into the open and give chase but for the moment we should try and steer any that made a break for the open back whence they came. If we saw Charlie sprint away we should screech, 'Holloa' or 'Gone away' as loudly as possible and point in the direction he had gone. If he ran back we should yell, 'Tally-ho back.' I'm very glad that hunting people do actually get to shout 'tally-ho' at some stage, but less glad that our first hunting friendship was jeopardised within minutes of its inception when Norman kicked Mary a glancing blow to the ankle as I slowed to pass through a gateway.

By nine o'clock we were trotting back to the kennels through a morning that was still amazingly quiet apart from the low groan of the motorway a few miles away. Passing children waiting at village greens for the school bus I felt like someone who had been out dancing all night, incredibly hungry and rather smug that I had the stamina to be going home just as the rest of the world was waking up. Yet as the master bizarrely bid us goodnight and we loaded up the horses to go home, I found that mingled with relief that I hadn't fallen off or been run away with was a flat grain of disappointment.

Cubbing is a wonderfully refreshing way to start the day. The outfits are a treat, apart from scary Laura the people seemed really friendly, and Norman and Ari hadn't disgraced themselves. But I had arrived expecting to be physically injured and morally offended and instead didn't really feel I'd been tested at all. The hounds, whose forebears were noted for having 'clean necks, beautiful shoulders, rich colouring, real fox-catching heads and legs more like a greyhound's below the knee', were undeniably handsome. But with their rather dim aristocratic expressions they looked like a bunch of public schoolboys flopping about in the junior common room rather than an elite killing force. Where was the outrage? Where was the blood?

TUESDAY 10 SEPTEMBER
THE COT

Some of the blood is in the scabs on the inside of my knees and the giant blister on Bee's arse. Crikey, my bum aches. If we are this knackered after a few hours of gentle rambling we're going to be completely done for when the fast stuff starts up.

Spotting us dragging our tired limbs around the yard, Jane, a sweet-natured financial analyst who keeps her horse in the stable next to Ari's, advised us to stop chasing foxes and save our powder for more elusive prey. Recently returned from her own honeymoon with a man she met when he bought a house across the village green from hers, she has taken on the role of our talent scout with relish, winkling out fresh male flesh in the neighbourhood like a half-starved bloodhound.

Today she directed us to a far-off hamlet to buy veal cutlets that she knows full well will be rendered inedible by our cooking. But the cutlets are irrelevant to the real purpose of our mission, which, she explained, is to admire the legs of the recently divorced butcher who sells them. He has thighs like Stefan Edberg's and a penchant for wearing short shorts in hot weather. Failing that, she thought it might be worth a drive through Pauntley to see a perfectly formed teenage farmhand haymaking with his shirt off. She's clearly going to be an invaluable consultant when our search for the barley baron starts in earnest.

WEDNESDAY 11 SEPTEMBER
THE COT

I'm impressed that so many of the farmers around here can summon the energy to operate their heavy machinery. Despite our efforts to entertain each other with unpleasant stories every day quickly degenerates into a losing battle to stay awake. Yesterday I caught Bee dozing in an armchair before we'd even had lunch. Fresh air is so incredibly soporific. When no one answers the Cot's phone after nine at night our friends assume we're out jamming with the local Morris-dancing troupe, little suspecting that we're either too comatose or too crippled to answer it.

Even the arrival of an envelope from Cathedine containing details of Archie, Cleo and Nell's school terms didn't impinge unduly on this afternoon's siesta. Bee is convinced it's some kind of oblique threat from Mum but we're too sleepy to decipher it.

THURSDAY 12 SEPTEMBER
THE COT

Things must be at a very low ebb in London. Orlando rang to tell us he'd been named by the *Daily Mail* as one of the top twenty most eligible bachelors in Britain but that despite his upgraded status he had no fish to fry in town and wanted to drive down to the Cot for supper.

When he said he'd be with us in time for drinks I didn't dare tell him that the closest we get to cocktail hour here is swilling back cider while we clean our tack in front of *EastEnders*. He was also unprepared for the standard of cuisine at the Cot. Frightened off trying to cook anything elaborate by the jam fiasco and tragically out of range of Abrakebabra, our nearest take-away joint, we shop mainly at the local garage and eat like people held hostage at a motorway service station. Apart from snacks of sweets and crisps it's fried breakfast all day, every day.

A worryingly horsey evening followed our dinner of poached eggs on a succulent bed of prawn cocktail crisps. Instead of filling us in on what we were missing in London, Orlando devised a high-stakes quiz with questions taken from *The Manual of Horsemanship*.

FRIDAY 13 SEPTEMBER
THE COT

I think he really means it about finding himself a nice country girl. He cranked himself out of bed at 5.30 this morning and came to the meet with us. Disappointingly for him, when we arrived the only other women in evidence were a group of car followers – a handful of plain-speaking elderly ladies who, along with their whiskery consorts, spend their early mornings trying simultaneously to knit, eat breakfast and keep an eye on the hounds from a fleet of beaten-up Vauxhall Astras and Nissan Sunnys. Undeterred, Orlando immediately started chatting them up and was soon being inundated with cups of tea and offers to meet their granddaughters in return for tickets to *Phantom of the Opera*. We left him trying to impress a couple of teenage girls wearing jodhpurs so tight they must have been sprayed on while their grannies measured him up for a hand-knitted woolly jumper.

Having won the scramble for Ari, I felt considerably more relaxed and able to enjoy the hunting scene today. As well as the small band of regulars we met last time there was a small girl on a Thelwell pony being towed by a rope from her mother on a bigger horse. The poor child was already sobbing and pleading to go home but was being barked at to 'stop that silly blubbing'. In whispers Bee and I renewed our pact to wimp out if either of us started feeling like her.

There was also Harold Morris, a genial bachelor known as the Galloping Headmaster, who manages to combine running Archie's prep school with an addiction to hunting that compels him to feed his habit at least two days a week. Harold won himself a friend for life when he called Norman a 'lovely type' and confessed to buying a succession of good horses from Barry Joyce. In fact, his praise for Norman went straight to my head and I spent a good deal of the morning lost in silent admiration for my horse as Bee rode ahead of me, convinced that he moves more smoothly, thinks more clearly and is far better looking than any of the rest. I was so busy admiring Norm's juicy backside and white-starred face in the small crowd of horses following Thomas Harvey that I didn't think twice about accepting when Harold suggested coming to watch Archie play in a football match next week.

But Norman was not the only talent out hunting. I can report confirmed sightings of Definite Peppermore Material. The first was Matt Heller, a tall, whippet-thin guy on a neurotic racehorse with a spectacular half-moon scar across his temple and his riding cap pulled low over a black eye tinged with magenta. Despite being an amateur jockey he had an even profile and a heart-stoppingly naughty smile of pearly white teeth that seemed to be all his own. We're talking about the best kind of bad news there is. Imagine Vinnie Jones on a horse and you'll be somewhere near it. He eyed us appraisingly all morning but didn't speak until we were jumping some upright wooden pallets on our way home. I was still thanking God that Bee and I had cleared them without a hitch when in a meandering Gloucester drawl he offered us his services as a black-smith. It's going to be a struggle to stop ourselves wrenching a couple of shoes off the horses the moment we get back to the Cot in order to give us an excuse to ring him.

The other Peppermore possibility arrived late aboard the lunatic horse that Laura Wallace had ejected from Monday's meet. He was Mark Bennet, a scruffy young fireman who lives only for hunting and gossiping about hunting and is famous throughout the Ledbury country for riding unrideable horses in return for a free day out with the hounds. We ran into him along the airstrip of a biggish house set in the foothills of Eastnor, literally I'm afraid given that Bee's brakes on Norman had worn out some time before. Just before Norm collided with the back of his horse, Mark unclipped his crash hat and, turning in his saddle, swept it off with an exaggerated flourish to reveal a head of curly teddy-bear hair, inquiring, 'Molly and Annabel Watson, I presume?'

Alas, this gallant gesture was cut short when he was carted off into an ash grove. The smart crack to his forehead from a low-hanging branch that followed was enough to cure Mark of chivalry for the rest of the season. Returning to chat to us, he jabbed a finger at Bee and said, 'You've got to get yourself a hairnet,' before turning to me and saying, 'Bit scrawny, aren't you?'

These delightful preliminaries out of the way, he proceeded to tell us all about ourselves. Thanks to the local grapevine he already knew where we lived and how much we'd paid for our horses, and now he began to relate everything, printable and unprintable, about the hunt. He was in the middle of explaining an intricate Venn diagram of which able-bodied women residing in a ten-mile radius of the kennels the huntsman had seduced when great excitement broke out. A vixen had bolted out of an enclosure of saplings with ten or so hounds behind her baying at a much higher and faster pitch than I had heard before. She hurtled across a potato field on our right but was quickly out-sprinted by a strong black and tan hound who lunged at the back of her neck and killed her instantly.

As the huntsman whooped in delight and the following hounds shared in the congratulations I was surprised I didn't feel more – well, more something. The kill happened so quickly it seemed as though nothing more dramatic had occurred than a team of grey-hounds catching up with a fake hare on a racetrack. There was hardly any blood, I never saw a carcass being chewed up and after barely a minute of praising his hounds in an ancient sort of yodel-ling dog speak that Mark told us originated from the ancient French commands used by William the Conqueror's Norman wolf hunters, the huntsman calmly gathered them together and moved on to the next covert. I had expected to feel repelled at seeing anything killed at such close quarters but was left strangely unmoved. If David Attenborough had been doing the commentary I could easily have mistaken the scene for one of the less gory clips from a nature programme explaining the pack-hunting skills of dingoes.

SATURDAY 14 SEPTEMBER
A MARQUEE IN THE MIDDLE OF CUMBRIA

Christy is hitched! A gold wedding band now nestles next to that magnificent crop of diamonds on her nicotine-stained ring finger and she has put all memories of being usefully employed behind her. Good friend that she is, she picked me out of the bouquet line-out (not a massive feat of athleticism given that in my heels I stood at least three inches taller than the unmarried competition) and hurled her spray of lilies straight into my outstretched arms. But despite this fillip I didn't spend much time trawling the reception for Mr Smith substitutes. I found myself glued to my mobile phone, worrying like some anxious new mother about whether Bee was looking after Norman and Ari properly. I don't think she bothers checking their feet for stones when I'm not around.

IN THE PINK

The honeymoon is over. After just one week of following the Ledbury we've discovered that the hunt committee is in high dudgeon. They are arguing about the only thing that matters in the country, the only thing that has ever mattered in the country, be it to cowboys carving up the Wild West or West Country smallholders disputing a boundary fence. Land. I never took Pa O'Hara seriously when he told Katie Scarlett that land was 'the only thing worth living for, the only thing worth dying for', but the destiny of a few acres next to Eggs Tump has certainly caused an almighty scrap.

This is more like it. Today's meet at Forthampton was electric with the dispute about who owns the grassy slope that the effluent from the hunt kennels runs on to. As we held up a large uncut maize field you could hardly hear the hounds at work for the sound of bickering about the minutiae of land law concerning how many years a farmer had to harvest an unfenced piece of land before he became its de facto owner. After pointing out the spot forming on my chin and telling Bee her tack looked grubby, Mark Bennet told us that opinion on this varied between seven years, twelve years and infinity. From what I could gather the row had been triggered by the environment agency wanting a reed bed to be sown to absorb all the dog pee draining from the kennels but very soon that was forgotten as people used the occasion to pick at the scabs of other ancient grudges.

We encountered grown men who won't speak to their neighbours because of a disagreement their long-dead fathers had over a winter grass lease. Equally there are individuals with opposing views on virtually every hunt matter you care to raise who remain firm friends because one of them lent the other's nephew a donkey for a while in 1962. In many cases people have forgotten exactly what they fell out about, remembering only never to forgive. We were treated to a ringside seat for a fresh bout of bloodletting as we passed Mark Bennet's father Duncan, a smiley hunt stalwart more Pepperpot than Peppermore in shape, who expertly guesses which way the hounds will be headed by watching them from his car. We have already learnt to recognise that the Field Master has led us to the right spot when we see Mr Bennet already parked there, giant hunting whip in hand and the next gate open for us to canter through. Today we came across him and Matt Heller the blacksmith having a shouting match that I couldn't quite follow about terriers and what each had said behind the other's back. It ended with Matt delivering the immortal line, 'I know my name might be oik with the Ledbury Hunt but I'm still judging a national terrier competition.'

Although we killed one fox, we passed two of his cousins lying squashed by the side of the main road and a third sunning herself in the tall grass where we parked the lorry. But what the day lacked in sport it more than made up for in scandal-mongering. We ended up pumping Matt Heller for gossip across a nasty barbed-wire fence that he had jumped but we didn't dare to. Hang duelling. By the sounds of it all they need round here is oil and they'd give the Ewings of Dallas a run for their money. We put the wildest rumours we'd heard about the Ledbury to Matt who looked bored they were such old news. Affairs, lesbian action and people being stabbed in their beds by their jealous lover's jealous lover are just what happens when this crowd get off their horses. By day a healthy section of the Ledbury's members have a reputation for riding for their lives in the hope that it's not their turn to be carted off in the air ambulance. By night they're making Jilly Cooper's *Riders* sound like a nursery rhyme.

TUESDAY 17 SEPTEMBER
THE COT

We waited in all day for someone to drop by and molest us but not a dickie bird.

WEDNESDAY 18 SEPTEMBER
THE COT

Still waiting.

By mid-afternoon we gave up and headed off to see Archie's football match. I don't know which was worse; watching poor half-starved Arch getting tackled by a Chinese day boy from a rival school who was twice his weight thanks to a diet of home-cooked chow mein, or the attitude of some of the matrons when I followed him upstairs with a cache of biscuits to hide under his bed. They were charm personified to Bee, but I encountered crossing and uncrossing of arms and 'about time too'-type sighing. If I didn't know better I'd wonder whether they were under the misapprehension that Archie is in fact my unacknowledged son and that my mother, alias his grandmother, kind soul that she is, passes him off as her own to make up for my deadbeat performance as a single mother.

September

THURSDAY 19 SEPTEMBER
THE SOFA, THE COT

At last!

The Ecstasy: Matt Heller is in the yard right now looking sensational. It's the first chilly day we've had but he's wearing a black wife-beater singlet teamed up with a pair of devilishly tight black jeans. Even with his farrier's apron on he looks like an understudy to Patrick Swayze in *Dirty Dancing*.

The Agony: I can't get anywhere near him. I'm nursing a severely swollen foot after Norman and I had a disagreement this morning about whether he was going to canter around Mr Yarwood's dressage arena and he bucked, slipped and then keeled over on to his side squishing my left leg underneath him. This means I am marooned on the sofa with a bag of frozen peas swaddled round my ankle, resigned to watching Matt through the window. Bee keeps going out to him with cups of tea and accidentally-on-purpose tousled bedroom hair. She's making progress too. When she came inside to fetch him a biscuit and suggest I might want to find the binoculars in order to get maximum enjoyment from the ripple of muscle along his tanned ribcage, I could swear I saw Matt reach into the glove box of his jeep and surreptitiously splash on some aftershave. By the time he had shod both horses Bee was referring to him as The Hellraiser, he had offered to cook her dinner and I had dragged the curtains closed to spare myself the sight of them billing and cooing.

At least I can stop wondering about my frosty reception from Archie's matrons. A letter came today from Cleo's school asking me as her guardian to give my permission and £37.80 for her to go on an art trip to Stratford. Game, set and match to the old woman in the shoe. Manoeuvring us into spending the winter in loco parentis is a stroke of genius on Mum's part. Normal relations have been resumed in acknowledgment of her victory and she rang as I was limping to bed, offering to swap me Norman for the pestilent Starry. Over my cabbaged body.

FRIDAY 20 SEPTEMBER
ACCIDENT AND EMERGENCY DEPARTMENT,
GLOUCESTER ROYAL HOSPITAL

My ankle turned into a black balloon during the night and the village doctor has sent me in here with a suspected broken foot.

The up side is that the crushed bone in question could be a metatarsal and I quite fancy the idea of racing to get it healed in time for the Opening Meet like Becks striving to regain fitness in time for the World Cup. The down side is that I've already been waiting for an X-ray for five hours and if the prognosis is bad I could be in plaster for up to six weeks.

I'm not sure that I can survive six weeks with Bee as my nurse. Ever since I refused to drive us to the meet this morning because my foot was too swollen to fit into my boot let alone operate the clutch pedal of the lorry she has been blisteringly unsympathetic. Whenever I ask for help picking up a prescription or getting to the hospital she mutters, 'Fuss, fuss, fuss' under her breath. For the last few hours I've been stranded in the waiting room without food or drink because she's gone to a job interview for the post of deputy catering supervisor at Newent Primary School.

September

SATURDAY 21 SEPTEMBER
THE COT

Good moods all round. My foot is not broken but I'm high on the nectar of really strong painkillers and Bee is reaping the benefits of photosynthesis or vitamin D or whatever good stuff the sun does to you before it gives you cancer. Did I mention that it's been gloriously sunny nearly every day here? In three weeks we've had a couple of hours of gentle, sweet-smelling showers that I'd categorise as refreshment rather than rain, yet it is just chilly enough each evening to make the mornings feel fresh and kill off most flies and wasps. We're getting brown from messing around outside all the time. Norm is already brown but he still likes to spend a large part of his day sunbathing.

If what we've experienced so far is the countryside then I'm glad I'm going up to London to march for it tomorrow. Orlando says I can travel up tonight and stay at his place provided I lend him *The Manual of Horsemanship* so that next time he meets girls in jodhpurs he's got more to say.

SUNDAY 22 SEPTEMBER
BAYSWATER

I came round on Orlando's sofa. Conditioned to struggle out of bed and make a start on the mucking-out by 7.30 a.m., I then lay awake for hours trying to summon the strength to get my act together for the march.

Feeling seasick just from the motion of walking and with my swollen left ankle drooping over my shoe, I couldn't face waiting patiently for hours in Hyde Park to begin marching with Bee and the rest of the Ledbury crowd and instead crashed the march at the Ritz. It was hard going. For every gamekeeper and impoverished farmer hesitating at traffic intersections like wary hedgehogs, there were two wannabe landowners strutting down Piccadilly looking as though they had lain preserved in ice since their Sloane heyday in the mid 1980s. Instead of setting out in their everyday clothes, many ordinary townies sympathetic to the countryside cause had got rigged up in plum- or mustard-coloured cords, cashmere scarves and jerseys and spanking-new Barbours or tweed shooting jackets.

My bog-standard jeans, trainers and sweater looking street smart by comparison, I limped along like a teenager on holiday with her parents – strolling an aloof few steps behind them in the hope that casual observers would think me not really with and certainly not related to such ghastly people. I realise I can only throw smallish Sloaney stones myself. Let's face it – I use words like ghastly and my background is so woefully more green welly than ghetto fabulous that when my sister makes a plan it involves ponies and baronets. But the haw-hawing and shrieks of headscarves greeting trilbys in a mesh of jostling old school ties reached such a pitch as we shuffled past the clubs of St James's that I itched to ditch the whole thing and drag my ankle off to Soho for sushi and an art-house movie.

Two hours later I was still milling around in Parliament Square. Where was Bee? I wanted to go home but the fifty-strong gang I encountered from the Ledbury hadn't seen her all day and she wasn't answering her mobile. Eventually I gave up and drove back to the Cot alone to find Norman furious that his dinner wasn't in his stable on time and dear old Mr Yarwood recuperating from a day of Olympian irritation. Having set off for the march in his stately Mercedes, he instinctively headed for Harrods, only to be re-routed around the entire perimeter of London by a series of diversions and arrive home five hours later having completely circumnavigated the capital.

MONDAY 23 SEPTEMBER
THE COT

Bee has given me the slip. She never returned home from the march and her mobile is switched off.

It's another blazing sunny day but I am inside reading the *Daily Telegraph* from cover to cover. The Swan Inn in Staunton is holding a quiz tonight that costs £1 to enter and has a jackpot of £198 with the big money decided by a question taken from today's *Telegraph*. I massively fancy my chances. Armed with an Oxbridge degree and a career in newspapers that included spending the best part of a year dossing about on the payroll of the *Telegraph*, I've a sneaking suspicion that the village wonks are going to be severely outclassed.

TUESDAY 24 SEPTEMBER
THE COT

One pound ventured, nothing gained. I flunked out horribly at the quiz after arriving badly flustered from mistakenly going to the pub next door. A deathly hush fell over the room as I approached the bar and ordered a vodka and tonic as my sort always do, my crisp pronunciation ringing around a room filled with mangy youths loitering around a geriatric pool table and a few broken arcade games. I may well owe my life, or at least my kneecaps, to the landlord, who said he expected I was looking for the quiz one door down and escorted me out past the toughs.

After two hours of brainstorming at The Swan a retired mechanic won the jackpot by explaining in minute detail the exact coalition of parties that had enabled Bavarian Edmund Stoiber to make the German elections such a close-run thing.

WEDNESDAY 25 SEPTEMBER
TITHE BARN, ASHLEWORTH

That wretch Bee has definitely skipped the country. There is now a long continental ringing tone on her mobile and she never picks up.

No matter. I have drawn up an aide-memoire of all the sensitive information she revealed during the bonding sessions of our first week at the Cot and spent a happy morning setting out with the hounds from Stonebow Farm, a collection of huge barns standing on the flood plain of the River Severn. I quickly learnt to pipe down about my hurt ankle once I realised that to the hunting crowd anything short of a ruptured spleen is pretty small potatoes. Anthony the whipper-in, whose job is to be the huntsman's right-hand man, was full of pills but nevertheless in the saddle less than a week after twisting his knee out of its socket. I was also out-injured by Barry Joyce who appeared aboard a feisty young bay with a pair of leather chaps protecting a shin fractured from being stamped on by a horse that got entangled in a jump.

Barry rides so beautifully he could outshine William Black in the effortlessness stakes. Norman, realising he was in the presence of his old master, went up and rather sweetly snuffled the sole of Barry's jodhpur boot and got his ears tousled in reply. Barry still couldn't make much headway with his name though – which is hardly surprising given that he seems to specialise in juicy big bays with slender plucked tails and black manes.

For as long as he was in Barry's sight, Norm behaved like a model citizen – standing stock still while I held Anthony's horse and staying calm when a herd of cows rushed at him. But once the boss departed he started upping the ante, tearing too fast across a ploughed field and doing a lot of neighing when there was a call for hush while we listened for a shout from the far side of a spinney. He redeemed himself entirely though when everyone was being squeamish about following Thomas Harvey over a crooked iron gate leading down to the river.

Ignoring the chat about how dangerous it was, Norm trotted up and pinged over. Barry had taught him well. One second I was staring dumbly at the top bar, the next it was a blur beneath me and I was cantering away feeling supercool. Alas, the reception committee on the landing side were less impressed than I'd expected. I was roundly scolded by Mark Bennet for jumping in front of Anthony the Whip, cutting off someone else making their final approach at the gate and nearly flattening a hound in the process. But I wasn't listening. For the first time in my life I had jumped a five-bar gate, an iron one no less, and all the castigation in the world couldn't change that.

When everyone got engrossed in sending terriers down a narrow pipe to eject a fox that was hiding there I retreated to the shade by the tithe barn to relive my gate a few more hundred times. Wherever Bee is lurking she can't be having as good a morning as me. The sun has got his hat on, a triumphant Norm is feasting on the spoils of the deep grass outside the lych gate . . . oh, and did I tell you about the socking great iron gate I jumped with twenty-odd people watching?

THURSDAY 26 SEPTEMBER
THE COT

The sum total of my achievements today was to sharpen the end of a bamboo stick into a delicate point to stab at the telly when I want to change channels. Ray Mears eat your heart out.

FRIDAY 27 SEPTEMBER
THE COT

It's taken a month but I've finally been swept into the orbit of the centrifugal force at the core of the Ledbury Hunt – their huntsman, Jack Nightingale. A man with a job description so archaic and politically incorrect that it is hard to believe he can exist outside the musty pages of a grand nineteenth-century sporting estate's game records, far less be in his early thirties and ride a motorbike in his spare time.

In a world of secretaries masquerading as administration assistants and dustmen rebranded as sanitation consultants, Jack is bluntly referred to as a servant and obliged to call the masters and other high rollers of the hunt 'sir' or 'ma'am'. I've never seen him actually tug his forelock but the subservience he's expected to show towards his employers would astonish the most junior of office gofers. Despite being a trained professional paid by amateurs to hunt the hounds, he is basically not allowed to disagree with the masters about anything. Except for a free cottage and meagre salary, he derives a sizeable part of his income from tips and favours earned from chores as varied as clearing up after the foot and mouth cull and blowing his horn at old ladies' birthday parties. On days when he's not hunting or preparing for hunting, Jack spends his time shooting ailing cows and skinning dead animals to feed to the hounds. Before long the European Court of Human Rights will no doubt draft legislation to save him from himself and the time warp he occupies so happily.

But the flip side of all this servility is that as the man in sole charge of the hounds and the actual hunting itself, in my view Jack is unofficially the most knowledgeable and important person in the Ledbury Hunt. Helped by a cast-iron ego, a quick sense of humour and an appetite for women so fearless that his current squeeze is Laura Wallace, he has exploited his situation masterfully. He is part ringmaster, part Jeeves. Most men in the hunt crave his genuine respect and many of the ladies hope to earn his occasional attention. We've been naturally curious to assess the Peppermore potential of the subject of so much talk for ourselves but thus far Jack has remained a distant figure. My only attempt to introduce myself to him was not a success.

Riding up to him during what I thought was a pause in proceedings one morning, I ventured, 'Hi, we haven't met. I'm . . .'

But I was cut off when he started growling at some undergrowth ahead of us and making strange cheeping sounds.

I tried again. 'I'm Molly Watson. I just wanted to introduce myself.'

He glanced briefly in my direction but responded in dog talk,

113

yodelling, 'Yip, yup, yup, yup,' over and over again until a stray hound emerged from the brambles.

'I've just moved here with my sister . . .'

But I couldn't finish this sentence either before another wayward dog distracted his attention. 'Burnish,' he shouted, his eyes scanning the fields and coverts beyond us. 'Burnish! Come on! Get back here.'

Mercifully the incident ended swiftly when he sent the pack on into the wood and trotted away chirruping encouragingly to his hounds, completely oblivious to my 'Nice to meet to you' shrivelling in the air behind his departing back.

This morning I got an unexpected second chance with Jack. As the hounds searched through a sweetcorn plantation near Murrell's End where the Leadon thickens to join the Severn at the southern tip of the Ledbury's territory, I stood engrossed in conversation with Henrietta Kiernan, an august matron from Castlemorton riding a retired event horse. Seeing a fox nip out of the crops, we both admired his pluck when he came into view again swimming across a fast-flowing stretch of the river a little way upstream, but, thinking ourselves miles away from the action, we carried on chatting about her son who had also escaped London and was looking for a job with a local estate agent. Barely a minute later the entire pack came screaming along the riverbank and threw themselves into the water in hot pursuit, closely followed by Anthony the Whip and Jack Nightingale shouting to each other about what was going on.

This was my moment. Smoothing my eyebrows and licking my lips I gathered Arian together and rode over to Jack.

'Hello,' I beamed, piping up helpfully. 'A fox just popped out of the sweetcorn and swam the river. He went in there, where the last of the dogs are crossing.'

For a few seconds Jack choked in silent horror as the word 'dogs' ricocheted over the barley stubble and rebounded mockingly off a low line of trees clinging to the brow of the hill behind us. Magpies cackled and other riders ducked and cringed as the echo of 'dog, og, og, og' reached their ears. I now know that hounds are hounds, never dogs, and that it's called maize, not sweetcorn.

But that's not all I know. In a loud and blisteringly eloquent bollocking superficially directed at Anthony but rightly intended for me and Mrs Kiernan, Jack beseeched the Almighty about just how effing and blindingly sodding stupid anyone would have to be not to head the fox and certainly the hounds away from the river or at least raise the alarm. With Anthony still in the role of bruised intermediary, the dressing-down got its second wind as Jack, his kindly young face now a constantly contorting damson splodge, yelled about the web of main roads on the other side of the river and there not being a bridge for miles.

I didn't stay to see the morning's mortifying denouement but I heard later from Mark Bennet that poor Anthony had been made to strip off and swim across the river to retrieve the hounds.

Forget oik, my name must be squelch in the Ledbury Hunt.

SATURDAY 28 SEPTEMBER
THE COT

And now it's ouch.

On cloudy days the nearest place around here with mobile phone reception is the bridle path that skirts the apple orchards.

Hoping to make contact with the outside world I hacked Norman up there this afternoon. But as I let him walk along while I stared at the keypad, Norm started to skip over the brambles and nettles bordering the path, then skip with twists, then twist with bucks. Just as '2 messages received' popped up on the screen I was jettisoned into a patch of thistles and he galloped off without a backward glance.

As he made a beeline for the main road with the innards of my handset crunched inside his right hind hoof Norm's life flashed before me. I was disconsolately making headway with his obituary ('Charismatic young bachelor's untimely death on A417 . . .', etc.) when he eventually reappeared, led by a young couple who had heard him galloping along the road and hurried out of their garden to catch him. I trotted home relieved that Norm's life was intact but dejected about the increasingly wretched state of my own.

MONDAY 30 SEPTEMBER
THE COT

Bee is back – and with Daniel's fingerprints all over her. I spy him in the empty doll-like expression on her face. I smell him on the Alitalia ticket stub found in a routine search of her handbag while she was out feeding the horses. That boy is on a mission. But he's not back in the ball game yet. To truly win her heart it sounds as though he's going to have to fight it out with a button.

Utterly laying waste to my attempts to feign lofty indifference about her presence on earth and her whereabouts for the last seven days in particular, Bee explained why buttons could give our life a purpose. She had heard a rumour on the Countryside March that you can spot the people at the inner sanctum of every hunt by the special buttons they wear. The really useful and respected followers in the field are awarded a set of buttons embossed with their hunt's crest or initials to replace the plain black ones most people wear.

Winning one's Hunt buttons makes getting hold of this year's must-have Prada sandals look like a shoo-in. Apparently it can take years of endeavour and countless applications of butter to the hunt committee members to earn those three little fasteners. But when we looked up the Ledbury in *Baily's* and saw that there were not just buttons with the initials LH stamped across them in elaborate gothic italics up for grabs but the chance of a choco-late velvet collar to go with them we knew we had to try. We don't have the first clue about hunting but Bee doesn't think we should let that put us off trying to snare ourselves some buttons.

Indeed, a promising fast track to learning about Hunt button heaven was to present itself at the farm within the hour in the form of Patrick Dickens, another master of the Ledbury and chief roué of this parish. Roué is probably selling Patrick a bit short actually. He's the closest thing the equestrian world has got to Hugh Hefner. Flirting with collecting his bus pass yet still about to take a woman half his age as his fourth wife, his conquests in the show ring and the bedroom are so legendary I don't know why I'm bothering to change his name to protect his identity.

In keeping with a man whose occupation is winning horse beauty contests Hef arrived to supervise this morning's cubbing in a horse lorry so luxurious I half expected Elizabeth Taylor to teeter down its steps looking for a film set. Instead a bay with a dimpled rump and a profile so perfect he made the rest of the horses look like mules tiptoed down the ramp and stood like a statue while Hef climbed on. When Mr Yarwood, hosting the sweep of the farm on Queenie, his huge black mare, introduced us to Hef I immediately understood how he has made a career of showing off. His tweed jacket could have been a tuxedo and in the pale dawn light it seemed as though a spotlight were following him as he scooped off his bowler hat to us. Although regrettably well over the Peppermore hill in energy levels, he had the easy manners that Jane Austen admires so much in her country squires.

After discovering that our speciality dish coincided with the hunting tradition of a fry-up to round off a morning's cubbing, we enticed Hef and the two whippers-in back to the Cot for breakfast. With the exception of Hef, our guests were surprisingly heavy going – partly because everyone was shy and partly because we didn't understand most of what they were talking about. Without our hats and whips and reins to occupy us none of us seemed to know what to do with our hands and it didn't help that the jam eruption had left us with only three plates and four mugs that weren't coated in blackberry gloop. Ken Unwin, a tenant farmer and the amateur whipper-in, gamely tried to engage us in a description of the hounds giving tongue along a heel line. But when I couldn't translate what he was saying and Bee completely failed to keep a straight face at the phrase giving tongue, we called a truce and sat in well-meaning silence shovelling in bacon and eggs.

7

October

TUESDAY 1 OCTOBER
THE COT

Bee is sitting at the kitchen table pinning down a copy of *Marie Claire* with one hand and sorrowfully fingering her invoice from the tack shop with the other. She says she feels like a bird of designer plumage attuned to migrating for the winter that's had its wings clipped and been told to hibernate in a mouldy old pile of last year's hemlines. I know what she means. With the leaves really beginning to fall, now is about the time when we would normally be having a glossy magazine fest before going out to transfer a large part of the new autumn/winter collections into our wardrobes. This year all our money is going on hideous hacking jackets, thermal underwear, string gloves and riding boots instead.

It's not the dramatic curtailment of our social life denoted by this change in spending patterns I lament so much as the beautiful clothes themselves. I feel actively homesick for the rush of

119

fanned heat and haughty sales assistants that used to greet me as I pushed open the glass doors of Bloomingdales. If I immerse my head deep in the unpacked daywear boxes and concentrate very hard I can sometimes pierce through the sweet and sour stink of glycerine saddle soap, hay, horsehair, sweat and molasses that pervades every inch of the Cot to detect a few evocative particles carrying the smell of impractical expensive clothes still clinging to the pretty fabrics inside. On a clear day Bee claims she can pick up the heady aroma of the Joseph store near South Ken tube station from the stack of her cotton trousers and silk shirts.

Unable to even window-shop for the stuff we'd really like to buy, we've begun to talk about clothes obsessively. So I was relieved to learn from Valentine Hopton, a dishy doctor I met out on Friday, that hunting has its label lovers too. Leicestershire and Savile Row tailors charge small fortunes for well-cut hunting coats and breeches, but he said that a cheaper and faster way to cut a dash is to purchase one of the old-fashioned riding hats that many of the hunt stalwarts wear.

These hats come from Patey – the same company who make caps for the coachmen of the Royal Household. In Dr Hopton's medical opinion they are little more than fantastically elegant, individually crafted, velvet-covered eggshells that despite costing around £300 do little to protect your cranium if you fall off. But, he pointed out, slipping on his own faded brown Patey, 'You can't put a price on vanity.'

I think it comes down to whether you are the kind of person who'd rather wear a beret or a cycling helmet to ride a bicycle. Given the miles I have tottered in murderous shoes I hardly think a few hard blows to the head will finish me off and so tend to favour a thin, wildly fashionable but woefully unsafe membrane that clings to my skull rather than an oversized modern hat that makes my head look like a giant mushroom. But Bee only has eyes for Hunt buttons and wants to stick with our ugly crash hats in order to concentrate all our efforts and resources on that campaign.

WEDNESDAY 2 OCTOBER
THE COT

Foxes killed: zero. Horses dead or injured: two.

This is the tally from an absolutely disastrous meet at the Playboy Mansion. The day was starting as usual with a few sharp words from Mark Bennet, this time criticising us for wearing the wrong sort of gloves, when the meaty chestnut gelding he was riding for a correspondingly fleshy local restaurateur reared right up on its hind legs. Five minutes later when it reared again and flipped over backwards Mark executed a perfect T.J. Hooker roll out from under its thrashing legs and led it off into a shed where it wobbled to the floor and died of a heart attack. After a mourning period that lasted for as long as it took him to get the dead beast's saddle off, he reappeared and stomped off to follow the hounds from the back seat of a Mini Metro.

We did have a jolly few minutes when a gelatinous old lady complete with curlers, housecoat and slippers wobbled out into her garden to scream her head off at Hef for letting the hounds on to her lawn. Beaming, he doffed his bowler, smoothed his sleek grey hair and, as her ranting climbed octave after invective-fuelled octave, raised a silvery eyebrow before leading us off at a canter into the misty dawn.

Little did we realise it, but this incident was actually to be the calm before the storm. As we crossed the next stubble field Hef slowed down suddenly and we all had to hit the brakes. In the mêlée of everyone careering into everyone else Norm suddenly squealed, hunched his shoulders in irritation and delivered an angled kung-fu kick that Eric Cantona would have been proud of to an expensive young thoroughbred. As blood started spurting from just below the horse's armpit, its rider – who was none other than Matt Heller – leapt off to inspect the wound and I launched into a torrent of abject apologies. But when Matt vaulted back on, his pert bottom wriggling its way into the saddle so delight-fully it would have lifted anyone's spirits, Bee and I assumed that was that and set off to catch up with the others.

How wrong we were. The first inkling I had that we were now caught up in a major diplomatic incident was when Mark Bennet rang up after lunch and didn't pass comment on my weight, hair-style or general turnout, asking instead if I needed a lift to deliver flowers to the injured horse's owner. Flowers! I didn't know who the owner was and anyway wasn't that a bit much considering that, unlike him, I hadn't killed an animal? Apparently not. From what Mark had heard I needed to launch an immediate damage limitation initiative. I learnt that all the time I was saying sorry I should have been walloping Norm for bad behaviour, to be specific Mark recommended 'three mighty whacks – no more, no less'. Worse still, I had then continued on my way instead of taking Norman off for an early bath of shame. It was imperative that I ring Henrietta Kiernan, my collaborator on the riverbank last week, who, it emerged, owned the horse that got kicked, to see if Norman had inflicted any serious damage.

A permafrost has descended between Mrs Kiernan and me since

our balmy morning of ineptitude at Murrell's End. I called her just as she was preparing to cart her nag off to the vet with a suspected fractured forearm. Shaking off my sorries, she informed me I should tie a red ribbon in Norm's tail to warn people behind me that he is now 'a known kicker'. It seems a bit harsh considering today was the only time Norm has ever lashed out but I'm intrigued by the rules on this. If one really did have a habitual kicker what kind of a daredevil would risk fiddling around by its back legs tying bows in its tail?

THURSDAY 3 OCTOBER
THE COT

I've been scouring my hunting manuals and it sounds as if Norm's hunting career may be over before it has begun. Get a load of this from Michael Clayton, a former editor of *Horse & Hound*. In *The Chase*, a volume interspersed with treacly accolades to anyone who happens to share an interest in hounds with a mention in *Debrett's*, he writes:

> If your horse has a tendency to kick others do not think that putting a red or green ribbon on its tail absolves you from bothering to avoid your wretched animal lashing out. A horse which develops the kicking habit is a menace – and ultimately you may need a bullet rather than a whip to effect a permanent cure.

A wretched animal? Norm? I can't bear it. It's like hearing the child that I thought was so sweet has been expelled from playgroup for bullying. Even if he dodges the bullet but has to wear a red ribbon Norm will be treated as a social outcast, forced to trail along at the back of the field, and I could be legally liable for anyone else he kicks. It seems ironic that this morning he carried Bee gently through the woods along Foscombe Ridge when if he chose he could gallop her halfway to Swindon, but is considered a marked man among the hunting crowd. We can defend him this time but what if his malevolent rear hoof strikes again? The recriminations, the shame and in a worst-case scenario the legal bills would all be far more serious and we would be left unable to hunt the horse who inspired this whole project.

The horrible knot of anxiety in my gut keeps tightening as word spreads. We've hardly met anyone around here, yet barely twenty-four hours on Norman's efforts are the talk of the valley. When Bee and I happened across one of the regular car followers on our ride we found he had already been fully briefed about That Kick by a groom called Heather who I'd never heard of. According to the grapevine the incident is being compared to the court battle that blew up a few years ago between two women members of one of the Herefordshire hunts. One lady sued for £13,000 after the other's horse unexpectedly fly-bucked and broke her leg and the dispute is yet to be settled although both still brazen it out at Saturday meets.

I had envisioned my role in a tight-knit local community as being all about drawing up rotas for dusting the parish hall and swapping flapjack recipes – not overhearing in the tack shop that some farmer near Upton has been telling everyone that I should take Norman out and beat him until my arm hurts. Worse still, like a scandal finding fresh momentum, a second round of gossip about how worried I am is circulating, prompting Matt to call and try to cheer me up. I can imagine many things Matt Heller and his muscular buttocks could do to brighten my day but filling me in on hunting etiquette isn't one of them.

This is no kind of life. Bee has gone to London for a party in the latest phase of Operation Tease Daniel, obliging me to stay at home and horse-sit. I've taken the phone off the hook because right now a call from Mum or one of the other inmates of the Cathedine Academy of Equestrianism offering advice on dealing with kickers would be the final straw.

FRIDAY 4 OCTOBER
THE COT

I'm considerably less miserable after some kind mots from Mr Yarwood at the hay barn this morning. He pointed out:

(a) Money talks on the hunting field. I am a full subscriber to the Ledbury and Henrietta Kiernan is not. Therefore Norman would have to trot round to her house and strangle her as she slept before he was banned from the hunt.

(b) There is a good chance that lots of people will have mistaken me for Bee so half the blame is unwittingly on her shoulders anyway.

(c) I am a girl who survived office politics so well I was nicknamed Molliavelli. A year ago a journalistic furore ten times worse than this would have left me unruffled. I must realise that country people are just as keen on unkind gossip and intrigue as townies and brave it out.

(d) Hunt buttons are still only buttons.

SATURDAY 5 OCTOBER
THE COT

Nell and Cleo's school is only a twenty minute taxi journey away – something they demonstrated today by turning up uninvited and with a coven of friends in tow after neither of my parents appeared to drive them home for the weekend.

They were genuinely outraged when we refused to subsidise a shopping trip to a discount retail warehouse near Oxford. As Cleo put it rather too piquantly, 'You sad acts must be loaded. You've got a lorry and a telly and everything and you haven't even got proper jobs.' We eventually settled on returning them to the boarding house via the pasty bus, an old coach parked outside Painswick that serves the most delicious trucker's grub I've ever tasted. The sisterly abuse, the aggressive panhandling and the certain knowledge that they already think of us as curmudgeonly old maiden aunts was worth enduring in return for seeing twenty-odd lorry drivers sitting agog over their greasy spoons as our table of lissom teenagers in full school uniform regaled them with tales of puppy love played out around the back of Woolworth's.

MONDAY 7 OCTOBER
QUIT SMOKING CALL CENTRE

I felt the first nip of cold in the air yesterday and, despite my reputation as a unutterably sad but prosperous act, I met a similar froideur when I read my bank statement.

Paying for our new riding gear and hunt subscriptions has eaten through another chunk of the book advance and although my glamorous accomplice has hung up her Selfridges customer loyalty card for the winter, the horses are profligate spenders. Their palatial stables cost almost as much to rent as the Cot, they barely go a month without a new set of shoes costing £50 a time and, according to the chap in the tack shop, when it gets properly cold they'll need to wear duvets at night and two £120 made-to-measure fleece-lined waterproof overcoats *each* in order to go outside during the day. With no gentlemen farmers keen to marry us, Bee's dinner-ladying career yet to hit the big time and Norman wilfully ignoring our cries for family to hold back on the seed hay, we are searching for ways to afford to switch the central heating on.

To this end I've just spent the last five hours working as a telephonist in a Stop Smoking call centre while a sweaty South African called Jason stood over my shoulder checking that I was reciting the ungrammatical spiel from the laminated card glued to my desk without hesitation, deviation or repetition. Most calls started with the person at the other end of the line, invariably a Glaswegian pensioner, choking through a five-minute coughing fit and ended when I crashed the computer trying to input their details after cajoling them to spend £250 on an hour of hypnosis that is 'ninety-five per cent guaranteed' to replace their cravings for nicotine with a longing to drink more water. Part of the way through my patter one of my fellow telephonists usually told me I was shouting so loudly they couldn't hear themselves or their callers speak.

Bee is teacher's pet. At lunchtime while I sneaked out to buy my first pack of Marlboro Lights in three years to cope with the stress, Jason showed her how to encode credit card details. At the end of the afternoon we were called into his office. Bee was begged to accept a full-time post. I was told that 'Working here isn't an IQ test, Molly, but you're very slow,' before being reassured that they needed 'special' people like me to work round the back stuffing envelopes.

Back at the cottage and delirious with joy, Bee spent her first week's wages ringing round all our friends to relay the IQ comment.

TUESDAY 8 OCTOBER

THOMAS HARVEY'S DENTAL SURGERY, TEWKESBURY

I spent her second week's pay on having my teeth looked at.

Soon after we moved here they started aching when I brushed them and recently the pain has reached a level comparable to round-the-clock root canal work. Yet when I first sat in the dentist's chair I did wonder whether I might be better off living with the constant throbbing along my lower jaw than seeking treatment in this surgery. The nurse was taking a telephone message from a farmer about some calves that had broken through an electric fence and there were so many paintings of horses and dogs on the walls that I was fully prepared for James Herriot to march in at any moment and take care of my toothache with a pair of pliers and a rasp.

Almost as bizarrely Thomas Harvey appeared wearing a little white smock and asked me to open wide. I hadn't really considered what masters of foxhounds do all day but my vague ideas involved them surveying acres rather than incisors. Reading my thoughts Thomas made it clear that dentistry is strictly his day job. As he peered deep into my mouth he dictated the layout of my teeth to his nurse along with postcards asking local landowners for permission for the hounds to meet at their farms. Then, having established that my teeth are being eroded down to two rows of rotten sweetcorn by an excess of cider in my diet, he told me the story of his hunting career.

Jamming one of those little mirrors on to my tongue with hands still shaking from four hours of cubbing before he started work this morning, he jerked his head towards a pastel sketch of a heavy-built grey horse.

'See that grey gelding above the filing cabinet?' he said.

'Yargh.' I nodded and then stiffened in agony as I jarred a decaying molar against the side of whatever instrument he was examining my teeth with.

'That's Murphy. The first hunter I ever owned. He's a brilliant jumper but a brute in the stable. He bullies all the others.'

'Argh a hee . . .'

'Then there's Scooby.' He directed one of his stainless-steel probes to an oil of a pale chestnut horse standing in an orchard. 'He's a real master's horse because he's only happy in front. Very good with rails but he can be a bit careless about wire.'

'Argh . . .' By now a small slick of dribble was running down my chin but we had two more horses and the story of how Thomas learnt to ride to get through.

Turning on a loud soldering machine to patch a place where my gum had worn away he had to shout to make himself heard. 'My wife booked us both a riding lesson for my thirtieth birthday present,' he yelled. 'She quite liked it but I loved it and once I went hunting for the first time I was hooked for ever.'

'Argh garse ee's a 'unting 'idow,' I replied.

129

'What's that?' he asked, taking the last of his machinery out of my mouth and passing me a glass of pink water to swill out with.

'I said I guess she's a hunting widow.'

WEDNESDAY 9 OCTOBER
THE COT

Bee volunteered to ride Norm at today's meet at Town Street Farm near Tirley, our first since That Kick. As a concession to Henrietta Kiernan we tied a green ribbon around the top of his tail to signal that he's a green or inexperienced horse and I agreed to station Arian on his heels to shield the rest of the followers from any stray blows. But even with these precautionary measures in place I still felt conscious of a cloud of ignominy on my shoulders as we trotted up to bid Thomas Harvey good morning.

Luckily we soon ran into Barry Joyce. He had already heard all about Norm's kung-fu effort and had come out all guns downplaying. Despite the damage we must have inflicted on his excellent reputation, Barry fought our corner brilliantly for us, laughing off any suggestion that Norm was a kicker and teasing Mrs Kiernan that Matt only got 'a bit of a knock' because he was so transfixed by my legs (if only) that he wasn't watching where he was going. In a quiet moment he urged us to take the green ribbon off Norm's tail the moment something else happened to grab everyone's attention.

We didn't have to wait long. The hounds are beginning to run on a bit more now and after a fast spin over half a dozen sets of wide rails that Norm flew and Ari cat-leapt over in a panic, we were faced with a really horrible jump. It was a trappy old fence made from an abandoned bedstead crisscrossed with barbed wire and set downhill in the poky end of a rutted field at such a sharp angle that there was no room for error. We've learnt to tell when a jump is proving tricky by the presence of a dozen or so horses circling in front of it like seagulls swooping down on floating carrion. Riders dive-bomb at the obstacle in a frenzy of flapping arms and legs, only to swerve away from it, swearing and whipping their horses, before looping back round again to have another try.

When we arrived at this one carnage was already in full swing. In common with William Canning, a master of the Ledbury who threatened to resign from the hunt after discovering a single strand of wire in a fence in 1889, Bee is phobic about barbed wire. Drawing up close to the jagged latticework of it swathed over the rails she turned as green as the ribbon round Norman's tail and was whining manically that she wanted to go home when Mark Bennet drew alongside on a pot-bellied brown mare he was hoping to sell Christy when she joined us. After a quick summary of why Norman's martingale didn't fit properly he started giving out advice on how to get over the jump. He was still explaining where to aim for and what speed to take the fence at when Norm cut him off in mid-sentence, loped up to the bedstead and, ignoring the horses lunging up and veering away from it, soared over taking his petrified jockey with him just as Henrietta Kiernan was wimping out round the side. As she landed Bee was greeted by a shout from Barry Joyce so triumphant it must have woken half the village up, 'There now, girls! Sure it's meat and bloody well drink to him!'

Arian was much less keen and it took two more attempts and the sight of Norm's juicy haunches disappearing behind a clump of willows before she scrambled over. Breathless from adrenalin and relief, we waited on the far side for Mark who had gallantly said he would 'pop' his mare over the bedstead once he had seen me safely across it. We saw him rush up to the jump but then refuse a few times before he tried again at high speed. This time the mare deviously ducked out to the right at the last moment and flung him like a rag doll over her head on to the fence. The bedstead was smashed to bits by the force of his fall and with her jockey lying limp and panting across the pile of barbed wire and rotten timber like a beached starfish, the mare saw her chance and bolted for home.

THURSDAY 10 OCTOBER
THE COT

Today is Bee's twenty-fourth birthday. Daniel gave her a set of La Perla lingerie. I gave her a confidential survey of her bum and thighs to assess how much of her cellulite his underwear is going to expose. She's looking pretty good. All this riding has given us both rough bobbly skin where our legs join our saddleworn buttocks, but far from spreading, our backsides are getting more toned by the day.

I wish I could say the same for our conversational skills, which have become as flaccid as our bottoms used to be. Most of the time we co-exist in a silent but cosy stupor. Too sleepy and relaxed to argue, we occasionally rouse ourselves into long discussions on topics such as whether to strike out an extra ten miles beyond the BP garage to shop at Tesco in Gloucester and how best to stop Norman belting round Mr Yarwood's favourite field, neighing like a maniac and leaving six-foot skid marks in the turf, the moment we take Ari out of it. Sometimes we just sit here so still that I can hear my hair growing.

FRIDAY 11 OCTOBER
THE COT

And then the rains came.

After six weeks of baking heat the weather has broken. It's blowing a gale and absolutely tipping down. I can't get over the smell of the earth gulping down the rain and the way the yellowing oak leaves hold their faces out for more water. The apples in Mrs Yarwood's garden are literally hurling themselves off the branches. It feels like we're in Africa, with a farm at the foot of the Ngong Hills.

Untroubled by the thought that everyone I know in London would just be starting on the first leg of their plans for the biggest night of the week, I went to sleep at 9.30 p.m. lulled by the insistent splatter of rain on the skylight over my bedroom.

SATURDAY 12 OCTOBER
THE COT

The novelty is beginning to wear off but the weather hasn't eased all day. Whatever combination of clothes we wear, just running across the yard to check on the horses gives us the kind of storm-force drenching I've only seen longshoremen and Royal Navy destroyer captains endure from the bridge in films set on the North Atlantic. The inside of the cottage isn't much nicer. There's an unexplained stink of wet dog and soggy clothes everywhere and the humidity is so extreme that every room feels moist from a clammy fug that I've only ever seen achieved before inside hot cars on cold rainy days.

MONDAY 14 OCTOBER
THE COT

Bee has headed off to save the world from nicotine poisoning.

I am lying in my dank bed reading a letter informing me I have been rejected for a part-time job in a country house that has been converted into a secure unit for the mentally disturbed in Redmarley. They want someone with an excellent pin-down technique rather than a passing fancy to work in Edward Elgar's former home. Can't say fairer than that. I intend to spend the day sampling the central heating in here with *Escape from Alcatraz*.

TUESDAY 15 OCTOBER
THE COT

I'm moving on to *Where Eagles Dare* today. Quite frankly, on non-hunting days when the weather's bad there's bugger-all else to do but absorb character-building stuff to prepare me mentally for my next outing with the hounds and deal with the mountain of correspondence I now receive from Nell and Cleo's school berating me for not attending parents' evenings and the like. Thankfully Archie's progress is signalled by an occasional thumbs-up from the Galloping Headmaster when I canter past him out cubbing.

First thing in the morning I wake Bee up and haul my astro-suit on over my pyjamas before going out to feed the horses. Whenever I encounter Mr Yarwood we exchange wry remarks about our respective hers indoorses lying about in bed while we begin searching for piles of horseshit buried in the sawdust bedding of the stables without so much as a cup of tea to fuel us. I then rush our horses out to graze before they convert their breakfast into a fresh load of manure for me to shovel up, and get back inside to Bee who is normally still in bed and feigning sleep.

She's eventually tempted out by promises of honeycomb on toast but once her metabolism gets going she can be prone to start bellyaching about how much she detests the call centre with its mindlessly dull work and pathetic wages. That's when I step in with some chat about how many thousands of words I wrote yesterday and how incredibly draining writing can be.

Once she's safely headed for Malvern I whip off the astrosuit, set my alarm clock and get back under my duvet. At four p.m. I'm roused from a heavy snooze and spend a frantic twenty minutes assuming a suitable position for the worker's return. I normally rotate between fixing it for Bee to find me trotting one of the horses along the lane, pushing a wheelbarrow loaded high with buckets and soaking hay across the yard or hunched over the kitchen table, chewing my pencil in such a dense cloud of creativity that I don't notice her arrival.

WEDNESDAY 16 OCTOBER
THE COT

I am seriously considering re-naming Ari and Norm Broad Sword and Danny Boy. In the meantime I have satisfied myself with giving them very military haircuts. The best horse stylist for miles, a tiny smiley girl called Sue who was sufficiently ahead of the local fashion curve to arrive wearing her own blue boilersuit, called by after lunch and braved the rain to give them a full-body Grade ll shave. This is called clipping and meant to make them look smarter and able to dry off quickly so they won't catch cold from sweating in chilly weather. The drawback is that for the rest of the time when they aren't sweating we'll have to keep them warm with loads of rugs and blankets.

Like every hairdresser I have ever encountered Sue gets her thrills from cajoling her customers into drastically short styles. Norman got away with a classic hunter clip but she said that hogging Ari, that is shaving all her mane off, would accentuate the curve of her neck and make her look 'less common'. I don't know about common but Ari certainly looks much less healthy. Without her mane she now has the perpetually startled, youthful expression of a cancer patient in remission.

THURSDAY 17 OCTOBER
THE COT

This weather front should have a title, like that wind whose name I've forgotten that sweeps through northern Spain and maddens townsfolk to the point of suicide. It's been pissing down almost without pause for the best part of a week now and if it doesn't stop soon I really think I will go demented.

Dad must be halfway round the bend already. He drove up to the Cot at dusk in a leaky fourteen-seater 'Sunshine Bus' he'd borrowed from the Cathedine daycare centre to escort a party of German lawyers and their hausfraus around the Cotswold antiques trail. Parking the minibus where it was most likely to get swept away by the swollen rapids of the Leadon, he locked his sodden charges inside it and came in for a sharpener.

Apart from a few more of his sheep dying of liver fluke the scene at home seems little changed. Archie has won another scholarship at school and has been christened Clog for his cleverness. Mum is launching a new double-pronged sales push for vacuum cleaners and rape alarms and Cleo and Nell are in disgrace after they ran up huge bills on their mobile phones by texting each other from adjacent bedrooms at night. The crunch came when Cleo was caught ringing Nell at peak rate from the kitchen after Mum asked her to go upstairs and tell her sister lunch was ready.

FRIDAY 18 OCTOBER
THE COT

Seven days of torrential rain has driven me to catalogue shopping – a habit I'd always assumed was reserved for unfortunates who are either housebound or afflicted with a taste for limited-edition Royal Doulton china figurines. Marooned at home all day once Bee drove to the oasis of dry air she calls work, I ended up ordering everything from sports bras to amphibious lace-up ankle boots called Muckers. I had to wrestle with myself to refrain from throwing in a set of Tupperware champagne flutes while I was at it.

SATURDAY 19 OCTOBER
THE COT

The rain lifted briefly for today's meet at Lackerby Park, an extensive country estate just outside Gloucester owned by a Czechoslovakian industrialist called Petroc Jevtic. After making his fortune in the tile trade Mr Jevtic moved to England and embraced country sports, in particular point-to-pointing. For this morning's festivities the jowly old man appeared very gamely on one of his young racehorses dressed in full Lester Piggott costume with stirrups so short that his limbs and spine were forced into a shallow Z shape. Possibly chosen to conjure up an image of a coiled spring, his pose reminded me more of a folded-up sunlounger strapped on top of a saddle. In any case it only served to make me even more impressed by Mr Jevtic. He has the look of a wizened downhill racer who should have hung up his skis years ago but is still having a crack at the giant slalom. After passing round a hip flask of schnapps he led the cavalcade up the lane before his horse whipped him through his own front gates and back to its stable. It was hard to tell whether this early exit was by accident or design but it looks like Lester decided to roll with it as we never saw him again.

There was also a man called Tony wearing gaiters and plus fours, who, in the absence of a horse to carry him, ran along beside us pulling a little dog on a string. The dog was a slower runner than its owner and liked to take its own line at things, generally one four or five feet across from Tony's chosen path, so that with the lead between them they provided a mobile tripwire that Norm couldn't resist occasionally chancing his ankles to.

It's amazing what a few tons of horseflesh and a pink coat can do for a girl's libido. All things being equal Tony is not significantly less attractive than Jack Nightingale, but relegated to the ground in an anorak he was too low to trigger even the faintest bleep on my Peppermore radar. Yet towards Jack I can sense myself developing the stirrings of a crush. I caught myself staring at him at the meet and swallowing with each flash of his scarlet coat when he takes the hounds into a wood. It's not so bad that I want to kiss him or anything like that but I hanker for a sign that I've made some kind of impression on him, even if only as an amiable fool. Judging from the way Bee whipped off her gloves for Anthony the whipper-in when he realised he'd forgotten his own, exposing the remnants of her manicure to the chilly wet weather, it looks as though she is not immune to the power of the pink coat either.

SUNDAY 20 OCTOBER
A FIELD OUTSIDE NEWENT

Those blasted Hunt buttons are still at large but we won our spurs as country mice today after deciding to visit our cousins who own a bookshop in Ross-on-Wye. Sadly we never made it to the premises where they crouch all day, pushing the covers of their new stock of novels very slightly ajar and giving the pages inside sidelong glances so as to follow the story while keeping the book looking brand new. And the reason we never made it is because, after years of careering round city streets hunched over my steering wheel in varying degrees of rage, I have become a rustic driver.

I think the syndrome must have crept up on me, which is appropriate because the main characteristic of rustic driving is an ability to clog the road by travelling at a speed that holds up everyone behind you but which is just a touch too fast for them to be able to overtake. Conversely, in a thirty-mile-per-hour zone where he can't be passed the rustic driver throws his weight on to the accelerator and burns along in low gear. I now drive at about forty-six miles an hour whether I'm approaching the zebra crossing outside a village school or on a straight stretch of the dual carriageway into Gloucester.

I also trundle about with my right-hand wheels firmly but inexplicably over in the path of oncoming traffic and am in the habit of sticking my arm out of the window and waggling it about instead of indicating when I'm planning to make a turn. As we learnt the hard way in Ross High Street, I can't reverse-park any more either. I can quite see how Mrs White bit the dust here. Even on a Sunday the roads are cluttered with motorists like me zooming around the busy parts of town and crunching their vehicles inanely back and forth next to vacant parking spaces while waggling their arms out of the windows.

But on the way home Bee showed herself to be even more acclimatised to the Ledbury lifestyle. After failing to park the car we abandoned Ross and had started back along the lanes when she spotted a sign at the gateway of a field that she would once have described as grooved but now correctly identified as ploughed. The placard read simply 'Free Spuds Here' and before I knew it she had made me pull over and was out there in the mud scratching about for potatoes. Bee Watson, the Dry Clean Only of a thousand manicures kneeling down in her Earl jeans and feeling through the newly turned soil for spuds with her bare hands! I never thought I'd see the day. But there she was, pausing to make her jumper into a sling to carry her haul of King Edwards back to the car. She didn't even scream all that loudly when an earthworm attached itself to her wrist.

October

MONDAY 21 OCTOBER
THE COT

Even with Jane's expertise and exhaustive knowledge of local male talent to assist our search, over the last few weeks the quality of the marriageable meal ticket specified in part four of The Plan has been gradually and dispiritingly reduced. The sad truth is that no one seems to fancy us.

TUESDAY 22 OCTOBER
SOUTH KENSINGTON, LONDON

Cancel that. Mr Smith rang.

He wondered if I fancied a drink. The thought of feasting my eyes on a slightly undernourished version of Michelangelo's David instantly made me feel very thirsty indeed. I had a lightning-quick bath, left Bee in full charge of the horses and drove for over three hours in return for a couple of vodka tonics and an unobstructed but alas clothed view of him that lasted for fifty-one minutes. The tax levied on those fifty-one minutes was that I was obliged to spend them fielding his queries about my life in what he called 'the cuntry', all the while bracing myself for the moment when he broke it to me that he had a gorgeous new girl-friend.

The moment never came. Hallelujah. So she doesn't exist. Or at least not in my world. Yet.

WEDNESDAY 23 OCTOBER
EAST DULWICH, LONDON

I've totally capitulated to the daydream that there's still a chance Mr Smith might one day see me in my hunting gear and not be able to help himself. Which is why I'm at Patey being measured up for a hat by placing my head in an inverted pincushion where all the spikes grip my skull and show its exact shape.

You would understand why I'm entrusting my brain to £295 worth of glorified papier-mâché if you could see how elegant I look. The low brim and sleek finish over my ears has done wonders for my profile, somehow making my nose look straighter and my chin less chubby. As with yachts, trains and cars we devised the most aesthetically pleasing riding hat at least fifty years ago and should probably have left it at that.

THURSDAY 24 OCTOBER
LADBROKE GROVE, LONDON

Katie threw a dinner party in my honour last night, mainly to collect her winnings from those of my friends who had bet that I wouldn't last a month of what they have taken to calling my Year en Province.

Her cooking, or rather the caterer's whose cartons she hid behind the freezer, was a welcome change from the Cot's perpetual breakfast bar. But she made me wear some of her clothes because mine kept making her wheeze, and once she noticed my hands were stained with Cornucrescent, a smelly brown jelly I've been rubbing into Norm's heels to make his toenails grow stronger, I had to eat with washing-up gloves on.

It was good to see everyone but I'm surprised by how easily I've forsaken them in favour of my own little universe beyond Gloucester. Moving out of London is a bit like forgetting to watch a soap opera I've been glued to for years. It's still a treat to catch the occasional episode but I'm no longer completely up to speed with who's doing what with whom and am increasingly less interested in new characters in the storyline. My only recent shared experience with my oldest friends is being frustrated by delays caused by leaves on the line. They were all whingeing about the Tube running slower than ever after windy nights while in Ledbury at the moment the big nuisance is falling leaves burying the scent of the fox in many coverts.

FRIDAY 25 OCTOBER
THE COT

Pathetic news. Mark Bennet dropped round unexpectedly for a drink soon after the six o'clock news and caught me already dressed for bed. In New York I simply undressed for bed. Nowadays Miss Marple would look a vamp beside me in my floral nightie, towelling dressing gown, woollen scarf and sheepskin slippers.

Mark had come to canvass for our votes at the hunt's AGM next week at which he would be standing for election to the hunt committee. The way he told it, the battle for committee places sometimes reflects a more profound struggle being played out in the cauldron of pride, prejudice, sex, spite, ancient feuds, vested interests and sheer bloody mindedness that is internal hunt politics.

As with so many skirmishes in the Ledbury, at the heart of the fray lay Jack Nightingale. In the opinion of many members of the hunt Jack is a world-class striker playing for a Second Division club. After a glittering stint as whipper-in at the Quorn, the very smartest pack in Leicestershire, he came here to hunt hounds about seven years ago and despite having not yet turned thirty immediately caught a record $61^1/_2$ brace of foxes in his first season as huntsman. As meteoric rises go Jack's makes Michael Owen's footballing career look sluggardly. His supporters feel that as a respected but inescapably modest pack that only hunts two days a week, the Ledbury should be thrilled to have netted one of the best huntsmen in the country and be doing everything they can to delay his inevitable departure to a more prestigious, three- or four-day-a-week pack.

However, there is a rival sect that would like Jack ousted from his job *tout de suite*. They object to him partly because he doesn't measure up to their memory of their own relatives when they ran the show, partly because he's a cocky little son of a gun likely to rattle cages and partly because his style of hunting is not to their taste. I stopped listening for most of the technical stuff but in a nutshell they don't like his Leicestershire method of letting the lead hounds run on when they pick up a fox without waiting to marshal up the whole pack and set them off together. This posse seem to favour Ken Unwin, the amateur whipper-in, to become huntsman in Jack's place. Whether he would be any good at the job is a matter of speculation given that he's never tried it, but he would be free – a boon for the cash-strapped hunt, which currently provides Jack with horses, grooms, a cottage and a salary.

Now here's the rub. In the malleable and ever-changing

maelstrom of alliances and coalitions within the hunt nobody knows for certain whose side anyone else is on. Mark assured me that a vote for him is a vote for Jack. But even he can't be sure whether a vote for his two rivals, respectable ladies from long-standing hunting families who do tireless fund-raising work organising hunter trials and social events, is necessarily a vote for the pro-Ken Unwin faction. All I know for sure is that I would never have suspected any of this bad feeling out hunting this morning when in crisp sunshine we skirted the Frith, a dense wood on the westernmost tip of the Malvern hills, and gasped at the nearly 360-degree wraparound views across the Ledbury Hunt's glorious domain with the hounds spilling out across it.

SATURDAY 26 OCTOBER
THE COT

Matt Heller and Anthony the Whip appeared at teatime, and after ascertaining that 'Little 'Un', as they have taken to calling Bee, was at home came up with an elaborate pretext for gaining access to the Cot. Apparently they needed me to write an account of their recent digging adventures for *Earth Dog, Field Dog*, a publication that I had never heard of. Two hours, four hundred words and a bottle of vodka later Bee's daywear was undisturbed, she had had her boots professionally polished by Anthony and declined the offer of having her toes sucked by Matt. I, on the other hand, was au fait with the innermost workings of a Kangol drill and had been told I was a good sport. It's the story of my life.

In the Pink

SUNDAY 27 OCTOBER
THE COT

Boy. They really know how to do weather out here. An oak tree is lying uprooted outside the front door after being tossed like a matchstick across the field when a freak storm hit last night. Ignoring a forecast of clear skies, the Leadon has flooded so much that the lane towards Redmarley is impassable and a power cut shrouds every house between Gloucester and Malvern.

I've been counting the tins in the store cupboard and wondering how long we can last cut off from the village before hunger drives us to make a leathery broth from boiling up the horses' bridles. But Bee says the climate outside is pretty calm compared to the mayhem she and her friend Rosie endured last night at a Rugby Club Ball. The edited highlights of what they christened the Ugly Bug Ball, an event held by the organisers of an annual springtime extravaganza called Death By Cider that would make Miss Whiplash blush, allegedly included:

(a) A girl wringing the beer out of her little black dress in the loos and putting it back on to re-enter the fray.
(b) A gang of boys needing medical attention after drinking flaming Drambuies that were more like infernos in a glass.
(c) A discussion overheard between the bouncers about whether Royal Jelly really is bees' spunk.
(d) Mark Bennet on the dance floor. Word is the boy's got rhythm.

146

October

TUESDAY 29 OCTOBER
MAYFAIR, LONDON

I'm up in town to submit myself to inspection by the in-crowd and collect the gold necklace Daniel is giving Bee to replace the last one he gave her that got lost somewhere between the potato field and the Ugly Bug scrum. Not just jewellery but replacement jewellery – the Beezer is back in business. I'm hoping this latest gift has a good resale value now that the lorry's tortuous progress through its MOT has taken us through the last pennies of the book advance before we've done any proper hunting at all.

Last night, after getting a free and ultra-gamine haircut that without its trainee stylist creator on hand to arrange makes me look uncannily like Anthony the Whip, I dropped in at my friend Lucy's private view. Although I have lost two inches around my hips from all the riding I really struggled to find something to wear that didn't expose my still flaccid ankle, the bruises all over my knees and shins and the scratches across my neck. I eventually found myself sweltering in a corner wearing a long woollen dress and staring gormlessly at her landscapes for fear that somebody would strike up a conversation that might lead to me having to explain how I filled my time. For, after a couple of abortive chats which ended with my acquaintance making his excuses and running off stifling his screams, I realised that The Plan wasn't playing well with the boys. I think it's the whole pony thing. In male eyes it turns me into a toothy, pearl-wearing gel with two black Labradors straining at the leash and knickers made out of waxed jacket material.

But as I killed time in W.H. Smith waiting for my train home I discovered that I have nothing to worry about in the bristle stakes compared to some people. *Horse & Hound* has compiled a

147

list of the horsiest people in Britain. But the name-and-shame campaign appears to have backfired. Ample-buttocked readers have been clogging the switchboard lobbying for their favourite riders to be added to what they misguidedly assume is a roll of honour. Dad will be spluttering into his cornflakes for days when I tell him about this.

WEDNESDAY 30 OCTOBER
HEOL-AP-FIN YOUTH HOSTEL, HAY-ON-WYE

Weehee! I'm going up up up up upupupupupupupupup!

THURSDAY 31 OCTOBER
THE COT

Forget potatoes. Some hitchers that we picked up yesterday directed us to a sheltered stretch of common land just below the Black Hill that should be signposted 'Free Drugs Here'.

In it we found swarms of people armed with plastic bags tiptoeing gingerly over the turf, frequently pausing to stoop to the ground and finger their way through individual blades of grass like dexterous clerks searching for a crucial file. There are some crops that still have to be harvested the backbreaking way and magic mushrooms are one of them. The camaraderie amongst the pickers, who ranged from farm labourers and schoolgirls bunking off double physics at the comprehensive school further down the valley to semi-professional dealers who'd driven all the way from Essex in search of organic gear, was great. Due to unusually mild frosts there were so many mushrooms for this time of year that far from being warned off someone's patch as we had expected, people stopped to explain exactly what we should be looking for.

A poetic man from the electricity board, who was wearing his company tie wrenched down over one shoulder like a beauty queen's sash, said that like Wordsworth's daffodils, magic mushrooms grow in golden hosts. No taller than our little fingers, the tiny flaxen sombreros on very delicate blonde stalks are indistinguishable from other noxious little mushies that would make us very sick indeed except for the puckered nipples on the very tip of their heads and the dark undersides to their canopies.

For the first twenty minutes we both stared dumbly at the grass, failing to find anything that looked anything like a mushroom. Then Bee spotted a minute, partially furled fairy-sized umbrella and we were off, probing through the secret world of vegetation barely an inch high for hidden villages of mushrooms. By lunchtime we had picked well over five hundred between us and walked back to the car park of what must be the only upland youth hostel in Britain to be turning customers away in late October for further instructions.

Delia Smith would be impressed by the versatility of our haul. A pair of students from Manchester University who make a pilgrimage to Hay Bluff every year told us that magic mushers go well in cakes, in honey and with soup. You can also make tea with them or you can do what we did, which was to dry them out in record speed on the fan heater vents under the Renault's windscreen and shovel them into our mouths by the handful. Then sit in the back and wait and complain nothing was happening and wait and sit some more, rather crossly now, and then suddenly be laughing and laughing and laughing from a delicious euphoria that came bubbling up from nowhere like hiccups. That's what a dose of thirty-odd magic mushers makes happen for a couple of glorious hours. People's jumpers go funny colours and things shrink and expand a bit as your perspective warps but you don't feel hyper, or think a ghoul is chasing you, or crave more or feel like you'll never be able to sleep again. You just laugh and laugh and laugh and all for free.

My face was still hurting from laughing at last night's AGM of Ledbury Hunt Limited. It could be due to my Ready Brek glow of champignon good cheer but after all I'd heard I couldn't detect the faintest whiff of venom in the air at the meeting in a room above the Feathers Hotel in Ledbury. The only indication that there was ever disunity in the ranks was a mention in the minutes of last year's meeting that the hunt's new chairman was chosen for his reputation for being 'very good at stopping people fighting'.

With the exception of one man, who had opted for an ambitious Vegas-wiseguy look in a beige suit with such a high nylon content people's hair went static just walking past him, the favoured style amongst the men was for tweed jackets and polished brown brogues finished off with lashings of corduroy. But because of their mud-splattered ties, ruddy outdoorsy faces and roughened hands they didn't look anything like the bogus marchers I'd spotted. Most of the women had puffa jackets and trousers on – rather shaking my belief in all I'd heard about their allure and athleticism in the bedroom.

The proceedings started with a roll-call of the fallers, that is all the supporters of the hunt who had died recently, including a progress report on a local jockey who was now walking again after being badly mangled at a point-to-point nearly two years ago. Then

Hef took to the stage with a school report on each of the five horses kept for the hunt servants, including a scathing assessment of one new acquisition who is still 'not quite as brave as he might be'. What was pretty routine stuff for the rest of the room was an absolute eye-opener for me. I had no idea for instance that the hunt owns arable land bequeathed to it years ago and operates a number of quid pro quos with supporters who carry out plumbing and maintenance work on its properties in return for rough shooting, or that its spare cottage brings in a reasonable £14,000 a year. Surprisingly, the Ledbury's finances were actually improved by the foot-and-mouth epidemic that stopped any hunting at all taking place until the end of December last year. But the £28,742 that the hunt has in assets was quickly dwarfed by the £24,000 needed to put in the infamous reed bed to soak up the kennel effluent and the major repairs required to Jack and Anthony's unheated cottages that the treasurer described as 'an apology in this day and age'.

Softened by cider and the lullaby quality of the Gloucestershire accents around me, my eyes swivelled up to the ancient beams holding up the ceiling and I began to turn over in my mind how remarkably little the talking points of these meetings must have changed over the Ledbury's nearly two-century-long history. Of course nowadays busy roads hamper the hunt and the occasional strands of wire that so disgusted masters in the past have come to plague nearly every hedge in its country. But as the speakers bemoaned the problems of both wet and dry ground, thanked people for walking hound puppies over the summer, chivvied them to pay their subscriptions on time and returned again and again to how crucial the generosity and support of farmers was to the hunt's survival, I imagined an eerie thread of similar speeches echoing down the years.

But that thread snapped and took my reverie with it once we came to elect the new committee members. Due to the substantial numbers of incoming landowners and smallholders in the region who are opposed to hunting, the Ledbury can no longer allow every local farmer to vote at its meetings for fear that the proceedings could be infiltrated and packed by opponents of the sport. I had assumed everyone in an area as sleepy as this one was either indifferent to or supportive of their local hunt but that much has definitely changed. After quite a lot of posturing and flushed faces amongst the farmers it was agreed that everyone in the room would be allowed to vote on the prospective committee members.

And so it came to pass that Mark Bennet failed to win a place on the committee by only one vote – a vote that could have been supplied by Miss Annabel Watson if she hadn't wanted to spend her evening giggling like a maniac in the Cot with the rest of the mushrooms.

8

November

So this is it. November the first. The day of reckoning has arrived.
At eleven o'clock this morning our Opening Meet will mark the
official kick-off of the British fox-hunting season.

Propelled from our beds by excitement as much as unease, we
got up at dawn and bathed Norm and Ari from top to toe in special
anti-dandruff tea tree oil shampoo and conditioner. I think Norm
rather fancies himself as a dandy and realising beauty is pain
stoically endured a cold rinse under the hose and an equine bikini
wax as I pulled clumps of hair from the soft skin at the sides of
his tail. He let us burnish his coat until it shone like mahogany
and held his head still while we braided his mane and forelock
into a dozen little plaits, rolled them into tight balls and sewed
them fast as specified by *The Manual of Horsemanship*. He nibbled
the small of my back in gratitude when I painted his toenails with

hoof oil and proffered his chin to be snipped free of whiskers.

When we'd finished, the only part of him that still caused concern were the flashes of pale hair around the ankles of his hind legs, which we discovered to our horror are called white socks. Bee says she would never have let me buy a horse burdened with wearing white socks for life ('So common') if she'd known, but I'm trying to think of Norm's ankle togs as being more of a Michael Jackson than a dodgy Italian waiter-style statement. Ari was much more troublesome. I think she's done all this before and knows what's coming next. Too wound up to eat her breakfast, the churning of her stomach had turned its contents into a gassy spinach soup that spurted out down her back legs and tail each time we scrubbed them clean.

By the time we had tacked them up in their sparkling saddles, leather necklaces called breastplates and their bridles each sporting a gruesome new bit, a gag for Norm and an evil-looking contraption called a Kimblewick fitted with a hoop to scrape the roof of her mouth and a chain to jam her jaws shut for Ari, it was nine o'clock and time to make a start on our own toilette.

It was difficult to know where to begin. Should we wear big sports knickers for comfort? Something tasteful in case we found ourselves ending the day in hospital like the record-breaking seventeen riders who reportedly were carted off there after the last opening meet? Or skimpy lace G-strings in the hope that the Ledbury lived up to its Jilly Cooperesque reputation? Then there was the Visible Panty Line conundrum to consider. At length we opted to abandon our knickers altogether and instead go commando with only opaque tights beneath our breeches. A chap I'd met out cubbing with another pack a few weeks ago swore that if I got up close and personal to a hunting man once the season began I would more than likely discover he was wearing hosiery as well – partly for warmth, partly because after a hard day in the saddle tights allegedly act like a poor man's Viagra.

The big decision made, we squeezed and eased and pinned and buttoned ourselves into by far and away the most expensive and wildly flattering outfits either of us have ever possessed. Our riding boots alone had cost over £350 a pair but the bespoke sheaths of glossy black leather that made our legs look so fantastic were worth every penny. I have never felt so sexy in an outfit that didn't expose an inch of flesh anywhere apart from my face. Seeing Bee buttoning her black hunting coat up over a yellow waistcoat I twigged why the look worked so well. As she stood, thonged whip in hand, her bottom and thighs showcased by skin-tight white jodhpurs rising out of spurred boots, she looked at once wanton but also proper to the point of being prim with her hair in a net, the soft skin of her throat pinned away underneath the folds of her creamy white stock and her chest buttoned into a thick black corset of a jacket. The only spoiler was the crash hat that once in place gave her the silhouette of a lollipop on a black-and-white-striped stick.

It was only when we could tear ourselves away from the mirror to gulp down a bit of breakfast that we realised we were exhausted just from getting ready for the Opening Meet. My fingers ached from all the plaiting and my left shoulder throbbed from carrying countless buckets of hot water out to the yard but I was still far too jittery to follow Bee to the sofa for a five-minute power nap. Instead, I went out to start the lorry. He was not keen to come out to play. After checking that his water, oil, fuel, battery and radiator situations were all as they should be and giving him a number of kicks in the guts I could only deduce that the pesky machine had stage fright.

So the longest day in our hunting careers became forty minutes longer as we were forced to hack to the meet at Corse Lawn, a country house hotel several miles away owned by a man with a voicebox jammed on shout mode that had earned him the nickname Whispering Dennis. Very sweetly the Yarwoods came out to see us off, telling us we'd be fine but to steer clear of the many other riders who wouldn't. Beyond expecting there to be a few more people out than the couple of dozen we had got to know cubbing, I hadn't really considered other riders. But as we trotted along the wide grass verges to Corse Lawn lorry after lorry came past us bursting at the seams with every kind of steed from swanky thoroughbreds to hairball ponies and we realised that today was going to be very different from hunting as we knew it.

Even though it was beginning to rain so many people had turned out to see the meet that cars were backed up along the road for a good half a mile each side of the hotel. When we arrived we couldn't get anywhere near the sweeping drive where piles of canapés and punch were on offer because of the sea of horses and pedestrians milling about. Where had these hordes of fit horses and pristine jockeys been hiding all this time? It seemed as though you only had to glance behind a tree or lift up a stone to find yet another plaited hunter and its immaculate rider ready to join the party. Queasy with dread at the sight of what looked like well over two hundred horses improvising a chaotic re-enactment of the Trooping of the Colour, I made Bee tie the green ribbon in Norm's tail. His heart had started beating like a bad boy again and even Ari's eyes were popping out of her head as Thomas Harvey, magnificent in a pink coat fastened with four gleaming brass Hunt buttons, made a speech welcoming everyone to the meet. Then after a final successful pounce at a tray of sausage rolls and a gulp of stirrup cup, Jack Nightingale tooted briskly on his horn and we were off.

My initial sensation as we swept up the lane in a deafening clatter of horseshoes and the sizzle of warming blood pumping through a multitude of arteries was of being in a swarm of locusts. Packed knee to knee with the riders each side of me, I could neither steer nor see anything in any direction except clouds of steam rising from the mass of horses all around me. The cavalcade was pushing forward so hard I worried that if Norm tripped he would get trampled to dust. As we slowed to turn into a flat clay field to wait for the hounds to draw the first covert and the swell of the horses pushing behind us shunted into his rump I felt Norm hunch up in alarm and prayed he kept his cool.

Praying wasn't enough. As I went through the gateway his infamous right foot shot out and clouted Bee hard on the shin of her new boot. Remembering correct procedure I began to deliver the recommended three mighty whacks to his arse. Big mistake. Huge. The moment my whip made contact with his buttocks Norm squealed with indignation and then totally lost it. Suddenly he was galloping round the field like a madman, his usually supple neck stuck out like an ironing board, his teeth clenched so hard round the bit that standing up in my stirrups and yanking back on the reins with every ounce of strength I had elicited absolutely no response at all. At one stage he veered full pelt towards a spindly bit of hedge with car followers and kids on bikes waiting in the road on the other side and I really thought that in his fury he was going to plough through the lot of them. Thankfully he changed tack and belted full steam back towards Ari before jamming on the brakes and going into a maddened bucking fit that was accompanied by a series of high-pitched mews and squeaks.

By now the entire Ledbury Hunt and its retinue was stationary and watching me with interest as I circled wildly round the field, calling weakly to Bee to please, please help me. She played the role of the injured party with impressive theatricality, taking care not to spare the crowds a twinge as she doubled over in her saddle clinging to her leg. When it felt as though Norm had dipped marginally below the world land-speed record I became aware that I was being shouted at. Someone was yelling at me to stand still and keep behind the Field Master. What? Like they didn't think that option hadn't already occurred to me as preferable to hurtling around the field, preparing to die either from my internal injuries or embarrassment.

After what must have been another thirty seconds but felt like a lifetime I detected a hiss whenever I passed one of the acquaintances I'd made cub hunting. It was Hugo Hammond, an affable town councillor, who finally stage-whispered, 'Drop the whip,' loudly enough for me to hear. Looking up, I saw that in my fright I was still holding my right arm aloft, whip above my head, poised to deliver the second and third blows to Norman's bum. For what seemed like an age I couldn't persuade my fingers to loosen their grip on the handle but at last it fell from my hand and Norm grudgingly allowed himself to be pulled up next to Ari.

I slumped traumatised in my saddle, hoping that Norman dropped dead of a cardiac arrest before Thomas Harvey issued the inevitable order for me to be sent home and waiting for Bee to say something soothing. It was a while before the muttering of the three-hundred-odd spectators died down enough for me to realise that she was bent double not with agony but laughter. Just as she was expressing some fake remorse for finding her sister being nearly killed amusing and congratulating me on managing to stay on, Mark Bennet rode up in hysterics to amend his earlier rule about whacking kickers. Apparently some horses won't tolerate being beaten. No shit, Sherlock.

In the long moments of waiting for news of my expulsion from the hunt I have never missed London more. Oh to be trapped in a Tube strike now that November's here. I remembered with fondness the hundreds of hours sacrificed to traffic jams, yearning for the chance of travelling too slowly rather than sickeningly, uncontrollably fast. I thought wistfully of the insidious rudeness of strangers on the streets that would statistically have one day boiled over into my being mugged, an assault that would have been a trifle compared to the ordeal I'd just been through. Damn this healthy outdoor stuff. I longed for that dry feeling in my mouth after I drank the city's tap water and the certain knowledge that the tiny crumbs of filth in the air that stuck to my shirt collars were also becoming lodged in my lungs. If this were London I could hail a black cab and exchange Norman for a credit note at the shop where I bought him. Heck, I could trade him in for ten pairs of Manolos or a few hundred thousand daiquiris. As the drizzle turned into sleet and bloody Bee and bastardly Mark persisted in unrelentingly seeing the funny side of Norman being revealed as a psychopath, I pictured myself safely restored to SW10, my riding gear replaced by the latest fashions, my current torment still souring my sleep but at least providing me with a batch of bite-sized anecdotes to bring out at dinner parties.

But I was not to get off that easily. To my enduring astonishment the masters decided to grant Norman a stay of execution and instead of sending me home pretended not to have seen his antics at all. Looking like the star of a costume drama in a silk top hat and swallow-tailed coat aboard a huge grey horse with a hefty neck so arched that it looked as though it had cavorted straight off the

Bayeux Tapestry, Hef even swept off his hat in greeting and managed to say with a straight face that he was honoured to welcome us to the Ledbury Hunt. Nor was I able to send myself home. Bee refused to honour our pact about wimping out, claiming that if I stuck it out on Norm I might win my Hunt buttons, albeit posthumously, and when I tried to wimp out by myself Norman reared up in protest. He really is the pits.

Before long the hounds picked up the trace of a fox on the other side of the main road and we chased it for a mile or more towards Eldersfield before coming back in a big arc and circling round again. In terms of speed and danger, the handful of simple wooden fences and patches of galloping that made up the rest of the day never came close to Norman's tantrum, but we did see some pretty spectacular accidents. Hunting is a bit like an off-road car rally in which the drivers wear morning suits, their only form of speed control is handbrake turns and while they all want to get in front of each other they risk disqualification if they race past the pace car a.k.a. the Field Master. Like any kind of motor sport, things only really started getting interesting when it came to overtaking. We saw horses barged into gateposts and trees by faster-moving traffic and riders jumping barbed wire rather than queuing for a safer wooden rail in their quest for pole position.

Nervous of Norm kicking anyone else, we stuck to the back of the following pack with the dive-bombers, who included a pony with a distinctly size 18 figure and a fittingly stout girl on its back that reversed at speed over the lip of a deep drainage pond and only just managed to claw its back legs out. At most jumps we ended up catching the horse of an endearingly optimistic garden designer who, perpetually anticipating a bold leap from his mount, launched himself into the air only to land solo on the other side each time.

But by far the worst fall came from the most unlikely quarter. A couple of hours into the day when driving icy rain had hosed at least half of the mounted followers back home, Hef followed Jack Nightingale over a wide but innocuous waterlogged drainage channel between a ploughed field and a patch of kale. For some reason his white charger tripped into the ditch, caught its foot in some wire lurking in its depths and turned somersault, hurling Hef, top hat, tails and all into the mud and then landing on top of him.

Despite having broken his nose and fractured his neck, Hef's immediate concern was for his teeth. As he lay concussed and choking on the surge of blood streaming down his face he was heard to shout for Dean, a carroty Irish bruiser who rides his more rebellious horses and generally acts as Terry to his Arthur Daley. Jumping off his horse to assist, Dean, who comes out hunting sporting a large gold earring as well as a bowler hat, refused to let anyone take his boss away until they'd found his caps.

Accordingly, Hef wasn't carted off to open the Ledbury Hunt's account for the season at Gloucester Royal Hospital until his dental crowns had been fished out of the ditch. I have never ascertained whether, fractured vertebrae notwithstanding, he went home to shower and change before presenting himself at the casualty department for fear of frightening the nurses with his bloody clothes or because they might have defrocked him and perhaps discovered a pair of 15-denier American tan support tights cradling his groin.

At two o'clock (could we really only have been hunting for three hours?) the pink-coat brigade changed on to their second horses of the day so as to have fresh tyres and a full tank of fuel in case an afternoon fox led us into the fast lane, and Bee and I started to make new friends. My favourite was Harry Langmead, a silver-tongued, silver-haired charmer from Pershore with the deliciously lazy, appraising flirting style peculiar to Englishmen when it's all too late and they are happily married to the point of being out hunting with their wife Christine on a pair of matching greys. Mr Langmead had a flair for not saying anything particularly risqué while still being an absolute tonic for a girl's morale. He deduced our knicker situation at a glance and laughed off the assertion that I had joined the Ledbury in order to research a book. 'It's husbands you girls will want to be researching,' he said, before running through a checklist of what we should be looking out for. As the Ledbury's own Capability Sliproad who made his fortune from landscaping motorways he thought an alliance with a country squire was very much yesterday's breakfast. What we needed was new money or at least a man with the prospect of making plenty of it. He would consult his files and see what he could do for us.

An hour later there were fewer than a dozen riders still out. We shared Mars bars and hip flasks and filled each other in on the various bumps and scrapes of the day. Bee's and my reports foundered for not knowing anyone's name or where anything was but like sympathetic hosts in a foreign country the other riders strived to include the pair of strangers in their midst, explaining the nuance of a joke about a particular farmer or why the hunt couldn't ride through a certain pheasant drive. As the light faded I was still unsure of the names of the woman riding a stallion with a fantastic Farrah Fawcett hairdo crammed under her hat and the jug-eared man who bossed Mark Bennet around so mercilessly. But I felt the first sinews of friendship stretching out between us in the dusk like a silken spider's web.

If I'm beginning to sound tired and emotional then who can blame me. I had been in the saddle for nearly seven hours and endured more exercise and adrenalin in that time than the sum total of activity over the rest of my life. Exhaustion had flattened Norm's trot to a listless jog as we rode abreast with Thomas and the whips just behind the hounds. Apart from our chipper huntsman, only Ari, ears pricked and tail still swinging, looked game for more as we swung under the willows and alders back along the damp sleeping lane to Town Street Farm. Watching Jack lead the troop of hounds in, each dog responding to its name when he called and thronging adoringly round his horse's legs or tiptoeing up to rest their paws on his saddle whenever we paused, I felt the familiar creeping feeling of the hots blossoming in me. Admiring the way the sleek dark horse that had behaved like a maniac a few months ago was trotting meekly beneath him, I absorbed his broad shoulders, his compact riding style and the gentle curve of his hairline above his collar.

As anyone who has pined for a pug-ugly football star or a supremely talented but acne-blighted tennis champion will attest, there is something intoxicating about men who excel at physical pursuits. Even when they aren't actually executing a perfect triple axel, effortlessly hitting another boundary or slam-dunking a basketball, they still bear the lustre of us all knowing that they can. Whatever the magic, maddeningly alluring ingredient of physical courage alloyed with coordination is, Jack has got it in spades. And, dammit, he never so much as glances in my direction.

The farmyard was a hive of activity as grooms led mud-caked horses away to their lorries, the terrier men loaded up their quad bike and supporters mobbed Jack, offering him nips of whisky, cajoling, questioning, hoping for a joke or a warm word. But, fatigue etched all over his face, he was barely able to respond to their compliments and I began to have some idea of the immense pressure on him to show a couple of hundred people, many of them paying over £60 for their day's hunting, a good time from a sport hostage to the vagaries of weather, scent, geography, luck, parish politics and a host of other factors – like Norman's mood – that he can't possibly predict or control. Thomas Harvey, who as master is responsible for the front-of-house duties of the theatre that is a fox-hunt, didn't look much fresher.

But at least their work was done. Good old Mr Yarwood came to collect us in his lorry to spare us hacking another five miles home in the dark but we still spent the next two hours outside with the cold hose scrubbing every last sod of heavy clay mud off Norman and Ari and then checking their legs for cuts and thorns, towelling them down, putting on their night rugs, preparing their hay, fetching their water, plumping up their sawdust beds, bandaging their aching limbs and boiling up a hot barley gruel for their supper that makes the Cot smell like a family of Ukrainians are subsisting in it.

We barely had time to get the tack inside, pull off our own filthy boots and get out of our sodden jodhpurs before I was back out in the yard, giving the horses more hay and water, an extra layer of duvets and mucking out their stables one last time. I finally tottered back across the yard, hardly conscious of the sleet that had started up again stinging across my wind-scorched face. I was too tired to eat, too tired to talk, too tired to know what I thought of my first full day's hunting. All I wanted was a hot bath to get me warm and ease the aching muscles across my shoulders. But in the sitting room I found Bee weeping. Between sobs she informed me there was no hot water and definitely no God. It was pitiful. We boiled the kettle, sponged the worst of the grime from our faces and fell, moaning softly to ourselves, into our beds. It was seven o'clock.

Sometime during the night I was roused shivering from my dreams by Bee slapping limply on the wall. Did I know if the hounds had caught anything today? Not a clue. In our excitement we'd forgotten all about Charlie.

SATURDAY 2 NOVEMBER
LONGDON

Call an ambulance. Everything hurts. Every limb feels like chewed string, every movement is a struggle. Both my elbows are locked fast at 90 degrees as though I've been carrying a heavy tray around all night. My stomach muscles are so knackered that I can't stand without first rolling into a kneeling position and using a piece of furniture to pull myself up with like a toddler. Even lying down doesn't stop the slow pulsating aches seeping up and down my legs. Bee is as bad and having particular problems with her knees; one's horribly swollen and the other won't bend at all, bestowing on her the kind of gammy-legged hobble hard to achieve without having seen action at El Alamein.

In our weakened state we probably shouldn't have accepted an invitation for tea at Mark Bennet's ancestral home a few miles from Longdon. Like natives immune to tropical diseases, the male inhabitants of Five Oaks Farm are the most hale and hearty specimens imaginable, thriving in an environment of flamboyant mess, as strong and cheerful as young cattle. I consider them a living advertisement for never bothering to wash your hands after you go to the loo. Built on a treacherous marsh that was uninhabitable until the nineteenth century, Longdon was described as follows by the Reverend Symonds, Rector of Pendock in 1881:

It was silent as the grave, save the call of its wildfowl and the croak of the frog. There were mires, tall rushes and sedges and boggy places which would engulf a man if he slipped in and cover him up to the day of doom in black peaty slush.

From the look of the Bennets' farmyard there has been scant progress since. The place is such a mess there is something majestic about its decrepitude. All the barns are in the final stages of falling down and ripped pieces of tarpaulin and discarded grain sacks flutter around in the breeze like autumn leaves. Mark's hunters live in ramshackle stables fashioned from barricades built with whatever seemed to come to hand, be it a garden gate and a wilting line of string or the rusting fuselage of a jet aeroplane. Howling dogs cower in pens beside stacks of rotting silage and everything is covered with a slippery, smelly glaze of goose guano.

But if you hold your nerve past the decades-old detritus that leads up to the back door and hold your nose through a boot room pungent with the aroma of washing powder fighting for supremacy with an indigenous gamey stink, you reach an oasis of cleanliness and civilisation marshalled by Mrs Bennet that extends through the rest of the house and front garden. We spent much of the afternoon in her kitchen. There, holding our aching bodies against the Aga and feasting on tea and fruitcake, we were introduced to a hunting ritual almost as important as the opening meet – that is, spending the following day scouring the newspapers for photographs of oneself at said opening meet. There was a brilliant picture of Hef in his topper in the *Telegraph* and an even better one of Jack Nightingale in *The Times* that Bee is convinced shows the back of her head and half her arm in the far distance. But best of all was a piece in the *Independent* describing Mr Bennet as a 'rotund Hogarthian figure' which he was pretending to be incensed about. Surprisingly there was no evidence of any anti-hunting protesters at the meet at all.

It is hard to convey how obsessive the Bennets are about hunting. All conversational gambits lead inexorably back to patches of woodland with names like Howlers, Hacklers, Netherton Furze and Hospital Wood and the progress of the hounds through them or the legendary day Jack chased a fox the best part of seventeen miles from Ledbury to Hereford. If someone crops up in conversation who can't ride or is allergic to dogs their condition is explained in hushed tones of regret normally reserved for the victim of a tragic twist of fate or calamitous accident. After hours of unflagging hunting talk we headed out in Mark's clapped-out transit van, a crudely painted plastic fox stuck resplendent on the bonnet, to the hunt's Auction of Promises at Welland Court.

One of the best things about people who spend lots of time outside in the damp is that for some reason their newly washed skin smells as fresh as a baby's. Even as the crowd we found congregating in the hall got busy with the merlot and rolled Golden Virginia, they never entirely lost their wholesome whiff. But as I made my way through the ranks of tweeded backs and rosy faces all the chat was again only of hunting – mainly about how rival packs had fared with their opening meets, especially the South Hereford, who chalked up a brace of broken ankles and a lady knocked unconscious in a pile-up on a slippery lane. An overdose of hunting discussion, tiredness and the steady flow of cheap plonk on to our couple of slabs of fruitcake combined to give Bee and me a bout of bidding fever.

The auction had scarcely begun when I managed to bid against myself for a day's trout fishing and buy a couple of tickets to the racing at Cheltenham. Then Bee inadvertently found herself in contention for a week in a holiday bungalow on the Isle of Wight. She managed to get out of that but became entangled in a trip to the Kilkenny hounds in Ireland with Mark Bennet. Distracted by teasing her that she was going on a Peppermore mini-break, I ended up paying what everyone assured me was the bargain price of £160 for a night of passion with the stallion at stud at Eastnor Castle which the auctioneer relished explaining had to be for Ari rather than myself. How much of a desperado do I look?

Probably not much more than I am. When the auction ended our bidding fever degenerated to plain old fever. Bee went up to Hef, grabbed him firmly by his neck brace and kissed him full on the mouth while I gawped dumbly at Jack Nightingale up on the podium until at last Mark took me up to talk to him and he asked me how I was. To answer Jack's question I was quickly the colour of a tomato with third-degree burns and unable to string two words together. A tense pause descended as all available mots deserted me. Then, panicking that Jack might get up from his chair and walk off, I blurted out that I wanted him to come to the hunt ball with us.

The pause returned, but longer and tenser than before as I began to comprehend that I, who had just wobbled through my first ever proper day's hunting, had invited the Ledbury's huntsman to his own hunt ball, an event that didn't take place until February and was probably bound up in as much impenetrable ritual and custom as the rest of the sport. Backtracking hastily from what I suspected was some massive failure of etiquette, I said I expected he and Laura had already made plans. But my declaration was already out there. Jack has the type of unblinking, sewn-on-looking eyes that you find on soft toys. As

I spoke his dark pupils had rocked forward in their sockets. Now they gradually narrowed and sank back into place before he nodded vigorously and said yes.

Yes. Yes. Yes! It felt like the word had been winched down from the ceiling in letters ten foot high and spangled with fairy lights. Their brilliance was soon subdued by the tense pause that drifted back over us like persistent fog as it became abundantly clear that we didn't really have anything much to say to each other. But who cares? I have until 7 February to find the mots capable of captivating Jack Nightingale, and in the meantime I can warm myself through the cold months ahead with the thought that I have a date with the enfant terrible of Eggs Tump.

SUNDAY 3 NOVEMBER
THE COT

I limped out to feed the horses with a hazy recollection of making a fool of myself and a crystal-clear image of Bec making a fool of herself last night.

Having a fairly strong idea that she's a laughing stock hasn't quashed her appetite for Hunt buttons though. To that end we delivered some honeycomb and a get-well card to Hef and then set off to cover ourselves in brownie points by jump-judging at the Ledbury's own hunter trial at Gadbury. Jump-judging may sound important but we found it involved parking the Renault 5 beside a smallish log for the day and then peering out at it through pissing rain for hours on end in order to record which riders had cleared it at the first attempt.

Occasionally we heard the loudspeaker calling for the

ambulance to race to other jumps on the course and a couple of times a riderless nag belted gleefully through the finishing flags to a chorus of 'Loose horse!' but gripping viewing Jump 7 was not. Apart from one competitor who forgot all about it, in five hours the biggest excitement at our log was the arrival of our complimentary packed lunches. By the end of the day I was beginning to lose the will to live but to Bee our time there had been invaluable. A tractor had barely pulled us out of the deep mud at the gate before she began colouring in half a button each on a scrap of paper entitled 'Hunt Butt Chart' that bears testament to all her wildest fantasies and suspicions about our progress through the ranks of the Ledbury Hunt.

Back at the Cot she made a start on our tack in front of *El Cid* while I applied a lot of black eyeliner and set out across the yard with my head set at a droopy snowdrop angle to look up at Norman through my eyelashes and tell him that although there were still only two of us in the marriage I felt very let down by him. Restored to his relaxed self, he carried on eating his supper and pretended that he didn't understand what I was complaining about. When I explained what an imbecile he'd made me look at the opening meet and warned him that if he pulled that kind of stunt ever again he'd have to be sold to those nasty Black Beauty people, he blew stray oats unconcernedly around the bottom of his feed trough. Throughout my reproaches about him betraying my trust and not being the horse I thought he was he didn't even pause between pulling mouthfuls from his hay net.

If Norm had been a real man, any time now he would have been reaching for his car keys, telling me he'd see me around and not calling for at least a week. But held captive in a stable he was forced to hear me out. It was so refreshing to be able to whinge to my heart's content at someone whose only retort was to look bored and swish his tail around. But that's not to say I had things all my own way. I think what Norm was getting at with the strong silent treatment is that I can't make him do anything. Ours is a relationship, he seemed to be arguing, based on his benevolent responses to respectful requests for co-operation from me, his passenger. He was not in the business of being shown up in front of his peers by some girl with a fraction of his strength taking swipes at him as though he were some kind of dumb brute. While I stopped short of apologising to him, as I filled up his water buckets I did express regret that he was whipped on Friday and I left him for the night fairly sure we had agreed a truce. I won't wallop him again so long as he never goes stir-fry like that again and cools it on the kicking.

Just in case diplomacy isn't enough I've also taken the precaution of introducing a system of performance-related feeding in the tack shed. Following her faultless performance on Friday Ari is on generous rations of oats, a brand of horse cornflakes called micronised maize, chaff laced with molasses syrup and a helping of muesli garnished with a pulp of soaked sugar beet that looks like darkened coleslaw. Norm will be eating muesli and cod liver oil until further notice.

MONDAY 4 NOVEMBER
THE COT

We're back in the saddle again. This time for the Ledbury's first full Monday meet of the season. Slipping Mr Yarwood's tame mechanic £100 miraculously revitalised the lorry enough to chug us into the heart of the Monday country, which slopes from the hills above Colwall and Ledbury itself south-west towards Hereford, through the sheep pastures and oast houses of the small mixed farms around Dymock and Much Marcle where Fred West played as a boy and later buried his murder victims. Apart from the occasional grand country house now usually owned by Americans or townies and so prohibited to the hunt, the main sites of interest pointed out to us were a field where the Wests had kept a caravan and a quiet hedgerow bordering a turnip crop where the police had dug for one of their ill-fated au pairs.

Held in glorious sunshine at Cherry Tree Cottage, a modest little house built beside Hallwood End, a lovely big covert of oaks and beeches, today's meet was totally different to Friday's. Fatigue and the presence of Barry Joyce on yet another handsome bay combined to make Norm so docile he barely had a pulse. This meant we felt able to position ourselves very close to the kitchen door and swill down the port and sausage rolls emerging through it. In sharp contrast to the easy charm of Thomas Harvey, the Monday mastership is the preserve of Peter Evans, husband of Sally, the Hunt Secretary. Like Jack Sprat and his wife, Peter is skinny and unsmiling with a sour horse to match, while curvaceous, effervescent Sally was mounted on a classy but cheerful cob.

Very different too from the thrusters and pushers of Friday were the riders out today. No more than a couple of dozen horses turned up, ridden mainly by very jovial and comfortably upholstered women, more than a few of whom were grandmothers. The car-following fraternity was also much reduced. There was a yellow Ford Capri with a trio of retired farmers sitting across the back seat and a man in a string vest with binoculars slung round his neck at the wheel. But my personal favourites were a group of so-called Forest Gumps. This is the local slang term for slow-thinking people native to the Forest of Dean, a breed charac-terised by a cluttered expression caused by all their features jostling against each other in the middle of their faces.

We set off at a suitably sedate pace to draw the big wood and soon encountered the heartening sight of a man on a plump brown horse having even more trouble than I experienced at the opening meet. Spectacularly out of control, he pelted past us on the narrow track through the trees, scraping his spine on overhanging branches and hauling futilely on the reins. After clinging on for a few chicanes he gave up and curled into a foetal position before bouncing off an oak tree and skidding to a halt halfway up his horse's neck when it ran smack into the back of Harry Langmead's big grey. Hard on his heels and laughing uproariously were a handsome older lady with ravishing bone structure and a loud camp man on a chestnut.

This trio, known affectionately within the hunt as Two Queens and a Duchess, form one of the Ledbury's most engaging curiosi-ties. The Duchess is an adorable merry widow with a thirst for the chase and the contents of the drinks cabinet. The Queens are an antiques dealer called Andy and his boyfriend Nigel who keep their horses with the Duchess. Such is Queen Nigel's devo-tion to Queen Andy that he only took up riding in January and today was his first try at hunting. Seeing him trying to pull his concertina-ed neck out of his body protector and organise his petrified face into a smile of exhilaration as his boyfriend approached, I wondered whether his heart, not to mention his bones, would last the season intact.

Despite the much chattier and less competitive atmosphere, Mondays are not without their hairy moments. As the hounds were running after the second of the three brace of foxes they killed today, Peter led us over some sturdy rails into a coppice. Seeing Mrs Langmead pop over it I followed her on Norm, who flew the rails and then stopped dead with surprise when he saw the fat hidden ditch immediately beyond them. Luckily Ari shunted into the back of him and sent him on over the trench just as I was tipping forward into the quagmire. Sally Evans was less fortunate and was dragged face down along the brambly path with her foot caught in the stirrup after her horse tried to jump the whole thing in one.

It took until mid afternoon, when only a handful of riders were still zooming around a big conifer plantation, to make any headway with Peter Evans, a master we must win over if we're to progress on the Hunt button front. I misdiagnosed Peter this morning. He's not sullen so much as sick. We've already been warned about catching the hunting bug but in Peter I saw first hand the debilitating effect of the virus when it takes over your life. So great is his passion for fox-hunting that as well as running his own printing business he also works as a long-distance articulated-lorry driver in order to cover all the expenses for half a dozen horses and a full-time groom to care for them. Like most of the other masters he bears the physical scars of his fair share of nasty falls, the lasting effects of which he can control by taking increasing amounts of painkillers as the season wears on. But the hunting bug has triggered more serious harm to Peter's mental facilities. The infection has spread through much of his brain, meaning that virtually the only topic that animates him is hunting and his horses – a condition not helped by his co-dependent wife Sally contracting the bug herself. In the light of concerns that the hunting bug is an inherited syndrome it may be just as well that both the Evanses and the Harveys are childless. For although experts claim that with careful management and periods of recuperation during the summer months even people with full-blown hunting disease can live to a ripe old age, there is no known cure.

We left the Evanses at half past three, concerned that each new story about the amazing run the hounds had taken them on last year out of the very wood we were sweeping would break down our immunity to hunting germs and aware that Norm and Ari were flagging. Peter and Sally have seven horses between them for the season, while we're relying completely on our two. Hoping they go the distance, I gave Norm a well-earned scoop of sugar beet with his muesli.

TUESDAY 5 NOVEMBER
THE COT

It's a lovely clear sky for Bonfire Night. The Yarwoods' old stallion was frolicking in the gloam when I led Norm and Ari in for supper across fields covered with low wisps of mist. As I strode up the farm track flanked by the horses, our backs to the setting sun, our breath billowing up like steam through the cooling air and their ears pricked at the thought of their grub, I felt an unexpected feeling creeping up on me, so foreign and half forgotten that for a moment I struggled to identify it.

Happiness. That's it. I'm stupidly, bewilderingly happy. I haven't experienced this surge of elation since I was a child. When was the last time you were struck with a sudden simple conviction that all was well in your world, a blissful feeling all its own and unanchored to any recent digestion of drink or drugs or sex or good news? A sensation occurring for no apparent reason of the sun not just on your face but beaming right into your head.

WEDNESDAY 6 NOVEMBER
THE COT

It's still here even though Dad rang this morning to report that a large part of Archie's hair had been scorched off during the home-made fireworks display at Cathedine and to offer me an intriguing front-of-house job that eventually turned out to be a career traipsing bewildered foreigners around the front of his house.

I can't resist prodding myself to work out why I feel like this. There are the obvious pleasures of bunking off, of course. Who wouldn't feel chipper spending a good chunk of their day in bed reading *Catch-22* and making half-baked applications for a hardship grant from the Society of Authors while their sister slaves away in a Quit Smoking call centre? The time of year is also propitious. Exercising the horses, one of the few activities I undertake that resembles anything like work, involves trekking round a ravishing stretch of countryside still full of autumn colour, armed with an Ordnance Survey map to guide me on to camouflaged bridlepaths and a bag for collecting conkers in. Even the hours I spend each morning and evening shovelling muck around coincide neatly with the times of day when my London friends are braving the rush-hour traffic.

But the biggest factor has to be the effect that spending two days of each week fearing for your life has on your attitude to the other five. For hours at a time on Friday and for significant stretches of Monday I was acutely aware that if I didn't slow Norm early enough, steered badly, misjudged a jump or got plain unlucky with a hidden rabbit hole or a slippery stretch of road, I could get badly bashed up at any moment. For the bits when my brakes didn't work my body throbbed with dread, the way your fingers can if you stand near the edge of a cliff and contemplate how hard you'd have to hang on if you somehow ended up dangling over the sheer drop below. On the days when this isn't going on I'm so pleased to still be animate that my old worries seem absurd. Instead of fretting that I haven't got a boyfriend I loll in bed savouring not being interfered with and wondering what to do with the money I used to spend on getting my legs waxed. I don't care that I've had two evenings out in as many months. As I lunch on pasties instead of prosciutto I cherish every sign of life as I knew it passing me by and can't even get myself properly worried that my bank account will run dry by the end of the year.

FRIDAY 8 NOVEMBER
THE COT

It is accepted practice at the Ledbury that whenever a particular sort of leggy, statuesque woman of a certain age and deportment appears at a meet, an appreciative whisper goes round that she is the illegitimate daughter of the Duke of Beaufort. A generous coating of pale pink lipstick that seeps into the deep smoker's lines around her mouth combined with a handsome face framed with pearls and a mane of hair that has been expertly dyed to mask the grey is enough to make any lady an unwitting contender for this dubious honour. But the real sign of breeding is in her posture. Above her Barbour and fur hat should sit an invisible stack of books that she has carried erect since she was a deb.

Just such a candidate appeared on foot at today's meet and caused excitement when it emerged that in addition to being related to the royal family of fox-hunting she was writing a book about the sport. I was then wheeled out as the Ledbury's author in residence and encouraged to relate the essential themes of the season so far as I saw them. I knew what was needed – an off-the-cuff rendition of the hunting reports from various packs that now occupy up to nine whole pages of *Horse & Hound* at a time. There is an art to writing these accounts and no slim measure of skill in understanding passages of impenetrable non sequiturs that run something like this:

Godfrey and Venetia Whitehead generously hosted a meet of the Hawchester Hounds in the Vale of Pimpleton where an early thaw made for soft going and attracted a strong contingent of younger riders from the North Bottom Pony Club. After drawing Thistle Dingle, huntsman Tom Carter put his hounds in Amos Agony's bale stack where a customer was quickly afoot. Turning his mask west across the marsh this pilot took us on a rattling good gallop up along Roman Ridge before going to ground in the willow beds. A six-mile point in an hour and twenty-minute hunt or eight miles as we travelled. Fresh foxes intervened at Arse's Clump, and checking, hounds had to work it out over slurry before following a left-handed line behind the walled gardens at Brearton. Reunited, they were soon on better terms and rolled him over in a sown field bordering the lane that divides Chipchase Farm from the Flabringham country. A ferocious snowstorm saved the brushes of a further brace found in Bullerstock's Spinney that were given best in failing light before being accounted for.

An art that, alas, we quickly established I haven't mastered. Condensing the chaos of my hunting days into a tidy little item in which hounds run hither and thither across a landscape where every last thicket of stinging nettles and thorn bushes knows its own name is beyond me. All it takes is a few boggy acres of plough and a couple of casualties at a jump for the affairs of fox versus hounds to become as distant from riders like me, struggling to keep afloat in the heaving mass of muddy horses on their trail, as the relationships between allegorical figures floating about on the ceiling of a chapel. I can recall with perfect clarity the colour of the watercress bed in the meandering stream where one horse kicked another so hard that it fell over and half drowned its rider. I can tell you the exact expression on its rider's face when a clumsy Dutch-bred horse beached itself on the top of a fence and turned turtle on the road the other side. But my GPS co-ordinates and how far the hounds had travelled as the crow flies or the fox runs during these incidents remain a complete mystery.

Puzzled by my ignorance, someone asked me what kind of book I would be writing about the Ledbury if I didn't understand hunting. All in good time, my pretties, all in good time.

MONDAY 11 NOVEMBER
LITTLE MARCLE

I feel we're beginning to get the hang of things. We earned our first official bollocking from Peter Evans this afternoon but rather than shuffling off home to repent we've stopped off at the Trumpet Inn to celebrate.

Although he did rethink his initial impulse to kick Mrs

Langmead's Dublin Horse Show champion as we arrived at the meet, Norm set the tone when he started making eyes at the plates of sandwiches being passed round and ended up headbutting a whole tray of them across the yard during the Remembrance Day minute's silence. The rain started up soon after we reached the first covert, and bored of standing around getting wet, we decided to copy hunt stalwarts like Mark Bennet and Mary Clarke the milkmaid and make our own way over to see what the hounds were up to on the other side of the trees. Leaving everyone else waiting for the master to emerge from the wood we trotted down the lane and up an overgrown track where we found Anthony the Whip snatching a cigarette break. He fell in behind us and before long the three of us were belting full speed across a field so unmarked and green it reminded me of Astroturf. Quite by accident we ended up bang next to the hounds and in full view of Peter Evans but the wrong side of a high wire fence to reach him.

When, after much scrambling about, we made it back into the wood and rejoined the field at second horses, Anthony managed to melt away round the back of the kennel lorry as Peter Evans bore down on us. His style was more headmasterly than Jack's fury on the riverbank but his anger was as patent. Without permission we had trespassed all over the smallholding of a woman who has barred the hunt from her land. He would receive a furious phone call from her this evening and any hope of her relenting her ban would be lost. We didn't know the country or what was going on and it was basic good manners to stay behind the Field Master. All of this was true but the impact of the bollocking was much diminished by the sound of Anthony chortling in the lane behind us.

WEDNESDAY 13 NOVEMBER
THE COT

It looks as though New Labour really do mean business. At the State Opening of Parliament the Queen teamed up a pair of bifocals with her ceremonial robes to deliver a speech that included a promise to unveil a bill on hunting with dogs before Christmas. After twice voting to ban hunting since it came to power in 1997, and twice being blocked by the Lords, the Government has pledged to bring the matter to a 'conclusion'.

If my hunch about the hunting debate being embedded in a class war incited by the bizarre, outdated outfits that we find so sexy is correct, then Her Majesty had better watch her back when she brings today's regalia out for another airing. In fact, I wouldn't even say her grip on the throne is impregnable any more – Mum just rang up bemoaning the new bill and claiming it would all be very different if only she were in charge of everything . . .

FRIDAY 15 NOVEMBER
THE COT

Life at the Cot is proceeding in such a low gear as to be almost vegetative. The lorry is at the mender's yet again and since Monday's meet it has been raining with a soft but depressing persistence that makes it difficult to ever remember a time when it wasn't. The downpour has sprouted a crop of mushrooms along the damp patches under the downstairs windows, but without the strong winds of the last prolonged wet spell to accompany it has sunk us into gloom rather than lunacy.

IN THE PINK

SATURDAY 16 NOVEMBER
THE COT

Alarums. Lunacy has come in search of us. Christy swept through the Cot like a chain-smoking, Campari-swilling hurricane at daybreak, blowing the worst of the rain clouds off to Birmingham and Bee and me out of the doldrums. She arrived with Smartie, a small ginger horse with a resigned expression on its face and a star tattooed on its backside that she has rented for the season. She plans to divide her time between her husbandry duties in town and hunting with us.

Seeing her again made me realise what hartebeests Bee and I have become. While we now live in fear of our horses contracting colic, Christy still lives in fear of being sufficiently horsey to know what colic is and eyed the Poop Scoop with the same degree of bafflement and suspicion that Zsa Zsa Gabor would show towards a cattle crush. When the coronet of trees planted at the tip of May Hill to mark Queen Victoria's Golden Jubilee disappeared into cloud we automatically reached for our waterproofs while she traipsed about the yard in suede court shoes and only a cashmere stole to protect her from the rain shower that reached us twenty minutes later. She has invested in a Patey hat and an exquisitely cut old blue hunting coat to match but doesn't even know how to tack up.

When she assured us that the deep end was the only place for her to start, we took her off to a rare Saturday meet at the Eades, confident of impressing her with the expertise we'd accumulated over a hunting career that now stretches to four whole days. It was a decision I began to regret from the moment we arrived at the pre-meet breakfast held at the bungalow of riding instructors Keith and Cathy Cooper, a house built on the proceeds of selling a showjumper abroad for megabucks. As Christy followed Bee and me inside, the stampede of men in her direction was so powerful we practically had to hang on to the kitchen units to avoid getting swept into the vacuum created by the blast of male bodies rushing from one end of the room to the other. Infuriated wives and girl-friends gripped radiators and door handles like Bond villains trying not to get sucked out of the windows of a depressurising aero-plane as their partners swarmed forward to roll out their best stories to a fresh pair of pretty female ears.

With Christy completely hidden behind a mob of pink coats offering to light her cigarettes and trying to top up her already brimming port glass, women who had studiously ignored Bee and me for the best part of three months began to pass the time of day with us. Biting ruefully into a mince pie I realised this sudden warmth was because we had been displaced by a greater threat. Christy was enjoying the kind of interest we used to merit before; fools that we are, we ushered her in as our replacement as the Ledbury's latest gatecrasher. I can't believe I didn't notice and enjoy it more when I was the girl providing the hunt with the new blood or fresh meat or whatever it is that I'm always being told it needs.

I made a lot of noise about Christy being a newly-wed but that just seemed to fan the flames of adoration around her. She's got just the right sort of petite figure that works best with hunting gear. Even Bee looked outclassed beside her. She's also funny. I think there may have been a time when people said that about me (kindly old aunts, acquaintances whose first language isn't English, etc.), but my incarceration in the Cot has not done my comic timing any favours. I felt as though I was up against Dorothy Parker. Mostly I stood blinking at Christy's dazzling repartee like an illegal immigrant seeing daylight after weeks spent languishing in the back of a freight container. When Mark Bennet told me with glee that when he introduced her to Jack Nightingale the air 'crackled with sexual tension' it was as much as I could do to stop myself garrotting him with a tail bandage.

Mr Yarwood appeared at the meet on Queenie looking brilliant in his pink coat. Sniffing the air authoritatively as Christy won yet more plaudits for rolling up cigarettes on her thigh with one hand while holding her reins, whip and punch glass in the other, he predicted the melting frost might give us 'a screaming scent'. I didn't have time to ask what that meant before the hounds went screeching off towards Longdon at a pace that would have had me screaming along with them if I'd had any breath in my body at any stage over the next three hours of breakneck galloping.

Hunting really should be on Extreme TV or one of those other satellite channels devoted to footage of dangerous stuff that you shouldn't try at home. A fox that must have been fitted with booster rockets took us on three huge circuits of what I think of as a very treacherous, extreme-terrain Scalextric track with seventy-odd horses zooming round it rather than a couple of toy Ferraris. Just as I was beginning to adjust to a speed that made my eyes stream and filled my ears with billowing wind, the jumps started coming. There were lots of rails at first but then came a great big line of pickets leading on to the main road that Ari took so big Bee nearly hit a van parked on the opposite verge. Water tanks topped with wire, gates, pheasant feeders, half-fallen trees, gaping triangular sets of bars called tiger traps; the onslaught never slowed and neither, miraculously, did we.

The closest thing I can imagine to the thrill of being on a horse that is clearing big jumps at high speed is zooming down an icy mountain slope on skis. Whether you are a demon on snow or having your first taste of the Alps, the sheer velocity you are travelling at is exhilarating but it's tempered by a need to concentrate so incredibly hard on what your body is doing that your brain empties of everything else. This morning there wasn't room in my head to feel brave or terrified or any other emotion beyond focusing on whether I should be sitting up more or trying to make Norm shorten his stride. But a cold head isn't the only way to cope with fifty jumps over five miles. Watching Christy leap alongside me without a care in the world, my guess is that a Campari cocktail, a considerate horse and innate panache could do the trick.

Also like skiing, when everything's going right for you out hunting you look and feel amazing, but part of the kick is knowing that in a split second it could all go horribly wrong. We got lucky this time thanks to Mr Yarwood's kindness in jumping ahead of us as an expert pathfinder but I saw Queen Nigel lying swooning from concussion as the Duchess and Andy tried to drag him out of the path of the merciless pack of approaching riders. When another horse turned somersault as we heaved over a narrow stile into deep plough, the hunt's front-runners scarcely gave it a backward glance but we decided to quit while we were ahead and came home at second horses.

SUNDAY 17 NOVEMBER
STAUNTON COURT

We're at church masking our disappointment that tins of baked beans feature more prominently than sheaves of corn in the

Harvest Festival display and thanking God for seeing us safely through yesterday.

MONDAY 18 NOVEMBER
THE COT

I'm getting increasingly concerned that Christy hasn't returned as promised from yesterday's wifely duties to tend to her horse or send us a handful of readies for doing it for her. I hate mucking out, especially for Smartie, an animal as shambolic as his owner. It is only because both of our bank accounts will be headed for the red when the latest cheques to the feed merchants clear that I'm willing to clear up after Smartie's filthy habits at all. He drinks far more than the other horses and then makes a point of kicking the dregs from his water bucket into his bed. He also likes to crap on his hay. In contrast Ari is nearly as fastidious as Bee. Disgusted that Smartie has bits of mud stuck to him where Christy didn't hose him off properly on Friday, she uses a small corner of her stable as a loo and is liable to sulk if I try to re-arrange her sawdust. Norm is somewhere between the two. Mainly he lies down a lot and tells the other two he's doing some thinking for a book he's working on.

TUESDAY 19 NOVEMBER
THE COT

That's eight barrowloads of muck she owes me now.

November

WEDNESDAY 20 NOVEMBER
COLWALL, NEAR MALVERN

We have been bidden to a frosty playing field to watch Archie playing hockey. Arriving for the closing moments of the match and anxious to make public amends for abandoning him when I gave birth at fifteen, we took him off with great fanfare to bulk up at the local Little Chef. Happily munching his way through a mountain of chicken wings, he worried Bee by bingeing on so much cherryade that he became delirious and terrified me with the revelation that by writing in a few snatched minutes when he'd finished his prep each day he'd completed seventeen chapters of his book.

THURSDAY 21 NOVEMBER
THE COT

The Good News: there's a gorgeous full-fat hunter's moon slung low over the drive and a beautiful trio of foxes playing on the gravel beneath it.

The Bad News: I'm only awake because I'm too annoyed to sleep after Christy rang to say that she'll see us a week on Friday without mentioning any rewards for our labours.

FRIDAY 22 NOVEMBER
THE COT

I take it all back. Norm woke up with a puffy ankle and is off games so Bee borrowed Smartie and very grateful for him we are too.

It was a scrappy day with lots of what Mr Yarwood calls 'road bashing', that is belting along the lanes in neighbourhoods where the hunt is not welcome to go across country. Charging along the roads I put some spadework in on my Hunt Hate. A Hunt Hate is the opposite of an office crush. Instead of whiling away the hours lusting after someone you wouldn't remotely fancy were it not for the convenience of them working at a desk a few feet away from your own, with a Hunt Hate you work yourself up into absolutely loathing some unremarkable person you ride alongside with outward equanimity year after year. Everyone has one. My Hunt Hate is a man I've never spoken to but the sight of whom causes bile to rise to my throat. A man who barges anyone who gets in front of him out of the way, yet when he falls off throws teddy into the next county if the rest of us don't stop and help him. I still fizz with irritation thinking how he rode Bee off at a gateway when we weren't even doing anything except filing through out of the way of passing traffic. I wonder who hates us. Bee's going to try and factor some names into the Hunt Butt graph.

MONDAY 25 NOVEMBER
THE COT

A foggy meet at Kynaston. It was very slow going although I did follow Davey Smith, an eighty-one-year-old daredevil who has hunted with the Ledbury since 1936, only missing seasons lost to war and foot-and-mouth, over a nasty ditch with corrugated iron in front of it. Davey hunts on an impressively low budget, first riding horses for his incapacitated friends and then inheriting the animals when incapacity deteriorates into death.

All the talk was about *Daniel Deronda*, the costume drama everyone had watched on Saturday night. The hunting scenes that I thought got the story off to rather a good start had totally failed to pass muster with the experts. Not only were they filmed in the middle of summer, but the actresses looked like they were wearing body protectors under their side-saddle habits and even more sacrilegiously the sound of hounds speaking (the warbling noise they make when they're on to a fox) had been dubbed over footage of them standing about at the meet. Mark Bennet was practically threatening to write to his MP about it.

TUESDAY 26 NOVEMBER
THE COT

The future is not looking very orange. After failing to even get an interview for a job stacking shelves on the twilight shift at Tesco desperation has set in and I am contemplating joining a pyramid selling scheme. The job involves hawking catalogues for air freshener and detergent to old ladies from the back of the horse lorry and the remuneration package is so meagre that I'll have to shift a staggering 7,000 packets of re-usable antiseptic wipes if I'm going to pay off the balance on my Patey hat that is now ready for collection.

In the Pink

It's 7.30 a.m. and steam is coming out of the lorry's ears as it climbs the bluff above Gloucester at less than eight miles an hour, so slowly that I can scribble this down as I drive. I've got a heavy load on board of what Bee thinks are brochures for incontinency knickers and Limescale-Ease. In actual fact it is the weight of Ari and Smartie. Christy and I had a last-minute invitation from the hunting philosopher Professor Roger Scruton to saddle up with the smart set at the Vale of the White Horse and she is treating me to an expedition to see how the other half live.

9.30 a.m. The lorry is yet to catch his breath but I have made it to a barn built on a flat grey expanse outside Malmesbury. Christy of course is late so I am sheltering from the bitter east wind with the Prof's groom and checking out the oppo. The Scrutons' horses are much bigger than ours but they don't look as nimble. A man with the complexion of an oatcake, who I think must be the Prof, drove past a minute ago in a swanky 4x4. He stopped and asked me if I was Christy and then if I was Christy's groom before continuing on his way up to a stone cottage and walking firmly inside.

10.15 a.m. Christy polled up just as the Prof's incredibly pretty and pert-bottomed young wife invited me in for breakfast. She's established an instant rapport with the Scrutons' two small children and was still coating their angelic upturned faces in fag ash and Campari fumes when I went to check out the books in the Prof's upstairs loo. There's a great fat brick on Roman law, a Czech–Punjabi dictionary and a book of children's stories written in French. It looks like he really is as clever as they say. The smell of browning sausages is mouth-watering but I think I'll take my time up here and put off the moment when I have to pit my lowbrow mots against his.

10.50 a.m. My first impression of the meet is that I should have emptied the entire contents of my make-up bag on to my face before setting out. Now that the Clinique all-weather stuff is gone we've been plastering our cheeks in Vaseline in the hope that most of the brambles will slide off them. But set against the golden 'I've got a house in Barbados' tans and powdered alabaster brows of the VWH ladies, our faces look like chipped red billiard balls. They have Knightsbridge-blonde chignons. We don't even have hairnets. Where they have mouths painted rosebud pink and accessorised with an ever-present Silk Cut lolling from their lower lip, I can feel the first ruptures of a cold sore. Even in the driving rain that stalked us all day, their mascara held firm and their complexions kept the unsmudged look of newsreaders'.

Apart from a lethargic fox killed within minutes of the meet, but not before one of the Knightsbridge blondes had bitten the dust, the scent was poor and so the hounds didn't get up to much. Their famous but now elderly huntsman Sidney Bailey controlled them with just the odd whistle but had none of Jack Nightingale's sense of urgency. Undaunted, we made the best of a slow day by finding our sport in the VWH riders, a friendly gang who must have been put together by central casting. The Field Master had one eye that didn't report for duty and the cap was collected by a barking, chain-smoking retired colonel with a Cossack riding style that I expect was honed in a cavalry regiment before the Great War. We were also quickly befriended by a young duchess on an immaculate grey showjumper who told us how worried she was about finding the money to pay for it in a manner that made it abundantly clear that her similarly recently acquired Austrian archduke owned half of Wiltshire.

The cast of characters also stretched to Joe Brassington, a jolly scruff of a man who couldn't seem to get his coat to do up. Between telling lots of jokes about an easily seduced barmaid called Lucy Lastic he was full of ancient wisdom about what was going on. Particularly memorable was the time he led us into a plantation of ash trees and got very overexcited about the way the magpies suddenly started chattering. Telling us that birds often mock a fox when it enters a covert and give its whereabouts away he threw his head back and yelled to no one in particular, 'Oi! Look lively. These magpies are swearing like f**k!'

Despite a valiant high-speed effort from the Prof at a tricky stone wall, the Peppermore prize went to a quiet fellow visitor who rode his classy slender chestnut like a dream and jumped hedges nobody else dared attempt. I temporarily forgot about the rain trickling down the small of my back and collecting above the fastener of my bra, when, as we nestled in a dingle, his chestnut gave Ari a love bite. But alas we got separated by an ill-tempered outburst caused when a gruff old farmer came haring up to a gateway totally out of control on a lathered great bull of a cob and crunched heavily into the back of a young dandy engrossed in conversation on his mobile phone. The dandy complained loudly and advised the farmer that he might have less trouble with his brakes if he removed his spurs. Offended, the older man said he'd gore his own horse with his own spurs as much as he f***ing well pleased.

The two sniped at each other for hours until at last as the day drew to a close at Charlton Park, the tawny family seat of an earl now sadly divided into flats, Dandy agreed to buy the unruly bullock. With much chat about how he would re-train the horse and teach it some manners he mounted it and was immediately carted off along an oak avenue. My enduring memory of the smart set is of the wily farmer with a cheque for £3,500 warming his breast pocket smirking as his dapper young customer disappeared across the park into the dusk, his horse stretching out its neck and into fifth gear.

FRIDAY 29 NOVEMBER
THE COT

The first lesions of the hunting bug are making themselves felt. After an all-night party in London last night Christy and I clamped our Patey hats to our throbbing heads and hit the M4 courtesy of her brother Alec and his company car to make it home in time for the meet at Town Street Farm, scene of Mark Bennet's drubbing earlier in the season.

The idea that Alec and Christy are in any way related is a source of continuing bewilderment to me. Apart from a dark thatch of hair that refuses to lie down Alec has always seemed like the archetypal slick young executive on the few occasions that I've met him. He runs a company selling specialist machinery for blasting old chewing gum off pavements that required lots of international conference calling from the car and if his sister hadn't grabbed the jacket of his beautifully cut suit and rolled it into a ball to use as a pillow for the journey down I have a suspicion he would have dangled it from a coat hanger on a hook behind the driver's seat. He's a nice enough guy but Christy says he's too hygienic to have sex appeal.

When we arrived at the Cot to find Bee just stirring, Christy, presumably still in the midst of a caffeine rush, leapt out of the car and said she was off to do the mucking out. Like a new convert eager to confess but not sure what to divulge once behind the monsignor's grille, she spent twenty minutes in Smartie's stable before emerging with an empty wheelbarrow and a stubborn ball of dung skewered on her spike heel and admitted she didn't know where to start. She's a brilliant antidote to *The Manual of Horsemanship* brigade. She doesn't give a monkey's about stable management, the boring grooming and feeding part of hunting. All she wants is an animal that's still standing when she leaps on to it at eleven o'clock every Friday morning. She can't tell if Smartie has got a puffy knee or a hot tendon and so long as he's still staggering about in view of the hounds she doesn't care. By Christy's reckoning Smartie is no more sentient than a sit-on lawnmower and she can't fathom why Bee and I waste our time coddling Norm and Ari. Like a man taking care never to discover where the Hoover is kept just in case he's called on to use it, she plays dumb if we teach her how to clean Smartie or his tack.

This morning she manipulated our yearning for Hunt buttons as brilliantly as ever and opted to stay inside and make toast while we, anxious not to be tarnished by association, swabbed the worst of the filth off Smartie. I know it's bristly behaviour but I just can't help it. Far more anal was Alec's performance at breakfast. He declined to sit down after noting the horsehair plastering the sofa, didn't touch his tea once he spotted scum marks around the cup and only dug into his cereal after rinsing his spoon under the hot tap. When we invited him to see us off at the meet he pleaded a conference with his suppliers in Walsall and hurried out to his car grinning nervously like a man escaping from a close encounter with friendly savages.

After last night's exertions on the dance floor Norm seemed very big and boisterous and so I didn't dare promenade him around the meet for fear of him giving someone his pesky right hook. I'm very glad we bothered rushing down though. Before I had a chance to feel too nervous a fox belted out across the meadows towards Bushley and we gave chase behind it. As the scores of horses fanned out across the big flat field I saw a fat khaki fortification coming into view. When nobody slowed, nobody veered towards the gateway and a battle cry of 'Get yer bats out!' went up, I realised the moment was upon us. We were about to attempt our first hedge.

Right up in the first wave of riders going freestyle at the thing, I saw Queenie launch bravely into the wall of green, Mr Yarwood's pink coat hover over it for an instant and then disappear. I calculated I was about twenty seconds from take-off. So much for emptying my head of erroneous thoughts. Shit shit shit. Was I going too fast? Too slow? What about Norm? He was gliding across the spongy turf as smoothly as ever but his head was very low down. Had he even seen what was coming? Perhaps I should shorten the reins. Ten seconds. What was this bat I was meant to get out? Did he need a kick? I could see the first fallers now. Five seconds. Was I straight? What should I aim for? Shit a brick. Someone had refused and was wheeling back across my path. Pull to the right. Right! I can't! I'm too scared to move. Where's my bat? Oh shit, oh God, oh shhiiiiiiit.

There was a horrible jolt and everything went dark. Then I opened my eyes and I was on the other side of the hedge and steaming up the slope to a set of double rails. Yet again Norm had taken charge, soaring over to safety so perfectly he didn't even touch the hawthorn fronds with his belly. My paralysis disappeared and I was soon slapping Norm's neck and rubbing his mane in gratitude. Seeing a splodge of pink as good old Mr Yarwood twisted round to check that I was over I waved and looked back for Bee. Alas, what was meat and drink to Norm had got stuck in Ari's throat. As Bee zoomed into the hedge Mary the milkmaid had careered past her to the left on a horse that refused and then threw her off. Blown off course but bold as ever, Ari did a huge diagonal leap over the hedge that deposited Bee headfirst on the top of it.

Leaving her rider for dead Ari galloped onwards to me and Norm. As she approached the field where the rest of the hunt were waiting for the hounds to pick up the scent again the chorus of 'Loose horse' was replaced by derisive howls of laughter and shouts of 'One of the Watson girls is off!' The jeers swooped and fluttered around my head as I led Ari back to where Bee was being retrieved from the hedge. They had noticed us at last. It might have taken an unscheduled cartwheel on to a hawthorn bush to do it but for the first time I really felt part of the Ledbury Hunt. People crowded round checking Bee was unhurt and explaining that bat is slang for whip. You get the bats out when a big jump is coming, unless you're riding Norm that is. To crown it all, when the hounds started up again Jack Nightingale dashed past, swivelled round in his saddle and winked at me. Bee says he's got a squint but she's mistaken. He winked, I'm sure of it.

9

December

Norm's ankle is hot and full of fluid again and he's got a nasty nick on his knee. Mr Yarwood said it was time to let him have some bute and gave me a couple of sachets of white powder of exactly the same consistency as cocaine to administer to him. Feeling bad about introducing a seven-year-old to hard drugs I dutifully went off and found my credit card and began chopping the stuff into two lines on a plank in the tack room. Then, wondering if the old adage about leading horses to water but not being able to make them drink applied to offering them narcotics, I asked Mr Yarwood for the best way to get Norman to sniff it. His eyebrows shot up into his scalp at the question and, looking suspiciously at my handiwork, he told me to sprinkle it on Norm's food. If he doesn't like the taste and won't eat it then I'll have to mash it into a paste and syringe it down his gullet.

TUESDAY 3 DECEMBER
THE COT

Oh Norm is eating it all right. He seems to be enjoying life on opiates. His leg is much better already and he has been going around geeing up all the other horses. Sadly my familiarity with recreational medication has done nothing to improve my standing with my landlords.

I have been spending much of the day listening to the radio and trying to peer through the snowstorm of our telly reception for details of the new Hunting Bill. I'd been expecting fox-hunting to be finished off in a style similar to the way its hounds slay their quarry – with a single fatal bite to the throat that would see the sport abolished entirely by next winter. But not a bit of it, now that Rural Affairs Minister Alun Michael has hunting's jugular exposed he is setting about destroying it with the legislative equivalent of a plastic picnic knife.

The Bill bans hare-coursing and stag-hunting outright but the future of fox-hunting will depend on individual packs convincing an independent registrar that they constitute the most effective and least cruel method of fox control in their area – an uphill task given that there aren't any accepted tests to gauge the supposed cruelty or utility of different methods of pest control. Yet ironically, being secreted into the bureaucratic machinery of Whitehall provides fox-hunting with its strongest lifeline. For if a particular hunt disputes the registrar's findings they can appeal to a tribunal set up by the Lord Chancellor – a process likely to take up to five years, during which time they can continue hunting. This fact has not been lost on Mr Michael's own back-benchers who, furious that he has 'botched' his chance to deliver a deadly blow to fox-hunting, are already plotting vengeance. In open revolt to the Prime Minister's preference for a 'middle way' of regulation, they plan to go in for the kill by amending the Bill to impose a total ban. Using the Parliament Act to override opposition to the amended Bill in the Lords they're determined to consign hunting to the history books by the spring of 2004 at the latest.

WEDNESDAY 4 DECEMBER
LONGDON

When I nipped over to the Bennets' to discuss all this with Mark, I found him glued to the sofa and singing along to a video of *My Fair Lady* with his father. They had been too engrossed in the latest round of internecine fighting within the ranks of their own pack to notice the publication of the Hunting Bill. The Ledbury are fiddling while Rome burns. So wrapped up are they in the shenanigans about who will be Friday Field Master next season that they don't seem to have spotted that there may well not even be a next season.

The crisis has been precipitated by Thomas Harvey, who, worried that he falls off too much and doesn't enjoy the pressure of being in charge, wants to stand down as master. This has opened the floodgates, with the usual plots for Ken Unwin to replace Jack Nightingale as huntsman, and spawned a myriad of new conspiracies. To my great surprise I learnt that it is normal to advertise for the post of master much as you would any other job. The remuneration of £50,000 a year sounded pretty lavish until I found out it costs far more than that to fund the hunt for a season.

But before they come to a decision about whether to seek applicants from outside the Ledbury country the hunt stalwarts are having a high time picking over the devils they know. The most important qualification for a potential master of foxhounds is that the person should command the respect of the whole of the rest of the hunt. In the Ledbury, and I suspect most other packs, this pretty much rules everyone out of contention.

Top of the list to replace Thomas is his predecessor as Friday Master, Billy Chadburn. Billy's personal motto is 'I likes to live dangerous' and most of the Ledbury's bravest riders have got a pair of broken wrists, a punctured lung or a dead horse to show for the time they attempted to follow him over some mammoth hedge or cruelly angled seven-bar gate. Aficionados say he is as impressive a man across country as you'll find anywhere in the big jumping shires around Leicester. The problem is following him. Billy knows no fear. A couple of years ago when thieves tried to steal his Range Rover he leapt on a scrambler bike and gave chase with such ferocity that he drove them off the road. Some feel he's also got an ego to meet Jack Nightingale's punch for punch, which could prove problematic.

THURSDAY 5 DECEMBER
THE COT

Panic. I have been invited to dinner with Harold Pinter, Britain's Greatest Living Playwright, and his wife Lady Antonia Fraser, Britain's Greatest Living Historian, by her son Orlando Fraser, Britain's Greatest Living, um, well . . .

Conscious that Orlando has probably billed me to his other guests as a feral oddity whose book will be a cautionary tale of what happens to civilised people once they move to the country, I spent the day refreshing my table manners so as not to do a Tarzan Lord Greystoke when the fish course and port decanter come round. I also tried to kick-start my brain by watching *Countdown*. But even after kitting myself out with pen and paper like a real jobsworth, the only anagram I could make out of NQTAOMDEB was MOAN. Jim, a retired mechanic from Bradford wearing a jumper that looked like a trifle with arms, got BOATMEN and the smug girl with the dictionaries and her even squarer friend managed ABDOMEN.

As if having an IQ in freefall wasn't bad enough, when I trudged out of the yard to do the horses I met Jack and Anthony on a quad bike preparing to do some earth-stopping for tomorrow's hunt. Nerves again got the better of my repartee and I was badly let down by my daywear. As Jack struggled to make pleasantries I couldn't risk looking at his face for fear of the flea bites he would see on mine. Cursing my mauve tracksuit bottoms and stunted gnome wellies, I tried to remember the last time I looked in the mirror. With all the wretched dropping in that goes on around here I shall be applying full war paint before going downstairs in the morning in future.

FRIDAY 6 DECEMBER
BAYSWATER

I was totally monstered by Harold Pinter last night. After quoting pieces of *The Homecoming* at me he got on to the topic of Iraq. He had recently been given a prolonged standing ovation at the University of Turin after making a vehemently anti-American speech when he collected some honorific bauble from the faculty there. In an effort to hold my own, I responded half-jokingly that that was all very well but he was hardly going to change the world with the support of the Italians and the few dinky tanks their laughable armed forces tool around in at ceremonial occasions.

He went ballistic, swearing and slamming down his fork. He looked to me like a venomous old rooster wearing a black polo-neck jersey. I should have been terrified and I probably would have been if I hadn't endured Norman's tantrum at the opening meet. As it was I sat at ease, thinking how little actual damage the literary giant shaking with fury on my left could do me. He couldn't drag me flat out across Hyde Park like a maddened bronco. He couldn't get his tongue over the bit, slip out of his martingale and smash me over the garden railings and into the oncoming traffic of the Bayswater Road. He had innocuous loafers on, not iron-soled shoes with stud nails coming out of them. If the worst came to the worst I would be brawling with someone shorter and scarcely heavier than myself rather than over half a ton of muscle. For all his wrath Harold even had fewer of his own teeth than Norm. And who was watching? Six, eight, ten people. I had survived a far more humiliating attack in front of a few hundred.

When it began to look as though Harold was going to detonate charred pieces of cashmere all over Orlando's freshly decorated dining room I was moved to the other end of the table well away from Britain's Greatest Living Crosspatch.

December

SATURDAY 7 DECEMBER
THE COT

At some point between boarding the late train to Gloucester and losing mobile reception outside Kemble, bravado got the better of me last night and I invited Mr Smith to come and stay for the weekend.

In readiness for his arrival tonight I'm working on a blowsy 'just good friends' routine but in the tiny hope that he leads me away from my prepared text I haven't been able to resist cleaning up the Cot, changing the sheets and waxing hair off great swathes of my surface area. I keep telling myself that this is just because hunting has endowed me with the firm but lean figure of a professional swimmer and he is one of the few people who will appreciate my new improved bum. I have lost four inches round my hips and my buttocks have tightened and sprung upwards in a manner so agreeable it's remarkable they've managed it without a helping shove from a scalpel.

I'm debating whether I'll get beaten up in the station car park if I wear full hunting dress to pick him up from his train. Perhaps I should compromise and settle on my long boots and some artificially distressed jodhpurs . . .

SUNDAY 8 DECEMBER
BLEAK HOUSE

Bloody, bloody hell. General Total Failure to get my bottom an airing.

The patchwork of green I thought I had put between Mr Smith

and myself buckled the moment he walked across the ticket hall towards me. I'd been prepared for a gruesome haircut or one of those slightly camp French Connection jumpers and blunt-toed boots men my age tend to drift towards if left to their own fashion devices. But I knew from that kick in the guts feeling of longing as he folded his long legs into the Renault's freshly hoovered passenger seat that nothing had changed at all.

By the time freezing fog laid siege to the Cot at dusk and we talked over a casserole bought from a lady in the village for me to pass off as my own work it became clear Mr Smith was resolved to only ever being friends. Knowing I was sunk I smiled along, inwardly preparing to spend the rest of the night twitching with desire on the wrong side of the paper-thin wall from him. In the small hours I even started to feel nostalgic for a time when I was in contention for the title of Molly Smith, eventually coming to my senses in the cold light of dawn and realising I could never have agreed to a marriage that would have made me sound like an apple.

But Mr Smith can't drive, can't ride and won't go outside in wintertime on non-essential errands so with Bee away on a filthy weekend with Odius Daniel I was stuck within scorching distance of him all day, trying not to relish the long-absent smell of his hair or be reminded of why we made each other laugh so much. When the decent weekend telly ran dry and he started to pack for his return to London I veered so badly off message I even cried.

The forecast is for sleet and snow with a wind-chill factor of minus 3 degrees that isn't expected to ease for days – the weather and my mood both.

MONDAY 9 DECEMBER
THE COT

We met at Crossfield Point, home to the Nelsons, the only family we've found around here who manage to combine an obsession with horses with gracious living. Their farm houses their string of point-to-pointers and event horses but it also has a tennis court, an indoor swimming pool and the look of a place where on Sunday mornings the occupants sit about in white towelling bathrobes reading the colour supplements in their conservatory. Katherine Nelson, a feisty girl, is the hottest romantic property in the county. If only we could find a Y chromosome for her Bee and I would join in the chase.

My gloom about Mr Smith lifted slightly when a lady visitor from the Beaufort got tipped off when we scrambled across a river. When she got back on Norm very nearly took her head off with an impromptu handstand and earned himself a number of appreciative glances in the process. The Beaufort occupies an important place in the Ledbury's sensibilities. As a four-day-a-week pack owned by a duke and granted the run of the Badminton estate they are far smarter than us but many people within our ranks are convinced that with their manicured hedges, smooth turf and relative dearth of barbed wire they are not made of stern enough stuff. There is ill-concealed envy of a pack so popular that like a fashionable nightclub they have to restrict numbers to the few hundred members of their exclusive guest list. I've heard chippier elements of the hunt, whom I suspect have never made it through the velvet ropes of a Beaufort meet but are rightly proud of jumping mangled iron bedsteads and untrimmed hedges off plough, refer to the Beaufort country as Miniatureville.

Part of me would quite like to see the Beaufort in action if only to gawp at Camilla Parker Bowles on the glossy bay that Hef has allegedly just sold her for £10,000. But it is not just the £150 daily visitor's cap that dampens my enthusiasm. My loyalty to the Ledbury makes me increasingly parochial. I don't want to meet the buff-lapelled grandees on the other side of Gloucestershire any more than I fancy a day in the Forest of Dean with the homely Cotswold Vale pack, known dismissively, somewhat unfairly, amongst some Ledbury subscribers as the ClipClop Farmers. Just as Manhattan once made me indifferent to the attractions of Beverly Hills, I now feel that I've got all the excitement and intrigue I need in this freezing diamond of farmland west of the Severn and north of the Wye.

As if to confirm this, Laura Wallace rode up and introduced us to Eddie Backhouse, a champion point-to-point jockey. A brawny hulk of testosterone, Eddie looks like one of the Bash Street Kids but this doesn't stop women treating him like a touring rock star. Mark Bennet once broke off from haranguing me about an undarned hole in my hunting coat to tell me enviously of parties where Eddie could hardly move for women, and occasionally men, lunging at him. When Eddie asked about my book and I joked that it was called *Eddie Backhouse: His True Story* he blanched.

I can fully appreciate what all the fuss is about. There's going well and going swell. Eddie has won the amateur version of the Grand National over the same Aintree fences used for the real thing and while most point-to-pointers stay at the back of the field he took his fractious black mare bang at the front, sitting out bucks and cracking jokes with a generous grin that actually did stretch from ear to ear. When Norm lost a shoe,

Bee saw her chance and left me to walk him back to the lorry alone while she braved the cold to do some more 'research' on Eddie.

TUESDAY 10 DECEMBER
THE COT

With Bee at the call centre I've slumped back into a stew about Mr Smith. Actually I can't get the Cot sufficiently warm to stew. I'm congealing about him.

WEDNESDAY 11 DECEMBER
THE COT

Hef appeared at the yard today wanting to speak to Mr Yarwood on urgent hunt business. But finding the farmhouse deserted, he allowed himself to be enticed over to the Cot and fed toffees until he spilt his beans.

The news is that the hunt must present a new team of masters to the committee by Sunday and Hef wants to be the godfather of any deal. His fall at the opening meet has aggravated an old injury in his neck but he is keen for Laura Wallace to take Thomas Harvey's place as master. Even slouching on our sofa with sweet papers clinging to his neck brace like dandruff there was no mistaking his authority. Bee called me into conference behind the kettle, speculating excitedly that if Hef could bend the mastership to his will then surely our six piddly Hunt buttons must be in his gift. We agreed to couch our request for buttons as an appeal for advice – and therein lay our mistake. Displaying rather a tin ear to the subtext of our questions Hef gave us a lot of good counsel about chasing foxes and men but made no button promises.

His policy is not to own up to anything unless you have no alternative. He admitted that years ago while on point duty watching out for a fox to leave a covert his horse committed the cardinal sin of kicking a hound. When he got off to look at the injury he found the dog was stone dead. Checking that nobody had seen anything, he then hid the dead animal in a bush and spent the next few hours ostentatiously looking for it, loudly joining the speculation about where it could have got to. He recommended the same treatment for men. We should never admit that we loved them if we could possibly resist it.

He left us deep in thought; Bee musing on those three little buttons, me on those three little words. I need to retract my decla-ration of love to Mr Smith in such a way that will provoke him into repeating them to me.

FRIDAY 13 DECEMBER
THE COT

I can hardly write. My hands keep getting knocked off the keyboard by the aftershocks of the most blissful experience of my life.

I get goose pimples just thinking about the deep notch I carved today. I left my mark, not in a bedpost but over the Stanks Hedge, an obstacle so infamous that it has been given its own name. Most hedges are just that. A nameless oblong of brambles you jump near here to get to there. But the Stanks is what's called a rasper, a hedge marked out and spoken about as though beyond it there be dragons as well as a hefty drop and a gaping ditch. The Duchess has an Icaran photographic montage of herself soaring over the expanse of blackthorn as dense and erect as a marine's flat-top, before her horse stumbled into the ditch and crash-landed with some force a metre or so further on.

We were on our very last run of the day when the whisper went round that we were headed for the Stanks. As we circled the tall patch of trees nearest the Upton road someone pointed the hedge out to me, lying a few fields away as still and watchful as a long brown alligator. The hounds didn't find anything in the covert and we could all have filtered round away from the hedge but it seemed to be baiting us, a gauntlet that had been waiting to be taken up all season. The first to rise to the challenge was Billy Chadburn, who launched his steed into orbit with a mighty clout from his bat worthy of Ian Botham's 1981 Ashes triumph. But when I saw Thomas Harvey swerve out to the left on his approach I wondered whether I should troop after Bee and Smartie in the gang of horses circumventing the hedge through a series of iron gates. Norm was having none of that though and I figured that if I messed it up badly at least I could put on a frail yet so very brave performance for Mr Smith when he came to visit me in Gloucester Hospital.

I set my sights on the spot where Mr Yarwood had cleared the hedge before me, got a good hold on Norm's face and gave him a few hard kicks as he cantered down the slope to it. A couple of strides out, when he saw the enormity of the jump, he cranked his head round to check that I really did want to take it on and then gathered himself together. Like a lumbering jumbo jet that leaves the ground just when you're sure there's no more runway left, Norm lifted up over the Stanks as the toes of my boots were brushing against its outermost branches. With a heave of hydraulics he hitched his legs up and we were airborne.

Then I was suspended, looking first at the gaping chasm of the ditch as it flashed beneath Norm's outstretched hooves, then at the grass beyond it and out at the stream of horses galloping into the woods ahead and above them the oaks, pinky-grey mist gathering like smoke in their uppermost branches. It could only have been a second, perhaps two, before Norm dipped, landed with a thud of hooves, bunched and bounded on up the hill. But that instant was worth every hour of the hundreds I've spent shovelling muck, cleaning tack and hauling hay over the last few months. In it Mr Smith and the tangle of emotions around him withered away until he took on the size and importance of a stick man in a cartoon strip. I plan to replace the photograph of him in my wallet with a snapshot of Norm that I can take out and stroke when no one is looking.

Was it better than sex? Well it definitely lost something in the fact that when it was all over and I was lying back in the saddle laughing and panting with elation Norm didn't roll over on to his elbows, kiss me and promise to do it all over again when he'd got his breath back. But the climactic ripple and the conviction that at least for a few moments God was in his heaven was right up there in the high nines. At any rate, when I drove back to the Stanks at dusk to pay homage to a set of hoofprints I thought could be Norm's and stand in the ditch with the hedge towering over my head, the frustration of not having jumped it herself maddened Bee so much she set off to London in search of Odious Daniel and her oats.

December

There's nothing worse than hearing the nitty-gritty of other people's sex lives but I think I'm on a roll. Ari jumped eight hedges in a row this morning before losing a shoe and having to retire from a day with a bordering hunt whose name I've forgotten in my jubilation. Mr Smith RIP.

The riding was nearly as gripping as my conversation with Queen Andy on our journey along the motorway to join the Langmeads' local pack. In all his queenly glory Andy had barely a nice word to say about anybody. That man has at times got a tongue so acid his teeth must want to hurl themselves out of his mouth to safety. Bee and I seemed to get his vote, although he warned me that our horses were looking too thin. The rest of the Ledbury he portrayed as either boring or bonking someone else's wife.

As we arrived at the meet he got on to the woes of being a middle-aged gay man – 'Honestly, darling, everyone but everyone is looking for something blond and twenty-five with a massive cock' – and I lost concentration so dramatically I steered the lorry into a shiny new juggernaut belonging to Dawn Wofford, head honcho of the entire Pony Club. I left her a £50 note but not my telephone number. I'm a huge fan of Andy's. He calls his horse a bastard whenever it refuses at a jump and when the hip-flask-toting twelve-year-olds who insist on going at the front of the field get in his way tells them to 'F**k Off'.

SUNDAY 15 DECEMBER
THE COT

My eternal student friend Hugh came to stay last night and started making noises about how Gloucestershire wasn't very rural any more so I took him off to meet the Bennets. I love seeing the effect of their farmyard on a new person. Today it was looking particularly special. Persistent sleet had turned the goose shit into pea-green slush and at one end of the tumbledown barns Eddie Backhouse was busy flattening a selection of rusting old cars and trailers with a JCB to give the place the look of a landfill site.

Hugh is celebrated in London for being JGE – Just Gay Enough. While not actually being homosexual, he is gay enough to form real friendships with women, dress well, eat healthily and watch romantic comedies without reverting to being a marriage-shy emotional cripple by the time the credits are rolling. Not surprisingly Mrs Bennet loved him. But I was worried that Longdon, a village where any amount of gay is probably enough already, might not be ready for him. When we moved on for lunch in a pub that he pronounced quaint in a very loud voice before declaring he was on a cleansing teetotal fast, I thought it would be a matter of minutes before he was just breathing enough. But instead Mark ordered him a steak and ale pie and quickly collared him to be our designated driver for the hunt ball.

MONDAY 16 DECEMBER
THE COT

I'm at home fielding calls from Bee and the other occupants of
the hunt bus who went to Parliament Square to protest at the
first reading of the Hunting Bill wanting to know if they've
appeared on telly yet. They haven't.

I've stayed here mainly because for all my new rustic habits at
the wheel I cannot stand travelling below a certain speed. Taking
five hours to get to Westminster via Cheltenham and Oxford
rather than steaming down the M4 in half the time is the kind
of thing that makes me so impatient I want to kill someone. I also
didn't want to risk being spotted siding with the tweedos by my
former workmates at the *Evening Standard*.

But when the phone stopped ringing and the news flashed
footage of policemen grappling with enraged ladies wearing headscarves jammed on like pith helmets I began to recognise that I'm
part tweedo myself now and wish I was there too. Otter-hunting
outfits were thin on the ground this time and apart from a handful
of pinstriped bankers who came down in their lunch hour to parade
briefcases emblazoned with Don't Ban Hunting stickers above their
heads, the protesters looked like an army of animated Beatrix
Potter characters. When someone let off fireworks mounted riot
police were unleashed on the crowd with hilarious results. The
throng of portly Mrs Tiggywinkles and their liver-spotted Jeremy
Fisher husbands surged forward to pat the horses and inspect their
tack. Bee later recounted a brilliant incident when one young
fieldmouse lookylikey refused to be pushed back from the entrance
to the Commons until she had tightened a police horse's nose-
band and had a look at a worrying lump on its off hind fetlock.

TUESDAY 17 DECEMBER
THE COT

Oh hell. The phone stopped ringing not because Bee and the bus posse were too busy fighting the good fight against the Met to call in, but because BT has cut us off.

THURSDAY 19 DECEMBER
THE COT

They are not the only people our cheques have started to bounce on. A letter has arrived from Forest of Dean District Council asking me to have another go at sending them payment for our £527 council tax bill. £527? We don't even have fifty quid. With the nation's smokers abandoning the call centre and clinging on to their cancer sticks to get them through the festive period we won't have any money coming in at all until the rush of New Year's resolutions summons Bee back to the phones in January.

For the first couple of days of penury we were actually quite amused about having no cash. Feeling like a method actor getting into the part of a rural pauper I turned my back on the silver-packaged Tesco's Finest aisle in the supermarket with the inner comfort of knowing Bee was bound to have some money stashed somewhere that she hadn't admitted to yet. It turned out she had been thinking the same about me. Thanks to Bee being used to a steady salary and me being used to turning to someone with a steady salary in times of trouble, even when we started to plough through the advance and then our savings I don't think we ever really believed the money would run out. And now it has.

FRIDAY 20 DECEMBER
THE COT

Why do I bother recording our location any more? Of course we're marooned at the wretched Cot. We've had to cancel our weekend of Christmas partying in London because the handful of coins Bee managed to salvage from the back of the sofa won't buy enough petrol to power us past Windsor.

The only silver lining I can find in this financial cloud is that neither my parents or their schools will have been able to contact us about fetching Cleo, Archie and Nell at the end of term.

SUNDAY 22 DECEMBER
THE COT

Christy has just departed on a three-week African safari with her husband. I have just made myself a sandwich from Tesco's Value bread spread with nasty old butter. I am tackling this feast in the dark in a freezing cottage on the shortest day of the year listening to the rain lashing down on the skylights and gurgling up through the tack shed floor. Beside me Bee is swaddled in the woolly ruins of her daywear collection trying to read an encyclopaedia of fungus by candlelight to find out whether we can eat the mushrooms growing on the downstairs walls in a risotto of the horses' barley without poisoning ourselves.

In an hour or two we face the prospect of bedtime, a ritual that used to bring relief from the cold but that now involves bracing ourselves to lie in beds so icy that their sheets feel wet. We have implemented rolling blackouts to save on electricity, we are bathing once every three days to save on heating oil but I'm not sure what else we can do. Bee is pinning her hopes on Mum and Dad getting divorced and trying to buy our love.

MONDAY 23 DECEMBER
THE COT

Pigeon House meet, the last before we head home to Wales for Christmas.

It may be days since our own last square meal but stung by Andy's comments about his weight we've dramatically overfed Norm. I hadn't even swung my leg across his saddle when he leapt into the air and threw me heavily on to the road a few hundred yards from Pigeon House. Things didn't get any better when we arrived at the meet and I realised I had put his everyday exercise bit on his bridle, giving myself a strip of rubber instead of the usual levered steel nutcracker to stop him with. Then as I manoeuvred a vol-au-vent towards my mouth Norm rose up on his hind legs in celebration of the bit situation. I wish I could say I sat him like a pro, biting nonchalantly into the pastry puff while my horse paddled the air, but alas I hurtled to the ground without a struggle and squelched cheese sauce on to my already tar-stained backside.

After establishing he was boss Norm went quietly behind Ari when the hounds moved off into a steep copse to one side of the farm. Unusually the crowds of spectators stayed in front of the farm rather than rushing to their cars to follow the hounds' route, which meant that although they missed the spectacle of the hapless Galloping Headmaster smashing his glasses and losing his hat on a low bough they remained in prime position for the day's main attraction. What they had really come to see was our progress out of the wood and down the vale of hedges that swung back towards the meet and included the monstrosity that we had first seen in the photograph on Barry Joyce's kitchen wall.

The carnage was everything the viewers could have hoped for. There were three fallers at the very first hedge, one of them a speckled white horse that was badly winded and limped away with one foreleg horribly dislocated from its socket. To the bitter disappointment of the assembled crowds, when we approached what we now know was Barry's hedge the sensible half of the field went through a gate, reasoning that there was no need to damage themselves and their horses needlessly. Bee and I held back undecided but when I saw my Hunt Hate scramble over the hedge I knew I'd rather die attempting the jump than go through the gate. As I set off at it Norm kept gesticulating at the gateway and then ground to a halt in front of the hedge as a wiry boy on a point-to-pointer Fosbury-flopped across our path and into the ditch on its far side. I was circling back, rattled by my first ever refusal on Norm and in two minds about whether to take my bat to him for the second attempt when Ari came charging towards the hedge and cleared it in such fine style that Mr Yarwood later told Bee she 'ate it up'. Incensed at being over-taken, Norm mewed like a hungry kitten, spun on his heels and tugged me over in her wake.

Now here's a queer thing. After flying the hedge that she had joined the Ledbury to conquer, Bee was flushed and exhilarated but she also declared that she could now give up hunting without a second thought. For me every hedge hatches a fresh strain of the hunting bug in my bloodstream but as far as Bee is concerned it's mission accomplished. It would have been great if she could have had a photograph of her triumph but at least most of the hunt had witnessed her soar through the vale. She was happy enough to finish the season but the burning desire to take on the big country had died for her.

A few hours later she left early to meet the car that Daniel was sending down to take her to the ballet. I can't believe anyone would rather watch *The Nutcracker* (even if they knew their transport there was bankrupting their former boyfriend) when they could be starring in a bone-crunching drama of their own. I stayed out with Mr Yarwood, following him over jump after jump until eventually he stopped turning round to check that I was still in one piece. When I noticed the green ribbon was slipping from Norm's tail, shrugged off as he cleared everything in his path, I began humming the *Chariots of Fire* soundtrack and didn't stop to pick it up. I don't think we ever caught the fox who took us on such a whirlwind afternoon. I hope he dies in his bed, a grand old man.

TUESDAY 24 DECEMBER
CATHEDINE

It's turned out to be a very biblical Christmas Eve. We arrived back at Cathedine just as the lorry coughed up the last drop of oil in his tank to discover no preparations had been made for our arrival and there wasn't any room at the inn for Norm and Ari.

Cleo's excuse was that when they got a disconnected tone on our phone, rather than worry that we might be in trouble, the rest of the family assumed we had made other plans for the festive period. Instead of setting out to check we were alive and well, our sisters had ransacked the last of our daywear still stored at Cathedine and installed their friends in our bedrooms. While Flora and Nell grudgingly made up some beds for us we rode the horses bareback over the hill to our kinsmen the Talybont Watsons, who agreed to let us stable them in an open-fronted cowshed at the bottom of a precipitous slope.

Amanda Watson, whose neat stable yard has to contend with her husband Nick's Bennet-like mania for amassing poultry and letting them roam amongst a shambolic avenue of sheds crammed with his rotting collection of clapped-out cars, had filled the shed with a deep bed of straw for the new arrivals. But when we released the horses into their new digs gushing with thanks to Mandy for making everything so comfortable for them we were shown up badly by Norm and Ari taking a very un-Christian attitude to the proceedings. Norm nibbled at the locally grown hay before spitting it out in disgust while Ari stood by the gate wrinkling her nose up at the smell of cows. They looked so cheesed off that Amanda even offered to turf her nags out of their beds and let ours have their stables. We refused and, dressing Ari and Norm up in all of their indoor rugs and overcoats to brave the cold, urged them to remember their manners.

CHRISTMAS DAY
CATHEDINE

A very merry Christmas. Turkey and its trimmings are so much more enjoyable when one is actually hungry rather than full up on the contents of stocking goodies and our morning ride over the Black Mountains was just the thing for working up an appetite. The sun came out, the horses are so fit now that they tackled the steep climbs on turbo charge and, most valuable of all, exercising them gave us an alibi for not having to witness the family opening our presents to them.

There have been some rum exchanges of gifts beneath our Christmas tree in previous years. Flora once presented my parents with a signed photograph of herself and I remember my mother delightedly feeling the underside of an ironing board for the jewellery box she thought my father must have taped there, only to learn that what she thought was a joke was actually her entire Christmas present. But our financial crisis forced us to improvise our Christmas shopping to a degree that made those episodes look generous. I re-gifted my buxom sister Nell an old bra of mine she had borrowed in the summer and stretched so badly I couldn't use it any more. Bee made Flora a tape recorded from the radio and knocked my parents up a crayoned cardboard dial to show the milkman how many pints they want, despite knowing full well that they don't even have a milkman. I felt awful when I got a video recorder from my uncle in exchange for some foul home-made (and therefore blackberry-infused) biscuits, and all we could find for Archie was a fish-shaped ashtray and some scented bath oils.

To our relief there was an uncanny absence of cross words about all of this when we returned from doing the horses and all settled down to a cosy evening of Del Boy's Christmas Special in front of an open fire fuelled by remaindered paperbacks that Hay-on-Wye's second-hand booksellers flog off more cheaply than logs. The larder was full, the bathwater was hot, Bee and I had about £150 worth of goods apiece we could hawk to the pawn shop in

Swindon if times got hard in January. Except for aftershocks of the sharp stabs of yearning for Mr Smith when Odious Daniel and Chutney, Flora's boyfriend, rang up after lunch I was completely content.

BOXING DAY
CATHEDINE

No hunting for us today. We can't afford the cap.

FRIDAY 27 DECEMBER
CHEPSTOW RACECOURSE

Our highest-grossing day of the year to date. When Australians talk about betting like a Watson, an expression based on two legendary gambling brothers, they mean making the kind of wagers that would make Kerry Packer sweat. We didn't have much capital but we still managed to do our namesakes proud.

Bee backed the rank outsider Mini Sensation who won the Welsh Grand National after a steward's inquiry into how such a thing was possible and I cleaned up by sticking £20 borrowed from Archie's piggy bank on a dark horse called Ibal who romped home at 8/1. Even if Dad succeeds in levying his customary tax on all earnings entering the house we should have enough to pay our council charges and eat properly for a while.

The Chepstow crowd was very warm-hearted, agonising over each horse that fell and cheering when they staggered to their feet again. One lady even braved the biting estuary wind to express an interest in the outdoor jacuzzis some stupendously over-optimistic sponsor was showcasing at the entrance gates.

MONDAY 30 DECEMBER
CATHEDINE

The children's meet of the Brecon and Talybont Foxhounds dawned this morning with the time-honoured ritual of my mother having an epi. An epi, that is an emotional episode bordering on an epileptic fit, is what Pony Club mothers throw in order to dragoon children and ponies into action. It's the stage before they arrive at wherever it is they're going and start worrying about jack-knifing the trailer. By the end of the day when they turn for home the epi will often have subsided into a car chat. Car chatting over the hundreds of thousands of hours Mum and I shared driving home from horse shows and hunter trials formed the bedrock of our relationship when I was growing up. It was a time to talk horse in a major way, exchange secrets and have a good bitch about whichever members of our immediate family weren't in the vehicle.

Now I am supposed to be an adult with a lorry of my own I don't know if the car chat tradition is still alive in my family but from what I witnessed this morning the epi is still going strong. Tempers were running high because Archie wasn't helping get the ponies ready. Archie never helps get the ponies ready but I can quite see that that is no reason not to give yourself a migraine railing against the injustice of having a son who prefers to watch his mother and sisters slaving away from his bedroom window until it's time to go, at which point he brushes a few stray Coco

222

Pops from his chin and strides out into the yard like Toad of Toad Hall. When I left to get Ari ready Arch was putting on his socks in slow motion while outside Mum was shampooing his pony's tail and howling for him to hurry up.

Bee had gone to make merry with Odious Daniel so I had the choice of Ari or Norm for the day. Although I am a bit tall for her I opted for Ari because I think she needs a break from Norm. He looks like the kind of bedfellow who'd hog the duvet and she's obviously finding it irritating sharing the cowshed with someone who goes to the loo all over the place. I also didn't want to risk him kicking any small ponies carrying children whose parents know where I live.

I met up with Cleo and Arch on the back drive to Cilwych, a hill farm overlooking the River Usk, and we hacked along to the meet together. Cleo was riding the infamous Starry, who had recovered from her injuries and was looking rather exotic. She's covered with black and white splodges like the horses Red Indians ride in Westerns and despite a neat row of plaits and shiny tack seemed as if she was thinking wistfully about her Apache childhood on the Great Plains.

All Archie's ponies have names like MayDay and DamBuster and his newest steed was no different. Called Bombardier, he was a beast of baroque proportions with a back as flat and broad as a decent-sized picnic table, a thickset weightlifter's neck and a mouth that after twenty years of being hauled at had lost all sense of feeling. Bomb was really built for jousting and in wet weather wears a Lancelot-style oilskin hood as well as a rug to keep him clean and dry. This and my mother's efforts with the hosepipe mean he emerges on hunting days a snowy-white hairball who is the envy of all. Archie, I noticed, is well versed in the art of the bat. Because pulling on the reins is futile and his legs don't reach far enough below the saddle flap to make kicking very productive, he accelerates by brandishing a varnished bamboo pole he calls his 'whacker' around Bomb's flanks and slows by growling, 'Steady, Bomber,' at him.

Today's meet used to take place in Brecon town centre but after a long tradition of small ponies wiping out on the slippery road down past the cinema it has been rescheduled for safety reasons. Instead we were heading for Buckland, a gentle hill surrounded by rolling farmland that if hunting does get banned in the English shires could become the most sought-after fox-hunting country in Britain. The day was a very Welsh one. The main difference at the meet was that everything was much hairier. The hounds had longer, rougher coats then their Ledbury counterparts as did the ponies, and a disproportionate number of the foot followers.

We set off at a flat-out gallop during which most of the children overtook the Field Master and a couple even overran the hounds, but within an hour we were huddling on the backbone of a mountain in thick fog and freezing rain. Once the weather does this and the huntsman can neither see nor hear his hounds the most excitement you're likely to have hunting in the Brecon Beacons is discovering the soggy tracksuited corpse of some poor unfit accountant who never returned from his office's team-building and leadership course here.

Happy sending text messages to her friends sitting a few feet away, Cleo stayed out until the huntsman abandoned the day at two o'clock, by which time Archie and I had already weaved our way down the hill and home. Waiting for her to return I made a start on the long process of washing down, rugging up and feeding the horses alone. The last I saw of Toad was a noble figure, head down, whacker in hand, heading off across the cobbles to raid the biscuit tin and fire up the PlayStation.

NEW YEAR'S EVE
TALGARTH

No Good Boyo is 'havin' a do' and I'm going to it. Anything would be an improvement on last year when I rang in the New Year in the back of a car belting across St John's Wood to the eighth party of the night in an ongoing search for The Place To Be.

I'm taking along my friend Jess, who is now a fashion designer but grew up in the mushroom fields above Hay-on-Wye. She's flown in from Paris and has been saying she wants to 'go organic'. I hope that means what I think it means.

10

January

NEW YEAR'S DAY
CATHEDINE

The New Year is only nine hours old and already we are haemorrhaging cash. I am outside, still seeing in technicolour and trying to get Smartie to plunge his sore foot into a bucket of hot water in an effort to burst the abscess of molten black pus that is throbbing inside it.

Standing beside me is Tod, our local vet. Summoning Tod is like hailing a black cab disguised in milking overalls and a wolfish ginger beard. It's already cost me the best part of £40 to get him out here and the meter won't stop running while he waits for Smartie to brave the steaming water. Even while the horse is stamping on my toes and kicking over the bucket I can hear the ching-ching of pence totting into pounds on his bill. Tod is looking askance at my pop-eyed efforts with the hot water, stroking Smartie's neck and jotting his observations down in a notebook. Please may he not be writing AMITO, the acronym that Mr

Yarwood's veterinary son Richard claims is common currency in the profession. It stands for Animal More Intelligent Than Owner.

It eventually took an hour and most of my Ibal winnings for Tod to wrench off Smartie's shoe, pop the abscess in his foot with a knife, find the nail that had caused the infection, inject him with antibiotics, bandage his hoof and ram it into a crescent-shaped Wellington boot. During this time I was put in charge of the twitch, a device composed of a noose attached to a small stick that ensured Smartie stood still by inflicting more pain to his nose than the excavations could be causing to his foot. Tod claimed that winching the knot of rope ever tighter around the soft flesh of Smartie's muzzle was releasing endorphins to dull the pain but I'm not convinced. Bee has volunteered to constrict the perfect tip of her retroussé nose with a tourniquet fashioned from dental floss next time she has a Brazilian bikini wax and report back to me.

THURSDAY 2 JANUARY
CATHEDINE

Our departure to the Cot has been delayed by the lorry managing to get a puncture despite not moving for ten days. That machine is such a hypochondriac.

FRIDAY 3 JANUARY
CATHEDINE

We're missing a reportedly brilliant meet being held today at Welland Court, the home of Archie Smith-Maxwell, President and general top potato of the Ledbury, because my mother is worried that we'll skid on black ice.

Black ice? I don't think so. After barely a phone call to the Cot up until now I'm worried that she's suddenly claiming to be concerned for our welfare.

SATURDAY 4 JANUARY
CATHEDINE

Now the lorry keys have gone missing. I'm beginning to suspect a pattern of foul play designed to keep us captive here.

One unwelcome side effect of our extended stay is that Nell, my seventeen-year-old sister between Flora and Cleo, has started riding Norman out. Known as the J-Lo of Powys in appreciation of her juicy figure and determination to be a star, she's destined to become the next Welsh thing in Hollywood after Catherine Zeta Jones. But when she's not off auditioning for the National Youth Theatre or *Pop Idol* she stays at home and goes to Pony Club.

She's been without a horse since the fine summer morning last year when she walked out to the field and found it empty because Mum had flogged her pony for a small fortune to some punters in Bristol. But even though she's out of practice she rides like a dream. Watching her sitting easily in the saddle during Norman's bucks and cavorts as she admired the stooped, sheep-speckled shoulders of Mount Blorenge and the Skirrid Hill rising in the distance, my heart hardened. I resolved never ever to let her legs, blessed with a decade more spring in them than my own, stroll into Jack Nightingale's orbit.

SUNDAY 5 JANUARY
THE COT

We busted outta there but not without casualties. In the speed of our exit the luggage got chucked around in the back of the lorry and Norm spent the journey trampling on the video recorder and my new Patey hat.

We're all very relieved to be back at the Cot and Staunton has put on a fabulous show for our return. The Leadon has spectacularly burst its banks and then frozen in a ravishing deep hoarfrost that covers every last twig and power line with a furry white caterpillar coat of rime. We unloaded in a blaze of red sky that slunk behind May Hill and sent a sliver of moon out in its place as Ari threw herself down on her clean sawdust bed and rolled for joy at not having to share a stable with Norm any more.

MONDAY 6 JANUARY
THE COT

The big freeze has kept the hounds in their kennels for fear that the ice and hard ground will give them sore paws and driven the farmyard rats into the Cot.

We first heard them nestling up to the boiler when we turned it on for an hour yesterday evening. Then during the night when the central heating went off completely and the temperature inside the Cot dipped so low that our flannels froze on to the basin and ice spread over the inside of our bedroom windows, the rodents mutinied and stomped around the attic so loudly I needed ear plugs to get back to sleep. When Bee fell back into her pillows, exhausted from banging on the walls and shouting at them to keep it down, they went one further and ate through our Christmas presents stacked on the kitchen table.

I've detected the patter of tiny mouse feet in the night before but this was something else. I lost an entire Terry's Chocolate Orange to the rats' efforts to keep their blood sugar levels up in the arctic conditions. This mob hadn't tapped and unwrapped, they had munched through the whole thing, regurgitating tiny pieces of silver paper as they went.

As luck would have it Jonah and Vicky, my married accountant friends visiting from New York, dropped in for the evening and claimed to have a solution. It was ironic that every manifestation of The Plan terrified them but the rat problem left them completely unfazed. They toured the stables like zoo-goers entering a reptile house and finding bars rather than glass between themselves and the pythons. They shivered in front of the single-bar electric fire we have resorted to in lieu of central heating, gagged on a supper of non-organic bangers and mash and tried to explain the implications of the Enron scandal for corporate America to hosts who tussled like bear cubs over a stray fifty-pence piece that slid unbidden out from the clutter of unpaid bills, race cards and hairnets that covered the side-board.

At one point Vicky even caught my arm in the glacial tack shed and, staring at my coarsened face and swollen chilblained hands, asked me Oprah-style when I'd started drinking so heavily. She wouldn't believe that the scarecrow standing before her was what you get if you hardly drink at all, stop your gym membership and go out and live the healthy outdoor life Manhattan fitness instructors are always waxing lyrical about.

Yet our rat infestation was a trifle. The only part of rural life beyond a Martha Stewart colour chart that Manhattan had prepared them for was rodent control. The same couple who had been appalled by the local paper's coverage of the Newent Onion Fayre's children's shallot-eating contest brightly described to us how rats could jump ten feet, squeeze out of plug sockets, breed every twenty days and almost certainly would have already snuffled through our bedclothes as we slept. Before they left Jonah paged his PA and had her FedEx over what he promised was the best rat-catching equipment in all of New York City.

TUESDAY 7 JANUARY
THE COT

There is an undiscovered comic genius in our midst. Alec dropped in this afternoon on his way back to London from a trade fair in Bristol and offered to help out with Christy's share of the horse chores in her absence. Instead of admitting that his sister's usual portion of the workload was so small as to be immeasurable, we thanked him warmly but teased that he worried too much about his pristine business attire to risk exposing it to the hazards of evening stables.

The ribbing worked like a charm. After somehow fighting his way into my astrosuit he slid around the icy yard looking like a pantomime hybrid of Gordon Brown and Ken Dodd – the overalls ruched up around his knees to expose a few inches of mud-caked grey pinstripe flapping above a mottled expanse of shin that was rapidly turning puce with cold. The strain of hauling hay bales popped the top button off his shirt and his shiny brogues quickly became scuffed and waterlogged from shit-soaked sawdust and slopping water buckets. Once Smartie had trodden heavily on his foot the stitching on his left shoe gave way completely to expose the silken toe of a thin City sock.

Yet despite losing his favourite fountain pen down a drain and getting a noxious mustard-coloured blob of worming paste in his shock of black hair, he took his metamorphosis into a soggy shambles of his house-trained self in surprisingly good heart. We noticed he slugged down his tea without inspecting the cleanliness of the cup first and, after staying on to warm up in front of *EastEnders,* he eventually hobbled out to his BMW using my skiing gloves as improvised clogs. He even promised to come again soon. Bee thinks he considers helping out with the horses to be a good test of the mental resilience that will be vital if he's to make it big in business but I can't believe all that clowning around in the stables was practice for a 'when the going gets tough the tough get going with the mucking out' scenario.

THURSDAY 9 JANUARY
THE COT

Even in weather bitterly cold enough to eradicate all other bacteria the hunting bug survives. It's been ten days since my last fix and I really feel a need to get out there again. There'll be no hunting tomorrow as most of the Ledbury supporters will be turning out for Hef's wedding – as Barry Joyce remarked, if we cancel hunting every time Patrick Dickens gets married the government won't need to bother banning the sport at all. So to tide us over until the next meet we spent the morning working up a manifesto of mots and make-up worthy of Mae West and then drove to the kennels to deliver them and a Christmas tip of £100 that we can ill afford to Jack Nightingale.

Eggs Tump was unlocked but he wasn't home. We hovered in the porch for a while; me rummaging through the pockets of the brown stockman's coats hanging on the wall for mementoes, Bee keeping look-out and treading heavily upon my dreams by saying what sad behaviour this was. I was all in favour of casing out the entire Tump on the pretext of looking for a pen to write Jack a note with but was stopped short by a pair of wellies sitting watchfully on the doorstep with L. WALLACE felt-tipped inside them in steady blue capitals. Fearing to venture any further we stopped there and after much crossings-outs of variations on loads of love, love, love from, take me, best wishes and with thanks, settled on scrawling Happy Christmas Jack from Molly and Annabel Watson across the envelope of cash, jammed it in the door frame and drove home praying for a thaw.

FRIDAY 10 JANUARY
THE COT

Jonah's weapons of mass destruction have been laughed out of Ledbury by the plague of rats that have now grown into a thunderous herd that circle the loft space around the Cot all night. The special chicken-korma-flavoured cubes of poison haven't fooled them and the gluey floor tiles that they were supposed to stick to like flies on flypaper are unmarked apart from a series of long thin scratches where they glided across them like figure skaters.

There is some room for cheer though. If this book is starting to read like Jilly Cooper then the Jake Lovell character strolled into the plot today. I was in the tack shed trying to scrape rat-killing adhesive off the side of one of Bee's new riding boots when a tall, dark-eyed stranger with soft features and a sleepy grin walked into the yard and began talking to Jane. Dropping the boot I sped upstairs for my binoculars but was only in time to get a visual on him as he lowered himself into a green Honda Civic and drove away.

I did however catch sight of Jane dancing a jig of joy on the cobbles around the pitchforks and yard brushes. Even in winter when everyone else hides at home keeping warm and saving money, Jane busies about a grey landscape whose points of interest aren't churches or restored watermills but a village with a hunky vicar or a garage with a gorgeous and recently separated mechanic. Her unflagging zeal for our manhunt is like the enduring enthusiasm for the beautiful game that a footballer feels long after he has forsaken the penalty area for the pundit's sofa. Relating to Jane our disasters with Matt Heller or the latest sighting of one of the alluring handful of gentlemen farmers who always come out hunting alone is like conducting a post-match briefing with Alan Hansen. She oohs and aahs in all the right places and shakes her head before imploring us not to let ourselves down.

Discovering Jake Lovell had given her the look of a Second XI coach who has just signed Ronaldo for a snip. Jake is a horse masseur. He left Jane with a stack of poker-faced brochures about a special sort of equine chiropractic technique called McTimoney

Manipulation but a masseur is what he is and if his hands are strong enough to knead tons of muscle at a time I hardly dare imagine what he might be able to do to a girl.

SATURDAY 11 JANUARY
THE COT

Norman has brought it to my attention that he has a very bad back.

SUNDAY 12 JANUARY
THE COT

The Hunt button hound has been out to drinks with Hef and his new wife and returned full of gossip.

Before the first cork had popped the whole party was diverted to Evensong at Upleadon Church where Hef had a point to make. In the face of disapproval from the more devout members of the parish he had diplomatically opted for a registry-office wedding fourth time around. But you don't rise to be Hef without having a bit of front even where God is concerned.

After a flower-bedecked church blessing on Friday that was attended by all of his ex-wives, he was back in range of the altar again tonight with Bee and with his latest lovely bride in tow. Looking as benign as an overgrown chorister in spite of being none too deft at finding his way around a prayer book, the old sinner bellowed the Our Father, mimed all the hymns and smiled his critics into submission.

Still no dice on the Hunt buttons though, even after Bee nearly burst a lung shrilling her way through the descant of the Magnificat.

MONDAY 13 JANUARY
THE COT

Have I got breaking news for you!

We were settling in for an evening's telly-watching aching but sated from the slushy skid around Birtsmorton Common that was our first day's hunting this year when the telephone rang. I picked up expecting it to be one of my sisters trying to trade some of their unwanted Christmas presents for something I'd been given that they liked the look of.

'Hello?'

'Molly?'

'Yes.'

'It's Jack.'

Pause.

'Molly? It's Jack.'

Pause.

'Jack from the kennels.'

Cue the arrival of angels and archangels flapping in exultation. They fluttered up from the back of the sofa, swooped clockwise down over the sink, cleared the sideboard, banked steeply to avoid the telly and our hunting coats hanging from the curtain rail and then disappeared up the pistachio staircase to the open bathroom skylight. At last! Proof that Jack Nightingale has noticed me.

'Hello?'

'Oh, Jack! Hi!'

'How are you?'

'Knackered actually. Isn't it amazing how unfit you get from just a couple of weeks of not hunting? I'm sitting here eating a Pot Noodle in my pyjamas wondering whether I can even burble keep awake burble for *EastEnders* burble burble . . .'

'What are you doing on Wednesday night?'

Cue the angels again.

'Nothing. We never burble go out much. Just burble sit around like burble saddos burble burble . . .'

'Well a hunting friend of mine has just got engaged to a girl from the Pytchley country and we're having a black-tie dinner to celebrate. Would you like to come?'

'Great. I'd love to.'

'We'll see you at seven-thirty for eight then.'

Roll on many, many more angels.

It was only two hours later, when we'd jubilantly tried on every item of evening wear we own in every combination mathematically possible, that Bee asked if she was definitely invited too. Good sense and twenty-seven years of experience said that Jack wouldn't ask me to dinner and leave Bee at home picking at her non-existent spots, but it was a good excuse to ring him back and make some Cinderella jokes while he assured me that of course she was invited. It's sad news that this Peppermore-ish friend of his is headed up the aisle but then you can't make a delicious black-tie omelette without breaking eggs.

TUESDAY 14 JANUARY
TOP SHOP IN CHELTENHAM

I'm standing in the dunce's corner of the store beside the bargain basket of frayed bikini bottoms and broken jewellery being told by the assistant manager that my Switch card has insufficient funds to pay for a new pair of fishnets and a Wonderbra.

Coming only hours after the postman delivered a seven-word letter of thanks from my godson for the solitary jumping bean I gave him for Christmas and a request from the Visa people for a minimum payment of £218 to reach them by last Tuesday, I'm forced to concede that we're not just experiencing a few financial glitches. With Bee's services still not required at the call centre and me making little progress on the waiting list for a DSS hairstylist training placement, our household economics have hit such a bear market that what I hoped were hiccups may be the last palpitations before we go completely belly-up.

According to the Joseph Rowntree Foundation we are now absolute paupers. The Foundation states that people with a weekly income of £89 or less who are deprived of their basic human needs, such as televisions, outfits for special occasions, money to heat and decorate their homes and take an annual holiday with, are living below the 'absolute poverty level'. Admittedly we do have the solace of telly but otherwise I think we meet every criterion. Occasions don't come much more special than dinner with El Nightingale and I can't afford to buy underwear let alone a new outfit for it. The Cot continues to fester and refrigerate like a macabre science experiment and this enterprise stopped feeling like a holiday the first time we got bolted with along the dual carriageway.

Desperate times call for desperate measures. To get off the bread-
line we are going to have to join the antis. Rumours abound in
the hunting crowd of the Hunt Saboteurs Association paying
university students £50 a time to don balaclavas, pile into
minibuses and spend the day disrupting hunts from catching foxes.
Provided we don't see anyone we know I don't have a problem
waving a few protest banners and posing as a peacenik at meets.
Bee's keen too. She practised her estuary accent all the way home
and has decided that on saboteuring days she'll take on the identity of an orphan called Della. While she went upstairs to see
what her daywear boxes contained in the way of sabotage gear I
had a look at the organisation's website.

Holy Smoke. Fifty quid a day to join the ranks of the so-called
Bumpkin Harassment Squad really does sound like danger money.
I didn't think sports got much more hazardous than fox-hunting
until I read an account of sabbing. According to the saboteurs'
website two of their members have been killed while taking direct
action against fox-hunters. Page after page was devoted to stories
of sabs (calling a saboteur an anti seems to be as big a faux pas
as calling a hound a dog) being hospitalised for head injuries,
concussion, high blood pressure and dislocated limbs after being
rammed with cars and generally bashed about by hunt followers
while the police did little or nothing to protect them. Even if we
make it home in one piece, the website claims we could have
threatening phone calls and rockets posted through our letterbox
by hunt supporters to look forward to.

It's all a lot more muscular than I expected. Protesting at the
meet is the puniest part of a saboteur's day. After ringing local
papers to tell them the hunt has been cancelled we'll be out at
dawn unblocking earths and badger setts. Some sabs will go

undercover at the meet to find out where the hounds will draw first and phone ahead to the rest of us who'll race off to scare any foxes away from the covert. Other effective spoiling tactics are to set false trails and spray Antimate, a scent duller, wherever we think the hounds are heading.

At the very least Bee and I will be expected to blow hunting horns and run about the place mimicking the huntsman's dog talk. There was even a vocab section on the website to help with this last bit. Key phrases include 'covert-hoick', 'forrard' and 'leu-in'. It's all a far cry from Mr Yarwood's offer to play us his LP of hunting horns and hound song but I've sent off e-mails and SAEs to saboteur groups in Birmingham, Coventry and Bath in the hope that we can collect our attendance money without being in the front line of the sabotage operation.

WEDNESDAY 15 JANUARY
THE COT

Zut alors. I missed a phone call from Jack while I was out brushing Norm to a glossy sheen ready for his back massage with Jake Lovell and came in to find a message from him postponing tonight's entertainments indefinitely. For a moment I feared that word of my schoolgirl fantasies about him had leaked out to Eggs Tump but apparently the delay is because Laura has suddenly remembered she's got a doctor's appointment and won't be able to cook us dinner after all.

There's no denying the delay is a blow but at least I no longer have to figure out a way to dry-clean my little black dress with just the kettle and a boot brush to help me. There is also the consolation of being able to make the BT answering lady play back Jack's message ad infinitum. His voice is everything you look for in an avocado ripened north of the Wash; it has an initial roughness about it that soon gives way to a firm and unexpectedly indulgent core. Somewhere in his staccato delivery I like to think I can detect a faint, encouraging trace of nerves.

THURSDAY 16 JANUARY
THE COT

I want to table an amendment to The Plan. Now that Bee has slunk back into the clutches of what she declares is the new non-Odious Daniel I don't see why I must keep up the search for a barley baron. Instead I propose we marshal all our energies into a massive air and ground campaign to launch my seduction of Jake Lovell.

Jake can't offer us an exit from our financial woes but he has the kind of assets money can't buy. He's got soul. Unable to afford a horse of his own until he got his first student loan, and with nothing but his healing hands and his gypsy magic to help him, he's made a career from treating and competing other people's expensive animals for them. The hour and a half he spent massaging the horses this afternoon ranks right up there with the most pleasurable of my winter. Very different from the brash Peppermore material we've been fixated with, Jake ambles rather than struts. He's got a perfect Roman nose and dark eyes that shine green in sunlight. He also laughed so easily at all of my jokes that I began to wonder whether I am a comic genius after all.

I had worried that the McTimoney technique might be a quacky concoction of mood crystals and pan pipes but Jake's methods were much more physical than that. After feeling down Ari's spine with his beautifully tapering fingers he said she had a slightly cricked neck and her pelvis was lurching to the right. To re-align her skeleton he delivered a series of punches to the side of her skull with such precision that I am convinced that if he chose to he could kill a man with an expert flick of his wrist.

The muscles behind Norm's saddle patch were so inflamed and painful that Jake was surprised he had been jumping at all. Even after karate-chopping his vertebrae into line and flexing his ankles until I heard the joints snap into place, he recommended that Norm have the next two weeks off and gave me some hilarious exercises to do with him each day. These involve standing directly behind him, pulling his tail and leaning back like a water-skier to stretch his spine. It sounds like a surefire recipe for riling Norm into rearranging my face to match Barry Joyce's but at least it means Jake will be coming round to check on Norm's progress.

For once I'm satisfied that I acquitted myself well. I was much helped by Bee's absence at the call centre and a naturally flaw-less complexion achieved after forty minutes' work with a tube of gel-crème coverage foundation and a dusting of translucent face powder. Taking my cue from the photograph in his brochure I think I also scored points for dressing in an outfit of jeans, jodhpur boots and a chunky jumper that almost exactly matched Jake's own. But most encouraging of all was how sweet and self-effacing he was. We got on so well that selling my watch to cover the cost of Norm's next session seems like a good investment in my romantic future.

January

SUNDAY 19 JANUARY
THE COT

I should be feeling desolate. It's Sunday night, it's raining again and Bee is cutting my hair; hewing at it in the candlelight with the tack shed scissors we use to trim Ari's moustache and the greasy tufts in Norm's ears. But as I listen to the dull rasp of the blades against the tangle of curls straggling down my shoulders I feel like a small boat being cut free of its anchor. I'll be knitting my own shoes and mucking out with my bare hands next but I don't care. You see, I'm not going back. Not ever.

After Friday's meet the hunting bug has hatched out into a butterfly. I've often heard Ledbury old-timers talk about red-letter days of hunts so thrilling that they come perhaps only a handful of times in a decade, but I could never really empathise with their descriptions. Two days ago I discovered what they meant. It started when Bee very nobly offered to work an extra shift at the call centre and let me take Ari out for Christy's first meet back from Kenya on a cold and extremely blustery morning. With Mr Yarwood at the helm and Jack and the hounds on our heels, we hacked up to the meet at Corner House, Hasfield, a friendly dairy farm perched over the Severn flood plain where the resident family graze their hunters on the lawn when grass gets scarce.

It is a truth universally acknowledged that people in big houses skimp on meets. At one meet riders are lucky to get a whiff of port or a shadow of fish paste on a curl of bread and Bee was terribly dejected when a local chocolatier hosted the hounds without handing round a selection of his own caramels. In stark contrast to this meanness Friday's spread in the farmyard stretched to an endless supply of home-baked brownies, iced cakes, quiches, sausages, pork pies and Christmas cake. The result was that about sixty of us set off bursting at the seams to the top of the ridge above the Wickridge Motocross circuit and stood about digesting and warning one another that there wouldn't be any scent in the strong north wind.

Ari was in season and really flirting outrageously, squealing whenever Smartie came near and bounding at the jumps along the ridge as though she was on springs. Despite the wind the hounds picked up a whiff of a fox and we were soon belting over towards Corse Grove in the bitter winter sunshine with Christy, a layer of golden holiday tan being stripped from her face with each icy gust, somehow managing to keep her cigarette alight and Smartie on song despite the headwind. In quiet moments I talked Jake Lovell tactics with whoever would listen, but for the most part I zipped along trying to get a view of what the hounds were up to and guess where the fox would lead them next.

As we spilled down a steep hill towards Ken Unwin's farm I saw the other front-runners pile up at a mighty hedge with a ditch in front of it. Nothing warms the blood like witnessing one's Hunt Hate flipped off his horse like a pompous little pancake and instead of looking for a gate I set my sights at the hedge. Pushing the vision of Ari swerving away from that first, long-distant milk crate at Owain Llewellyn's farm to the back of my mind I set her on Mr Yarwood's flight path.

Ari has the jumping style of a Doodlebug. Once you light her fuse about thirty yards out from the hedge she sprints at it with a furious drumming of hooves, splutters, springs over just before her engines cut out and after an eerie pause plummets to the ground on the far side. The ditch on the take-off side made the hedge so treacherous that as I approached it I spotted Mr Yarwood and Valentine Hopton waiting on the far side to pick my ribs out of my lungs if it all went horribly wrong. The debonair doctor once saved Whispering Dennis's life after he turned turtle at the Stanks Hedge, rupturing his spleen and smashing his sternum and pelvis. The story goes that Dr Hopton pronounced his patient out of danger when Dennis showed sufficient pep to bite the fingers that were clearing his airways. Luckily for me Ari ripped over and with a relieved thumbs-up from the medical squad we pressed on.

Sadly Christy lost a shoe and re-opened the crater in Smartie's hoof soon after second horses but Ari was galloping on air by this point. We found a fox in the gorse-covered tumps between Hasfield Haw and the marsh and had to jump an unlaid stretch of hedge off the plough to keep on his line. Invincible, Ari was the second horse over, leaping clear alongside Keith Cooper's excitable piebald. As we watched the fox miraculously manage to sprint up the hill with the lead hounds literally nipping at his brush I was singled out by Thomas Harvey to hold the huntsman's horse while he checked where he had gone to ground. The only person happier than me to be nestled between Jack and Thomas as they debated whether they could leave their quarry for another day was Ari. She stood squarely to attention, satisfied that at last she was back in front where her days as Owain Llewellyn's master's horse had convinced her she belonged.

By four o'clock there were just a handful of us left drawing the ash plantation down along the river meadows in the waning light. But the day hadn't expended its excitements yet. I was standing chatting to Sally Evans and Debbie Jarvis, the smiley Farrah Fawcett lady on a stallion, when Billy 'I likes to live dangerous'

Chadburn rode up and asked if I would like to come on point duty with him. The invitation felt like a summons from the lord high wizard of a Masonic lodge to submit to a ghoulish initiation ritual. Billy in hunting dress is a terrifying customer. With his carnivorous teeth, wiry grey hair and pink coat skirting the tops of thighs fashioned after huge sides of ham, he looks like the wolf wearing Little Red Riding Hood's cape. He was on a giant chestnut gelding rumoured to be so evil that it would try to charge down any jockey who fell off it as they were lying winded from their fall.

When everyone went quiet and Mr Yarwood let his right eyebrow float upwards to the brim of his cap I realised Billy's offer was a test of some kind. Still vainly hoping Thomas Harvey might intervene and say I should stay with the field, I followed Billy behind the ash grove. We had barely got halfway along the side of the plantation when he turned to me and asked if 'that li'l carb can jump'. Ari snorted with indignation at being called a cob like a girl with a size 10 bottom whose boyfriend buys her size 14 knickers as a Valentine's Day present, but before I could answer he set his chestnut at a hedge sandwiched between a set of double rails. Thankfully Billy's chestnut smashed the back rail down and Ari sprang over behind him.

We then negotiated a narrow barbed-wire fence beside a gate before Billy pulled up, pointed to the far end of the track and asked me what I could see. Nothing. As I strained to distinguish anything in the haze of brown he explained how he could tell the low russet blob in the distance was a fox from the way it moved. We were like two people doing those Magic Eye pictures that with the right amount of focus will mutate from a swirl of patterns into a vivid three-dimensional scene. He described what

I should be seeing while I stared ineffectually at the messy palette of beiges and khakis in front of us. Only when the fox made a break over a drainage dyke and across a green field beyond did I spot him.

Jumping through a wide hedge after him we found Peter Evans, who had also seen the fox, holloa-ing to Jack Nightingale. A holloa is a funny thing. You are supposed to shout that word exactly as it reads so loudly that a huntsman embedded in an overgrown wood can hear it above the panting of the hounds and the rustle of the trees. But it's not just volume that's important; you have to yell it in the same tone as a tawny owl sicking up the remains of a mouse. Peter's worked brilliantly and in a minute or two the hounds had been gathered and set yelping on the line of a fox that ran straight to the river bank, leapt in and swam the Severn to escape them. The pause as we watched the small red head paddling towards the Berkeley country and safety enabled me to rejoin the field but by then the damage was done – I was hooked.

By the time Mr Yarwood and I turned for home in the dusk my right knee was aching so much from six hours of riding to Ari's short, marching stride that I couldn't rise to the trot and had to walk and canter the six miles back to Staunton. But the pain in my leg was dimmed by the onset of a high fever as the hunting bug took hold of me once and for all. When I eventually eased myself groaning from the saddle and began to tend to Ari in the yard I wouldn't have traded places with anyone in the world. I still want those brown suede boots from the Toast catalogue and an audience with Jack Nightingale, and probably in that order, but all I really truly care about is getting out there again as soon as the bute has worked its magic on Ari's puffy ankles.

MONDAY 20 JANUARY
NATIONAL WESTMINSTER BANK, LEDBURY

Hopelessly middle-class girl that I am, I can't fall in love with a place without wanting to cement the affair by buying myself a chunk of it to do up.

To this end I spent the morning waiting for my turn with the Lending Officer to find out about getting a mortgage on a derelict mill I've seen for sale in the estate agent's on the high street while Bee sulked outside in the car. It's not my trying to buy a house without any savings or prospect of employment that has convinced her that the hunting bug has made me delirious but my willingness to brave a public appearance with an unforgiving new fringe that gives me more than a touch of Down's Syndrome.

What she didn't know is that while the man in the mortgage department told me I didn't have a cat in hell's chance of becoming a stakeholder in the property boom, the bank did present me with a ladder out of our financial hole. Passing the time in the grey nylon web of the customer service atrium I found a leaflet on personal accident cover that informed me that for just seventeen pence a day the NatWest will insure me against all kinds of nasty scenarios.

If I lose either of my big toes or the finger of my choice I can collect £2,000 no questions asked. If an 'accident' left Bee and me each without the use of an ankle we would be quids in for £12,000. Even a little mishap resulting in the loss of sight in one eye or a withered arm seems tempting when it's worth up to £20,000 and you've got horses to feed, not a penny in the bank and still no offers of work from the Hunt Saboteurs Association.

I mean, can you think of a task you perform with your little finger that you wouldn't be prepared to use another digit for in exchange for £1,000?

TUESDAY 21 JANUARY
THE COT

Bee is being precious about her toes and has headed off to London on a fundraising mission.

She keeps saying The Plan was for six months not five years and telling me to be realistic about the chances of being able to stay on and hunt with the Ledbury. Her comments have a similar impact as I imagine the Smokers Die Younger wrapper on a packet of Benson & Hedges has on a forty-a-day man. They make perfect sense but are still insufficient to curb my cravings to forfeit my life expectancy and increasing amounts of my disposable income to my habit.

WEDNESDAY 22 JANUARY
THE BISTRO, CORSE LAWN HOTEL

I've just spent most of lunch, one hand clasped to my brow to hide my mongoloid hairdo, repeating every last detail of Friday's hunting excitements to Alec. I don't know what possessed me to spend the only date to actually materialise since I moved to the Cot talking horse through two crab salads, a salmon en croute and a steak tartare. If he had any sense he would right now be squeezing himself out of the cloakroom window to leave me stranded with a couple of crème brulées, the bill and, worst of all, the monotonous sound of my own voice ringing in my eardrums.

But the man is a martyr to good manners. Not only has he come back for another dose of mucking out, but he's showing no signs of regret that Bee couldn't join us and asking me endless questions about Ari and Norman. I'm having none of it though and intend to wow him with a lot of corporate speak and talking points about the international demand for inner-city chewing-gum-removal apparatus.

THURSDAY 23 JANUARY
THE COT

Jane's research has thrown up some terrible news about Jake Lovell. When he's not out setting female hearts alight and equine backs to rights, he lives in homosexual bliss with a fellow professional rider.

FRIDAY 24 JANUARY
THE COT

After a few days on the sauce Ari's ankle joints are still inflamed so there was no hunting for me today. Christy set out for the meet with Mr Yarwood's son Richard, leaving me at home to study the form for the race meeting at Cheltenham that I bought tickets for at the hunt auction back in the days of plenty.

January

I was throwing darts at the *Racing Post* when Mr Smith rang to invite himself down for the weekend. How is it that men can sense a girl staging a recovery a hundred miles away? To my great relief I found that despite a quick flaring of the emotional embers I was too miserly to give him the spare ticket I'm intending to sell to the Cheltenham touts in order to fund my gambling strategy.

SATURDAY 25 JANUARY
THE COT

When revolution comes my bet is that it'll kick off at Cheltenham racecourse.

The hoi polloi will rise up from the draughty concrete strip where they cling to the white rails of the home straight and storm the hospitality boxes of the grandstand. Watching boys from Cheltenham College sauntering through the crowds in outfits that would make Bertie Wooster and his friends look shabby I wondered why Bastille Day hadn't arrived at the Jockey Club already. If they ventured on to the streets of any major town in England I'm certain that these squadrons of floppy-fringed dandies would be toppled to the ground and have paving stones kicked in their faces. Yet at Cheltenham so long as they confined their movements to the paddock and the plush booths of the Tote they were hardly even jeered by the sans-culottes spilling out of the stands in search of a burger and a bookie.

I didn't stay long enough to see whether the mood amongst the racegoers darkened as their wallets emptied. Once I'd won

£360 quid on a £10 each-way bet on an unknown German hurdler called Moneytrain I floored it back to the Cot before my luck ran out.

As I made plans to distribute my winnings between the black-smith, the feed merchant and Sue the clipping lady I tried to remember what I would have done with a sudden windfall when I lived in London. It's odds on that I would have splashed out on a pair of new shoes for myself rather than two pairs each for my dependants. Then I'd probably have toasted my good fortune with a bottle of something fizzy and expensive.

As it is I haven't had a drink since New Year. We have one surviving bottle of Romanian merlot which we torment ourselves with each Monday night. The deal is that whoever correctly answers a question on *University Challenge* is allowed to crack it open. The cork has stayed intact for a month now, which Bee takes as proof that our brains are atrophying at an alarming rate. But I think they're simply making space for new data. Just as one forgets the finer points of Pythagorean theorem within weeks of sitting a maths test, I suspect the reason I can't make headway on anything but *TV Quick* these days is that my mental faculties are tuned in to judging at a glance if Ari needs more boiled barley and assessing the exact speed and distance required to meet a post-and-rails on a perfect stride.

I celebrated today's win by allowing myself a hot bath to show my minor digits that Moneytrain had won them a temporary reprieve, and a brief jubilant phone call to Mark Bennet. With Bee yet to be infected, he is the only friend I have who won't ask why the hell I don't use the money to switch the central heating on and can sympathise with the mental condition of a person who wants nothing more out of life than two days' hunting a week even if it means enduring an existence so crude that they are in constant danger of losing toes to frostbite and insurance scams.

SUNDAY 26 JANUARY
THE COT

Curiouser and curiouser. I've just got back from hacking Ari and Norm around the village with Alec. It was an absolute revelation to find that he was happy to accept a lift on a vehicle that didn't have an airbag fitted as standard and was able to keep his balance when Ari spooked at a dustbin and dragged him into the path of the oncoming traffic.

Sent on an adventure holiday as punishment for being hyperactive, Alec learnt to ride as a nine-year-old and still has the same rudimentary equestrian style he picked up on a bolshie fell pony all those years ago. He leans well back and steers by tugging the reins around with one hand like someone handling an outboard motor rather than a horse. His clothes are still atrociously smart-casual, but the horror of a pair of immaculately ironed chinos teamed up with a motif-laden golf shirt was mitigated by his claims that his other car is a Land-Rover.

Rather too well turned out and with the pudgy physique of a desk dweller, he's really not my type. But there is something undeniably appealing about spending time with a man who last night celebrated signing off the North American franchise for his pavement cleaners but yet also knows without being bossed exactly which brush to use to get rid of the mud that Christy had left caked to Smartie's tummy. I wonder if he's still in the

'Boy Meets Madly Efficient Female Marketing Manager' relationship his sister used to complain about so much.

TUESDAY 28 JANUARY
THE COT

A bout of mild sunshine has filled the birds with false hopes and put Norm in a terrifyingly joyful mood. When I attempted to ride him around the farm to the tweets of a premature spring chorus he bucked and did so many aerial swivels he pulled one of his new shoes off. He's either in agony or no pain whatsoever.

WEDNESDAY 29 JANUARY
THE COT

Jake Lovell came to have a look at him and says it's the latter. Jake's still lovely but now that he's off limits the best form I could manage was to wallow around the yard like a circus seal too full of fish to perform for more. Devoid of its imaginary frisson our chatter was slow and empty, although as he ambled away to his car I did have to suppress a last urge to give chase and implore him not to throw himself away on another man.

Anxious to work off some of my steam and Norm's sugar beet before Friday's meet I took him straight out on a hair-raising hack round Upleadon during which he shied so violently at a clump of dock leaves at the side of the road that we were nearly run over by a delivery van. I find these lonely skirmishes between the two of us every bit as rattling as a total breakdown of his brakes or goodwill on the hunting field. Once Norm's milometer tells him we are beyond the halfway point of any ride he starts seeing ghouls in every gateway and uses them as an excuse to bound forward towards his stable. Given his discipline issues the only safe thing to do is to sit tight and try not to rile him.

I sidestepped home and wobbled inside to recuperate over a bread and rancid butter lunch, little suspecting that graver perils were lying in wait in my inbox. Even absolute paupers like me have income tax bills to pay and in order to meet the Revenue's deadline on Friday I'd arranged to sell off the few pieces of furniture I brought back with me from New York. What possessed me to inform the gannets at home about this plan I don't know, but any fool could have predicted the consequences. This afternoon bought a cheery e-mail from Mum commending my good sense but informing me that it was too late. My parents had just completed their annual sweep of Cathedine for anything of value that hadn't been nailed to the floor and had already hawked my belongings to keep what she infuriatingly referred to as the 'mother ship' afloat on the choppy tides of the Inland Revenue.

11

February

I'm a God-forsaken square. This is the considered opinion of an influential section of Ledbury Hunt supporters, and even after letting Norman motor round Piper's End and Sarn Hill in a flat spin for the day I've returned to the lorry unable to shake off the hunch that they might be right.

My undoing was an attempt at this morning's meet to garner sympathy for the shoddy way I'd been treated by my parents in the general scramble to pay the taxman. As I related each roll and pitch of the mother ship the farmer standing at Norman's shoulder shook his head in incredulity, not, it transpired, at Mum's sharp practice but at my being registered to pay tax in the first place and my subsequent pathetically unenterprising reaction to the penury that this error threatened me with. As word of my folly spread quickly through the mounted field my financial worries were belittled in exactly the same way my bruised ankle had been disdained at the start of the season.

The Ledbury crew don't afford to keep hunting year after year on a shoestring without learning some tricks. One man told me the best fiddles start at birth. He has friends, grown men, who don't exist. Born in the cottages where they still live, their births were never registered, their mothers never collected child benefit or had them inoculated. As a result they don't appear on the electoral role and were never issued with National Insurance numbers. Without bank accounts or any kind of tax status they live entirely from grubby bundles of cash hidden in various jars and tins around their homes. Their cottages don't appear on the Land Register but when the worst occasionally comes to the worst their partners (getting married is frowned on as perilously official behaviour) pay council tax to the local bean counters at County Hall.

A jolly lady following the hounds on a bicycle told me that she'd had her suspicions about my fiscal prudence the moment I reached for my chequebook to pay her nephew for my first shipment of hay bales. She advised me to stop polluting the local economy with cheques, use cash instead and to contain my conformist urges to fill in every official-looking form that fell on to my doormat. Never having learnt to read she found this tactic came particularly easily. According to a passing rider, the answer to my cash-flow problems was blindingly obvious. If things were running up short Bee and I should stop belly-aching, find out what we were insured for and then have ourselves 'a little fire'.

MONDAY 3 FEBRUARY
THE COT

Bee spent the whole of today's hunt around Eastnor puffed up
like a blue tit on a frosty morning. Christy thinks this sudden
attack of the smugs may be due to the masters reinstating plaiting
for normal meets. According to Mr Yarwood, plaiting horses'
manes is a horribly dainty fashion introduced by the Victorians at
about the same time as they were getting worked up about the
sexual allure of table legs peeking out from under lace cloths and
has remained the bane of every groom's life since. Ari's skinhead
look precludes Bee from having to worry about plaiting but in the
absence of a groom Christy and I will either have to braid for
hours before each hunt as I did before the opening meet or be
told off each time for being disrespectful and scruffy.

No prizes for guessing which option Christy will go for. Our
Hunt button hopes finally dwindled into ashes today when, having
mistaken an old school blazer for her hunting coat as she crept
out of her marital bed early this morning, she greeted Peter Evans
at the meet with her hockey and netball colours blazing resplen-
dently down each sleeve.

TUESDAY 4 FEBRUARY
THE COT

I was musing on how best to set light to a lorry that rarely starts
of its own volition and trying to maintain a courageous
silence in the face of a final warning letter from the TV licensing
people when Bee casually dropped a postcard into my lap.

It was an invitation from a lord, scrawled on pale blue paper thicker than the plaster division between our bedrooms, asking Bee to join him for a day's hunting in Northamptonshire with the distinguished Pytchley pack. There are lords and lords and I waited for her to issue a caveat about hers being a dribbling old lecher with a Hapsburg chin, but Bee says although he doesn't grow barley he's a real live baron who comes equipped with youth, brains, a full stately and a heavenly body. A Peppermore with a palace! We may be plucked from the jaws of bankruptcy yet.

WEDNESDAY 5 FEBRUARY
THE COT

In the meantime Ari is being headhunted. Dorothy Baird, a bristly sounding woman from the Bicester who saw our 'cracking little mare' jump the monster hedge at Barrow Hill last month, rang up and asked how much we'd take for her. When I said Ari wasn't for sale she replied that she hadn't asked if she was for sale, only how much we'd take for her.

The general presumption round here that everyone who owns a horse is a vendor and all that is required is to agree a price is a shamingly canny one. Only Bee loves Ari more than me. Bold and brave but easy to stop and cheap to run, horses like her are like gold dust and because she's a mare we can breed more gold dust from her. But at the same moment I was thinking fondly of Ari's loyalty and courage, something very Welsh embedded deep down in my psyche made me say I wouldn't part with her for less than £4,500.

Horses born in Wales are a little bit like CDs made in Taiwan;

259

regardless of their quality you can be sure that their price doubled the moment they were exported to England. Just as Owain Llewellyn had made the best part of a grand off me, I found myself instinctively trying to take a couple more from the next person in line. My irritation at swooning so completely at the first overture was quickly superseded by annoyance at the brevity of the pause between me naming my price and Dorothy saying breezily that that sounded fine and arranging to come and try Ari out. I should definitely have asked for more.

Bee, convinced that we'll never have to sell anything ever again once her lord steps up to the plate for phase four of The Plan, is cleaning tack totally unperturbed by the bargain-cutting over Ari. She's strict about quashing all talk of hitting the jackpot but her cheeks are flushed with guilty excitement and when he agreed to come to our hunt ball at the weekend she resigned from the call centre in triumph. I caught her later in the quiet of the tack shed clenching her fists and mouthing, 'Yes!' through gritted teeth like a snooker player who's just potted the black in a crucial frame. When I asked why the lord was the man for her, she turned gooey and clutching a hoof pick to her breast started describing how her heart first skipped a beat when he whisked through the Corinthian portico of his south lodge and, on catching sight of the whopping sandstone façade of the main hall across an expanse of parkland, started grouching about the terrible burden of inheriting a house with over 700 windows.

February

THURSDAY 6 FEBRUARY
THE COT

Does stuffing ourselves on the forbidden fruits of shoplifted Tesco's Finest egg custards in anticipation of ensnaring the lord constitute counting our chickens?

Probably. But Dad's gone one better. In an ingenious attempt to economise he has suggested to Bee that she and the noble baron share a double wedding with Flora and Chutney.

FRIDAY 7 FEBRUARY
THE COT

The badgers must have heard that the Ledbury hunt ball is being held this evening. They kept us awake most of last night with their own festivities. An overexcited gang of them howled, flirted and feasted on the colony of snails that live underneath my window until dawn.

SATURDAY 8 FEBRUARY
OSTEOPATHY UNIT, GLOUCESTER ROYAL HOSPITAL

The only significant difference between the badger shindig in the garden and our own scrummage at Eastnor Castle was that the lady badgers didn't wear gold lamé evening gowns.

Hunt Ball: to Bee and me the words used to conjure up a magical night of glass slippers and courtly love set against a soundtrack of Viennese waltzes. Crouching in the Cot on miserable winter days when darkness descended at four p.m., we composed a fantasy of an evening in which I started the dancing with Jack Nightingale watched by Bee and her lord standing under a moonlit archway like the timeless little figures that would soon garnish the top tier of their wedding cake. The band would play till morning when we would slip away from the party through the dewy dawn, she to a Palladian mansion, me to that apology of a cottage at Eggs Tump.

Anxious for our townie friends to witness the crowning glory of our new roles as doyennes of rural life and equally keen to win plaudits with the hunt committee for bringing in a load of Londoners to contribute to hunt funds, we assembled a disparate party of twenty friends for the do. We have since learnt the hard way that there are some occasions that the very best management strategies can't control and last night's was one of them. Ball-going in the Ledbury country is a contact sport that ranks somewhere between the Charge of the Light Brigade and the Last Night of the Proms for expressing an archaic but enduring gem of Englishness in all its heart-warming and mildly disturbing absurdity.

The first major dent in our expectations came when we returned from a raid on the dressing-up box at Cathedine with two full-length ballgowns and had a look at our hunt ball tickets. To our amazement we learned that the organisers had chosen to copy the bizarre afternoon timing of the Oscar ceremony and summon their guests to Eastnor Castle's armour-adorned Great Hall for 6.45 p.m. While the credits for *Neighbours* were still rolling, two hundred or so hunt supporters squeezed themselves into their pink tail coats and best frocks and drove to a puddle-strewn car park at the back of the castle. After a bit of awkward small-talking they then sat down for a lavish meat tea.

Except, that is, for most of the guests at our tables. Not being attuned to the body clocks of a community with early-morning milking and stock feeding chores to do, our London friends had assumed like us that the ball would start at 8.45 p.m. rather than 6.45 p.m. As a result Katie and the most punctual of the visiting girls spent the first fifty minutes of the party getting out of their work clothes and doing their hair and make-up in the semi-darkness of a hastily commandeered minibus as it rocketed along the twisting lanes from Cheltenham railway station to Eastnor. They disembarked beside the moat of the pseudo-Gothic pile still spraying on deodorant, pulling up their tights and arranging their bosoms in the front of their dresses to be met by an extremely dismayed Mark Bennet. Expecting glamorous urban lovelies he was instead faced with an unwashed coven whose mascara and lipstick were so askew he thought some of them were in drag.

For all our mushy daydreaming Bee and I did not look much better. Our fashion choices for the black-tie extravaganza were severely curtailed by feet too chilblained to fit into high heels and faces permanently reddened by advance parties of broken veins that threaten to encroach right the way across our cheeks. With the hot water at the Cot on the blink again, we had had to leave our hair dirty and tease our greasy locks forward to cover our worst burst capillaries. Nor did our dresses do us any favours. Set against the elegant taffetas of the older hunting women and the slinky backless stretchy numbers worn by the girls our age, the moth-eaten, flouncy brocade outfits we'd plumped for looked like something Kate Bush wore on *Top of the Pops* in 1981. Once our shoulders were bared, our crimson faces perched like toffee apples on top of our pasty-white sticks of bodies and, as if that weren't gross enough, away from the gloom of the Cathedine attic I noticed for the first time that my dress had an unfortunate custard-yellow stain on the groin.

Leaving Mark to console himself with the cream of the castle's cellars we went off on a sweep of the local lanes. Every time we spotted a car with a man inside it clearly hopelessly lost and unable to get a signal on his mobile phone but choosing to concentrate on a road atlas rather than lose face by asking for directions, we discovered another missing townie member of our party. Bee's lord arrived by taxi some time later, tall, almost handsome but full of banter, and was quickly judged by a delighted Sally Evans to be as deliciously languid as anything the Beaufort could offer. Only Daniel never made it to the ball. He left a message on the machine this morning complaining that Bee had told him to head for Sudeley, a rival castle on the other side of the Severn.

Although our late start meant we had to plough through three courses in twenty minutes, dinner went surprisingly well. Over the fruit compotes I clocked Matt Heller telling Just Gay Enough Hugh what car he should have bought for that money and Katie and Mark Bennet discussing a Spanish fireworks festival that they'd both been to. Orlando had already massed a barricade of wine bottles around himself and Thomas Harvey's leggy girl groom and was trying to impress her with his views on the aids for counter-canter. At the other table the lord was sitting across the table from Bee in range of her giant blue eyes and tinkling laughter. Beside him two of the London girls were competing hard for a local point-to-point trainer's affections and beyond them, ignoring the rules about not drinking red wine in the Great Hall and not groping other men's wives, No Good Boyo had clamped a gnarled hand to Christy's leg and didn't let go until her husband applied pressure to the back of his wrist with a lit cigarette some time later.

But to be honest I could hardly bear to wrench my gaze away from the merry button-black eyes to my right. All winter long Jack Nightingale had haunted my days and my dreams, always galloping just out of reach into the next field or over the lip of a wooded hill. But last night, for twenty glorious minutes, I had him all to myself. And boy did I make the most of it. Bursting with laughter at his jokes and delivering a torrent of my own, I was soon sweating with the exertion of being the most captivating girl he had ever encountered and dulling the impact of my rancid hair and nasty yellowing outfit by making sure his glass never emptied of champagne.

But no amount of alcohol could save our fantasies from the dance floor. I knew Bee's daydreams had died there when I saw the girl who had imagined waltzing across a marble ballroom being flung around the slippery flagstones to the strains of 'Crocodile Rock' as icy rivulets of condensation dripped from the awning over the terrace on to her bare back. She broke off from composing her letter of complaint to the Trading Standards Authority when the rest of the hunt took to the floor though. It was hilarious seeing how the Ledbury's members all bopped like they rode. I couldn't contain my giggles when Jack pointed out Billy Chadburn, jubilant at being restored as Friday Master, cutting a broad-shouldered swath through the rest of the dancers and one hard-riding woman subjugating her partner with a stern look and a domineering pinch to his upper arm as though he was a disobedient horse.

But alas, I had laughed too soon. For when we eventually stood up and I dragged Jack in the direction of the dance floor I realised that I had been barking up the wrong-sized tree all these months. A bonsai tree to be specific. My crush, so carefully nurtured all winter long, evaporated before we had even made it as far as the disco when I realised that Jack was making conversation to my nipples and I could have rested my chin on the top of his head. Talk about a mismatched pair – Jack must be the best part of a foot shorter than me. Thinking back I realised that I've only ever seen him either on a horse or sitting down and was so taken up with trying to make an impression that I didn't notice his legs were the length of my arms.

Antonia did once mention something about the curse of seemingly charismatic men who 'go well' out hunting but who, once deprived of their horses, hedges and gorgeous costumes, are exposed as boring, balding, bow-legged little mortals you can't believe you ever fancied. Jack's not remotely boring or balding but I can't seriously pursue a man that I'll be tempted to perch on my knee. Releasing him to Laura Wallace's clutches before Mark Bennet cottoned on to my dilemma I retired to a sofa to watch Katie dancing in front of Jake Lovell and his boyfriend. She was thrashing about like a weak swimmer trying to precipitate a shark attack, furious that neither man was turning a fin in her direction.

I also witnessed epic scenes at the loos as hunting matrons urged their inebriated daughters up the steps to the cubicles to be sick in privacy. Magnificent ruby rings shining on their discoloured gardener's fingers, they clamped their hands on the girls' shoulders and bellowed at them to 'kick on' at the steps as though setting young thoroughbreds at a stiff hedge. Yet for all the usual party carnage of women falling out of their dresses and the wrong people being caught kissing in dark corners, the ball had an otherworldly atmosphere. Somehow it would not have seemed odd if we had been brought to a halt to hear a telegram telling us that the King was dead or his Empire at war.

What did seem odd was the music being wound down and the bar closed at midnight just when we were expecting breakfast to be served. It was the clash of body clocks again. Bee and I had expected to dance until four in the morning, while the early-rising owner of the castle thought that everyone should head to bed soon after the end of the *News at Ten*. Anxious not to face those of our London friends who had been at the ball for a mere three hours, we left the rest of our party to shamble off to B&Bs or the freckled arms of their newly formed local attachments and headed back to the Cot with just JGE Hugh and the lord in tow.

Bee's baron had cut an impressive figure at the castle. He had danced, he had joked, he had drunk too much and talked to everyone about everything from the dimensions of the Fernie hedges to why it's a travesty that Ole Gunnar Solskjaer keeps starting on the Man U subs bench. But he was strangely imporous too, somehow proofed against saying the wrong thing and resistant to red wine spills. The drunken excesses of the rest of us seemed to roll off him and while everyone else showed pretty severe signs of party wear and tear, he hadn't even worked up a sweat.

It took a romantic ride à deux on Ari and Norman to get his pulse racing. Given what a babe she looks in her jodhpurs it was good thinking on Bee's part to suggest a hack. Less clever was her failure to tighten Ari's girth. Half an hour after setting out she and the lord were cantering in tandem over the still springy turf towards Limbury Hill, a picture of togetherness, when her saddle suddenly keeled dramatically to the left. Alarmed, Ari sped into a flat-out gallop and bucked so hard that the saddle slipped right round under her tummy and with a final blow to her face from a loose stirrup iron poor Bee fell crashing to the ground.

For a girl who had flown the Pigeon House hedges it was a tame way to break her collarbone in two places and fracture her ribcage. As she lay winded and shocked from the shooting pains across her right shoulder she watched Norman add insult to injury by depositing the lord in a patch of gorse bushes at high speed. Nearly a pint of blue blood dripped along the footpath from Murrell's End as he left Bee with the horses and went in search of help for her and something to staunch his own nosebleed.

MONDAY 10 FEBRUARY
THE COT

Round One to Odious. He didn't dare brave coming to the Cot for fear of encountering me after all these months of trying to poach my glamorous sidekick, but his bouquet is bigger and more beautiful than the lord's and he managed to find someone to deliver it on a Sunday. I would have liked to have stayed at home with Bee for an extended literary critique of the messages accompanying the flowers but had a date of my own to keep. Encouraged by his ride on Ari last month Alec has decided to hire a horse and join today's meet near Colwall.

Waiting composedly by the mince pies for his rider to come and claim him, Hector, the dairy-fudge-coloured gelding Alec had rented for the day, cut a dash as the perfect specimen of a middleweight lady's hunter. He won approving looks for his square jumper's hips, the seven perfectly proportioned plaits lying along the crest of his neck and the generously sloping shoulder that would enable him to coast smoothly along for furlong after furlong once we started galloping. Emerging from his car at the other side of the meet Alec looked pretty hot stuff himself. He had on Mr Yarwood's old black hunting coat complete with Ledbury Hunt buttons, made-to-measure pale suede breeches and a pair of beautiful brown-topped leather boots. Checking a stock pin that was so straight he must have pinned it on with a spirit level, he picked up a silver-handled hunting whip with one calfskin-gloved hand, £200 cash in the other and went off to meet his horse.

But as he and Hector's handler were fiddling around with his girthstraps and stirrup lengths Alec realised he was missing a crucial part of his outfit – a hat. With just minutes to go before the off all he could do was gratefully accept the loan of a rather small and bright yellow crash cap that someone found in the back of a car. In an instant the hat transformed him from a Byronic hero to a dead ringer for Tweedledum. It flattened and fattened his entire physique so that where he had been well built now he looked like a pudding. Sadly it was a sign of things to come. Hector was a splendid animal but he was only 15 hands tall, significantly smaller than Ari and not designed to carry a man of Alec's height. He seemed to wilt under his jockey's six-foot frame. We had barely left the meet before people started laughing at the way Alec's legs hung down around his mount's knees and suggesting he might travel further if he traded places with his horse and gave Hector a piggyback.

I think it is fair to say that Alec did not go at all well but Hector could still have tried harder to earn his £140 fee. Over hill and dale the canary-yellow crash hat lagged a mile or so behind the rest of the Ledbury field. Quickly dubbed The Pustule, people kept pointing out Alec's head whenever he drew near. Occasionally, panting and trembling as Alec's heels dug into his sides, Hector would catch up long enough for his rider to be

abused by Mark Bennet for wearing another man's Hunt buttons
and having the wrong lash on his whip. The horse may have looked
the part but his athletic conformation did not dispose him towards
jumping any more than it did galloping. Even when Alec presented
him perfectly at a little post-and-rails and Norm went especially
slowly to give him a lead over it, Hector, ears pricked, would accelerate up only to slam on the brakes at the last minute, stopping
so late that his forelegs got entangled in the jump. Soon after Jack
Nightingale and the masters changed on to their second horses he
refused at some sheep hurdles even more violently than usual and
got his front feet completely embedded in them. Dismounting to
free Hector, Alec was repaid for his kindness by the horse barging
into him and stamping hard on the back of his ankle.

Powered on for another couple of hours by male bravado,
Alec at length admitted that the white-hot throbbing in his
Achilles tendon was beginning to overpower the appalling pain
where the yellow crash hat was biting cruelly into his forehead
and we turned back towards the lorries. Poseur that he is, I
think what hurt him most of all was watching our local doctor
shredding his brown-topped boot with a Stanley knife to free
his ripped Achilles tendon. But for a man who has endured a
day of utter humiliation he's in remarkably good spirits, trading
painkillers across the sofa with Bee and hatching plans to clone
Mr Yarwood's Hunt buttons for us. And he's never looked as
attractive as he does now stripped bare of his city polish – face
flecked with mud, hair sticking bolt upright with sweat, brown
eyes dull with tiredness, teeth purple from cheap wine and with
a deep red mark left by the Pustule stretching between his
temples that he keeps rubbing with palms blistered by his fancy
new gloves.

February

TUESDAY 11 FEBRUARY
THE COT

I have detected a staffing problem in our operation. We haven't got any. With Bee stretchered off and Alec restored lame but walking to the world of commerce my day went something like this.

4 a.m. Responded to a summons from the sick bay. Bee needed to pop another painkiller but couldn't reach the glass of water by her bed.

7.15 a.m. Rose and moved about Cot like a cat burglar, avoiding windows and keeping the lights off in the hope that the nags wouldn't detect any signs of life.

7.20 a.m. Busted. The horses must have got a visual on me as a furious kicking started up in the stables. Didn't stop until I rushed out with their breakfast.

7.30–9 a.m. Traversed the farm approximately thirty-seven times with half a dozen barrow-loads of muck, armfuls of dry hay and then soaked hay, stacks of feed buckets, empty water buckets, full water buckets, rugs and head collars. Trotted the horses up hoping at least one of them would be lame and therefore not require exercise. All sound. Damnation.

9–9.30 a.m. Took the one-armed bandit breakfast in bed. Informed her of labour crisis. She suggested ringing Christy for assistance and asked if I could bring the newspaper up when I got a chance.

10 a.m. Delivered bandit the paper and her post – a pile of Get Well cards and the first of what will no doubt become a rush of Valentines. Own breakfast interrupted by bandit calling down that my successor in New York was reporting poolside from Puff Daddy's party.

10.30 a.m.–12.30 p.m. Groomed and exercised the beasts. Saddled up Ari and led Norm from her right round Pendock and Bromsberrow in order to glide past Eggs Tump in a perfectly controlled extended trot. All in vain. My arm was nearly pulled out of its socket by Norm dawdling on Ari's heels in go-slow mode.

12.30–1 p.m. Untacked. Dressed Ari's scratches, massaged Norm's back and dangled off his tail. Rugged up. Mucked everyone out again. Distributed hay and water again.

1–2 p.m. Noted bandit apparently well enough to stagger downstairs and put *National Velvet* in the video but unable to make lunch. Much cheered by both Daniel and the lord offering to take the day off work to look after her.

2–3.30 p.m. Changed Norm and Ari into their outdoor rugs. Turned them out on to the sand pit, tacked up Smartie and took him out in search of a mobile phone signal in order to SOS his owner. Barely reached the end of the drive before he decided he couldn't go it alone and spun round for home making spoilt, girlie noises. Noticed it was either drizzling or hot tears of frustration were splattering all over the road as well as down my face. Picked up text from Christy that read POOR B. WILL

TRY TO HELP OUT SOME TIME SOON. PRAPS NEXT WEEK?

3.30–4 p.m. Free time.

4–5 p.m. Mucked out, soaked hay and made horses' supper. Put down fresh sawdust for their beds. Caught them, brushed them and picked out their feet. Changed them into their pyjamas.

5.05 p.m. Nearly sat down for a cup of tea when remembered hadn't mucked out the sand pit. Hate the way that I have to clear up every last turd those animals squeeze out.

5.10–6.30 p.m. Drove the bandit to the Outpatients Department to be told that she won't be able to ride for at least six weeks so her hunting season is effectively over. She took the news pretty stoically until the doctor mentioned the giant lump of gristle that would develop on her décolletage as her collarbone mended and the bloating effects of the drugs she'd be on while that was happening. Her face quivered and momentarily collapsed as she registered that it was hasta la vista house with 700 windows.

6.30 p.m. Congratulated bandit on convincing lady at chemist that she was too young to have to pay for her prescription.

6.45–6.55 p.m. Wasted approximately seventy-eight pence conducting a telephone conversation with a limp-sounding man called Sam from the Hunt Saboteurs Association. Disconcertingly he said all sabbing was unpaid and asked how much I could contribute in petrol money to any expedition before warning me that the group's activities were much curtailed this year due to many people thinking that fox-hunting is now as good as banned.

7–7.30 p.m. Gave my first and last bed bath.

7.30–8 p.m. *EastEnders*.

8–9 p.m. Found we'd run out of butter so baked the last of the free spuds and ate them with sunflower oil. Yuk. Tried to exclude from dinner conversation phrases like 'dead weight' and harrumphing calculations about the number of mouths to feed in this household versus the pairs of fully operational hands to provide for them. Registered only partial success in this effort once the bandit drew my attention to her no-losses clause in part five of The Plan and referred to this book as 'your opus' while making sarcastic speech-mark signs with her good hand.

9 p.m. Mucked out, fed and watered the nags for the last time.

10 p.m. Resolved to seriously mutilate myself if I have to do it all again alone tomorrow.

WEDNESDAY 12 FEBRUARY
THE COT

The worst possible solution to the staffing problem is on its way here right now. Mum is coming to take Bee back to Cathedine for some TLC and a full debriefing of all my secrets and she's threatening to deliver Nell in her place.

The Ledbury men are going to think they've got Lucy Glitters, Surtees's dashing heroine, made flesh on their hands if I let Nell anywhere near Friday's meet at Eldersfield. For 384 pages of *Mr Sponge's Sporting Tour* the reprobate protagonist clings to his bachelordom like a limpet to a rock until he and Miss Glitters cross Sir Harry Scattercash's frosted country in epic style. At the finale of a run on which they left the huntsman and the rest of the field far behind them as they cleared every rasper in their path stride for stride, 'a something shot through Mr Sponge's pull-devil, pull-baker coat, his corduroy waistcoat, his Eureka shirt, Angola vest, and penetrated the very cockles of his heart. He gave her such a series of smacking kisses as startled her horse and astonished a poacher who happened to be hid in the adjoining hedge.' Half a chapter later he and Lucy are married and expecting a little Sponge.

I can already picture the sickeningly triumphant scene of Norman carrying Nell gracefully over the Pigeon House frighteners and into Jack Nightingale and every other Ledbury man's heart. The huntsman, smitten, pausing to plant the vanquished fox's brush in Nell's bonnet, erm crash hat, and eyeing, à la Sponge, 'her lustrous eyes, her glowing cheeks, her pearly teeth, the bewitching fullness of her elegant tournure'. Then the final sunset capitulation on the hack home as he thinks of the masterly way the seventeen-year-old hottie rode the run and, delighted to learn she is over the age of consent, finds himself struck by 'a something quite different to anything he had experienced with any of the buxom widows or lackadaisical misses whom he could just love or not, according to circumstances, among whom his previous experience had lain'.

I want to retract last night's threats of self-harm. Shovelling shit round the clock would be a pleasure compared to sharing the load with a teenager so peachy I'll feel like a wrinkled, souring old plum beside her. But now that Nell is already in transit to give up her half-term in order to come and help me out I don't really see how I can stall her.

THURSDAY 13 FEBRUARY
ROSS-ON-WYE BUS STATION

Thank you, God. Nell is more like J-Lo than I could ever have hoped.

She flounced off home this morning, glossy ponytail still smarting under the final affront of asking to borrow some shampoo and learning that the bandit and I have been reduced to washing our hair with soap. An evening in a household with grainy terrestrial telly channels instead of MTV and no mobile reception had already taken its toll on the homebred diva's temper, but I think it was my performance as her hunting stylist that really made sure Nell would spit the dummy before long.

In an effort to fill the subdued Britney-free hours of yesterday evening I scouted around for an ensemble for her to wear to Friday's meet. It turned out that due to the bandit somehow smuggling her long leather boots and hunting coats out of the Cot under the bedclothes, Nell was restricted to some old jodhpurs, my boxy wattle-and-daub hacking jacket and some brown rubber galoshes topped with sagging brown gaiters that stopped halfway up her calves. Looking at herself in the mirror without the compensation of her natural elegance on a horse

276

she trembled with disappointment. All it took then was for me to shimmy upstairs to deliver my ode to her ratcatcher look in my exquisite Patey hat for her to start perusing the bus timetable.

FRIDAY 14 FEBRUARY
THE COT

I returned with Norm from a very fast day over the marsh at Long Green to find an article ripped from a back issue of *Country Life* jammed under the lorry's windscreen wiper. Its contents totally vindicate my unkind treatment of Nell.

The page is given over to a description of Molly Long Legs, a racehorse bred from Babraham and a fox-hunter mare, painted by Stubbs in about 1762. According to the commentary of her wild eyes, flared nostrils and flattened ears Molly was 'trouble' – a highly strung beauty in the habit of being tricksome. After winning two good races for the Bolingbroke stables she never made money and became a brood mare.

When I stopped sulking over the fact that a long-dead horse executed her version of The Plan with far more success than Bee and I have managed a tender thought struck me. Had I just received a Valentine?

SUNDAY 16 FEBRUARY
THE COT

Nobody has come forward to claim Molly Long Legs. So after a sweet-scented weekend of traipsing about looking my fragrant best in Bee's kidney-rupturingly tight jeans, I'm back in my astrosuit and concentrating on Ari's hair and make-up for Dorothy Baird's try-out tomorrow.

According to *Baily's*, to triumph with the Bicester Ari will need to look like £4,500 worth of horse that can 'gallop, jump flying fences, stay, and get through the deep'. With this in mind I've shampooed her from head to foot and plucked her tail into a long slim style to accentuate her bottom, the engine room of any horse, and make her look more aerodynamic. I've painstakingly picked the matted hair and scabs from her legs and fluffed her thighs up with chalk powder to look extra strong. For her face we went with a blue rinse that old ladies use on their hair to give her a bright white invincible look. Still tense from not hunting on Friday she looks like a highly toned jumping machine with the stamina to gallop all day.

The more I titivate Ari the worse I feel about letting Dorothy Baird anywhere near her. Seeing the mare pleased by all the attention and looking so good I'm reminded of a young girl preparing for what she thinks is a party, little knowing she is being beautified to be the bride in an arranged marriage. But with Bee and her call centre earnings gone, the only way I can think of to save Ari is to sell Norman, which is an equally awful prospect. I rang William Black for advice and he told me I had to focus more firmly on the money. He is bringing on a trio of young horses at the moment called New Washing Machine, Sitting Room Carpet and Two Weeks in Portugal.

February

MONDAY 17 FEBRUARY
THE COT

I've just come in from doing the evening feeds and putting the horses to bed with tears pouring down my face. Any minute now I'll put Sinead O'Connor singing 'Nothing Compares to You' on the stereo and lose it completely.

Ari is sold. Betrayed for the sake of five thousand pieces of silver, tack included. By this time next week she'll be the lawful chattel of Dorothy Baird. I've felt nauseous from intense pride mingling with regret ever since I watched Ari nobly carry Dorothy, sawing at her mouth as she banged about in the saddle, over a high narrow stile into the beech woods behind Haffield House that everyone but the master and a handful of thrusters had to make a detour round. After reluctantly shaking hands on the deal I tried an 'I know not what I do' defence on Ari as I loaded her into the lorry to go home but she rejected it with a bat of her blue-tinted eyelashes.

I've got to try and pull myself together and be more like Captain Ronnie Wallace, the legendary huntsman known by his peers simply as 'God'. He recorded the death of his first pony when he was nine years old with the starkly unemotional diary entry: 'Magpie, bay mare, 13 hands, was destroyed, 18th April 1929.' Ari hasn't died. I keep reminding myself that Bee and I are no great shakes as riders and she's going to a very kind home with a lady so knowledgeable that she dropped famous hunting names of her acquaintance into the conversation like depth charges and lectured me at length about how to cut back proud flesh from puncture wounds and gashes.

But no matter how much I think of the lovely big stable and seventy acres of meadow awaiting Ari at her new home I can't forget the sight of Dorothy Baird riding her. As arranged marriages go Ari is about to tie the knot with a sweet lady, but a lady now in her fifties nonetheless. Dorothy won her Hunt buttons and bought her Patey hat well over thirty years ago. In the meantime she's had a number of bad falls that have rendered her hunting style crucifyingly sedate for a busybody like Ari. She doesn't want to jump and intends to train Ari to trot along at the back of the field, which seems like a terrible waste.

TUESDAY 18 FEBRUARY
COLWALL, NEAR LEDBURY

Remember, remember if you're feeling even slightly maudlin not to sit next to Barry Joyce at the hunt supper.

After spending the day punching minus figures into a hot calculator in a desperate attempt to count up enough beans to buy Ari a stay of execution, I only went to the dinner because I thought being pelted with eggs and abuse by the hippy couple who turn out every year to berate the hunt supporters as they congregate at the village hall would take me out of myself. Thanks to Barry's efforts I am ending the evening wrapped in Norman's fleece-lined raincoat bivouacking on the outfield of the village cricket pitch, awash with vodka and well into the first swerve of a major bender that has given me the bright idea of making random late-night calls across Oxfordshire in an attempt to guess Dorothy Baird's number and tell her that the Ari deal is off.

His nose pulsating like a beacon with every invigorating tipple, Barry spent the evening convincing me that the end is nigh for the life that I have so recently fallen in love with. In a rambling eulogy to hunting that even the arrival of a guest speaker and an after-dinner game centred around sliding pound coins at a bottle of whisky couldn't stem, he reminisced about his boyhood in County Cork where children learnt to ride as they learnt to walk and horses were a religion, central to most kinds of work and the only form of play that mattered. He said that over his lifetime he had witnessed the countryside reduced to little more than a public park for town-dwellers to stretch their legs in and the horse world limited to a sanitised leisure industry. The demise of fox-hunting will sever the last bond between riding and rural life for ever. The jumps at the Grand National are getting smaller with every passing decade, for many people riding means nothing more than tooling around in the enclosed space of a dressage arena and with hunting gone point-to-pointing will disappear too, meaning that only a tiny fraternity of professional jockeys will still be able to test their courage and risk their necks in high-speed horse chases. The sport is already in its death throes. The best any of us can hope for is a fatal fall to finish us off before the end of the season and spare us from witnessing its last gasp.

WEDNESDAY 19 FEBRUARY
THE COT

Barry is quite an orator but six Anadin Extras, a hot bath and a look at a history of fox-hunting has brought me back from the brink of despair. Bee's broken bones and Ari's impending depar-ture no longer symbolise anything more than the moment of ill-fated exhibitionism and months of financial fecklessness that caused them.

Nostalgia seems to be an integral part of the fox-hunter's condition. In every era hunting's past is portrayed as uniformly glorious, its present state deteriorating alarmingly and its future prospects catastrophic. In 1930 Charles Frederick decried the advent of the motorcar as threatening the death of the sport and suggested 1914 as a time when fox-hunting was supposedly equipped with more foxes, hounds, horses and money than ever before. But a generation earlier Delme Radcliffe was wringing his hands in despair at the advances of 'the monster' of industrialisation into rural England and writing, 'How far or in what manner this trebly accursed revolution of railroads may affect the breed of horses and fox-hunting generally it is impossible to say. The speculation on the subject is of too painful a nature.'

But I'm not ready for the last rites yet. I'm not beaten in my quest for Hunt buttons and so help me God if I don't get myself kissed in the bushes at a hunt ball one of these days. Unencumbered by any memories of how much less spoilt rural England and the hunts that ran across it were a century, a decade or even a year ago I don't think the countryside is beaten yet either. Each time I throw up after using a heavy stone to pulverise the skull of one of the rabbits that occasionally lie along bridleways agonised by myxomatosis, or endure what I feel are 'hark at madam' glances between a couple of the staff at the local beauty parlour when I ask for a bikini wax, it feels as though life out here is quite primitive enough.

The arrival of a parcel from Alec put the seal on my good mood. Along with a letter make-believing that he enjoyed his excursion on Hector, he sent a family pack of chewing gum wrapped in a £50 note. He's trying for a pavement-blasting contract in

Gloucester so the money's mine so long as I undertake to spit all 120 portions of Juicy Fruit on the floor of the Eastgate Centre.

THURSDAY 20 FEBRUARY
THE COT

I'm comfort-eating my way through Ari's last days. With a vast cash injection just days away I've armed myself with a third credit card and cleared Tesco out of handmade ravioli, raspberries, cream cakes and hair conditioner. Along with the novel sensation of my stomach being full, I've got that light-headed feeling that goes with knowing you're going to feel miserable any time now.

Although I'm haunted by the image of anyone else riding her, I can't bear to hack Ari out any more and I feel guilty going through her daily stable routine when out of sight in the tack shed I'm embalming her bridle in oil to keep it supple and sorting through her rugs and bandages in readiness for her departure. If I don't guard against it I find myself captivated by a mannerism or tilt of her head that reminds me how desperately I'm going to miss her. Most of the time a sensible inner voice, the same one that yesterday sanctioned me splashing out on luxuries like freshly squeezed orange juice and a decent bottle of wine, stops me from going out to watch her and Norm playing about in the sand pit. It's very important this voice doesn't get contradicted, which is why I haven't yet told Bee that Ari is sold bar the cheque signing.

In the Pink

There is an old hunting dictum that says, 'One goes hunting to please oneself; not to astonish others.' It is utter nonsense of course. Jack Nightingale, the Ledbury hounds and the most competitive of the hunt's members drove halfway to Birmingham today to shock and awe the Croome and West Warwickshire Hunt with the keenness of our pack and the daring of our riders across their country. Rumour has it that the Croome have spent weeks bulking up their hedges and nailing top rails to their fences in readiness for what is euphemistically called a joint meet but is to all intents and purposes an undeclared hunt-off.

In order to avoid my biceps being exhausted by driving our heavy lorry to the meet I accepted a lift with Mr Yarwood and arrived with fresh arms and in great style at a triangular oasis of undisturbed jumping country hemmed in on all sides by motorways and their feeder roads. The meet was the closest thing to a *Hello!* magazine photo shoot that hunting is ever going to manage. Instead of the usual tired-looking sausage rolls to eat, a marquee-cum-delicatessen had been erected at one side of the so-called farm where we met. This was farming à la Victoria Beckham. Apart from the hangar full of horses and the vast sand exercise arena visible behind the Mercedes lined up on the forecourt the place had the look of a red-brick *Footballers' Wives* starter mansion.

If hunting in the faster parts of the shires is the preserve of Old Money, the Ledbury is the domain of Not Much Money and hunting in Wales is the home of 'no ruddy money whatsoever', then, by the look of some of the people who had come to see us off, the Croome are rubbing shoulders with Spanking New Money.

Mingling with the familiar russet huddle of tweed were some very exotic birds. Where normally one beheld woolly jumpers and filthy old trousers, today flashed scatters of sequins and nail varnish. I spotted a woman in a faux-leopardskin coat helping her friend unplug her stiletto heel from the soft mud around a gateway. Even the tentative sunshine emerging from weeks of sulky drizzle had the glimmer of studio lighting.

In keeping with the socialite atmosphere of the meet we hung about seeing and being seen for the best part of an hour – long enough to eventually track down Christy. She had caught a lift with Mark Bennet and spent every minute since her arrival warming her blood with him at the bar. There had already been a minor port-induced panic a little earlier when neither of them could remember what his horsebox looked like or where it was parked.

Mark Bennet had borrowed an extremely smart grey horse from a hapless fresher at Hartpury College. His steed cut a dash at the meet but very nearly buried him in the first test of the Ledbury's mettle – a hefty young hedge that the Croome fence-builders had spiked with brushwood.

Like a relay team who know they have an individual gold medal winner in their ranks, every Ledbury member at the hunt-off had the reassurance of knowing that however badly we ourselves fared over the Croome's stiffest obstacles our hosts could never hold a candle to the likes of Billy Chadburn and Laura Wallace once they really began to travel. So it was at that first fence. The pair of them took it together, ostentatiously turned towards one another in breezy conversation as Laura's grey mare and Billy's venomous chestnut crunched through the tall fronds, leaving a nice dent in the brushwood for the rest of us to jump through.

Each time one of our number fell off Billy distracted attention from the casualty thrashing around in the mud and silenced the gleeful Croome shouts of 'Loose horse' by cantering past a line of them queuing to take some simple rail fence and soaring over the unlaid hedge beside it that they had long ago deemed unjumpable.

We did have a fair few fallers though. David Harper, one of the silver-haired gentleman farmers hunting out their dotage with the Ledbury, came a nasty cropper at the bullfinch, Mary Clarke's cob collapsed with leg injuries in a boggy piece of woodland and Mark's grey had to retire when it skidded right over on its side trying to gallop round a slippery corner. When we turned down the line of hedges that the Croome had prepared Christy and I had a few troubles of our own. We stuttered over the first few of them until, hearing a cry of 'Big ditch!' as we approached the fourth in line, we got the bats out to disastrous effect. Incensed by the weakest tap on his shoulder, Norm made a bound over it that was so big I very nearly fell off backwards, while Smartie put in an almighty buck that catapulted his belabouring jockey over the hedge without him and then jumped over by himself to give chase to Norman.

For the next few seconds I clung to Norm's plaits, desperately feeling for my stirrups as he and Smartie raced neck-and-neck around the steep-sided field on the landing side of the hedge. Round and round the grassy velodrome we went, beginning to lose momentum as we climbed the hill only to pick up speed again on the perilous descent. Towards the end of each lap Christy, blood simmering nicely by this stage, tottered out to try and catch Smartie and each time was nearly mown down before fleeing back to the safety of the hedge.

It was precisely the kind of situation that at the start of the season would have frightened me to my core but today I felt impatience more than terror. We were getting left behind. With each dizzying lap I could see the hounds swinging far away from me across the jumble of set-aside fields and plough until eventually all that was left of them was an occasional muffled note on Jack's horn. After half a dozen circuits of hauling without success at Smartie's bridle as well as my own knitting of martingale, breastplate and reins I decided I stood a better chance of stopping Norm if I could head Smartie away from him and steer for some trees.

The easiest way to do this was to take swipes at his face with my rubber-coated bat during our ascent of the bank. It was only when the blows across his nose made Smartie swerve away to the inside of the racetrack that I realised the loose stirrup I had shoved my foot into with so much relief was attached to Christy's saddle rather than my own. For a moment I felt an agonising wrench on my left leg that jiggered the old scar tissue in my ankle, tore up past my knee and came to bring its full force on the delicate sinews under the soft flesh of my inner thigh that attach my leg to my hip socket. For a nanosecond cartilage duelled excruciatingly with leather before the stitching on Smartie's stirrup leather, weakened by a winter of never being soaped or repaired, gave way and we parted with groans from both sides.

There is probably some hunting term like 'hackle forrard' for what Christy and I embarked on next but I think it is most accurately described as plain old trespassing. Guessing that the hounds were a mile or so away but roughly parallel with us we turned inside the loop the rest of the hunting field had taken and took an uncharted direct route across country. We crossed it tentatively, avoiding paddocks with pregnant ewes in them and trotting up to check the landing side of each hedge before we attempted it. We missed the kill but with Norm jumping as boldly as ever we crossed poky little wire-strewn stiles and the odd gate to make it back to the action in less than twenty minutes.

Rejoining the two-hundred-strong throng of horses trotting through a ford to draw the next covert without so much as a twitch of exasperation from his meaty brown haunches at who might be riding close behind him, I felt as though Norm and I had finally got the hang of hunting. For the first time I felt sufficiently relaxed to actively enjoy myself while I was on board rather than in retrospect from the safety of the Cot. After spending an estimated 335 hunting hours gripping my saddle in what I now saw were varying states of alarm, I had learnt to expect the unexpected rather than dread it.

Saturated with confidence I set off on what looked like being the last run of the day, immediately steered Norm into a rabbit hole and piked over his head into a puddle when he stumbled and pulled off a shoe. Noticing my aching coccyx and my horse mincing along in a Harlem shuffle Mr Yarwood advised calling it a day and walking Norm back to the lorry before his foot or my back got any sorer. Leaving Christy to fight our corner with the Croome, we headed back and soon found our path blocked by a low wooden fence standing probably less than three feet high but decorated with a strand of barbed wire running barely an inch above its top rail. It was all that stood between us trekking half a mile back to the meet or having to walk three times that distance.

Jumping on the way home from hunting is apparently seen as seriously bad behaviour but the fence was so very small and the drive home so very long that it didn't take much to persuade Mr Yarwood to give me a lead over it. The next thing I knew Queenie was standing unhurt but shaken in a tangle of wire, her abrupt landing having thrown her rider well clear of the obstacle. Mr Yarwood fell in a neat but hurtling human projectile, balled up with his spurred feet sticking out like stumpy wings from a double-tuck position that Russian gymnasts like to dismount the high bars with.

SUNDAY 23 FEBRUARY
THE COT

Bee has heard about Ari's sale in the worst possible way. While we were out with the Croome my mobile, without permission from me, dialled hers and left an extremely long and disjointed message of clip-clopping noises and snatches of conversation. Tormented partly by the idea of us all out hunting while she still can't take her arm out of its sling and partly by how much Vodafone were charging her to listen to the entire capacity of her voicemail in one go, she sat at home revolted, enthralled and utterly power-less to end the call. Apart from an evocative humph as Norm launched over a jump and plaintive mutterings from me for him to please slow down, the only other things she could make out were me telling Thomas Harvey an embellished version of her accident and regaling various other people with the news that Ari was being traded with much regret but a huge profit margin.

I had expected anger, tears and recriminations to the effect that I was no longer her sister but it seems that I am alone in being hopelessly sentimental about the horses. Head-hunter that she is, Bee wanted to secure the best possible 'package' for Ari. I would receive a list she'd drawn up of the mare's likes and dislikes through the post tomorrow and I was to get an undertaking from Dorothy

Baird to abide by them. She also insisted that I get written confirmation that we would have first refusal to buy the mare back from Dorothy if she ever decides to sell Ari on and reminded me that under the terms of The Plan she was entitled to £378 of the proceeds of the sale.

MONDAY 24 FEBRUARY
THE COT

Glad tidings! I am chopping up a laminated piece of card with comments like 'Won't eat cod liver oil', 'Hates dressage' and 'She'll act like she's going to bite when you put her rugs on but don't worry she's just pretending' typed on it into a celebratory confetti. It's taking for ever because I keep pausing and looking across the yard to admire a familiar shorn white face that is nuzzling Norm through the bars of his stable. Ari is not going anywhere. She has failed the vet's inspection in spectacular style.

Dorothy Baird arrived to collect her armed with an officious, thin-lipped man. Charged with giving Ari and her kit the once over before I took possession of five thousand big ones, he made me strip her of her rugs and eyed her up as witheringly as a Yorkshire housewife deliberating over a sub-standard gammon ham. Still expressionless, he then gave Ari a series of flexion tests. These consisted of holding one of her legs bunched right up under her tummy for a minute or two, then dropping her foot to the floor, smacking her on the bum and watching like a hawk as she trotted off to see if she was sound on it. The findings of these flexion tests were that Ari is lame on a staggering three of her four legs.

The way the vet described it, it's a minor miracle she's still standing. When she hopped into trot on her first hind leg Dorothy's face fell, when the other leg failed she backed away towards her car, and once her off fore had been judged 'a bit poky' as well she called a halt to the vetting completely, bade me a sympathetic goodbye and drove off with her banker's draft unviolated. The vet brightened considerably at this point, introducing himself to me as Melvin and explaining in microscopic detail how Ari has spavins in her hocks, a degenerative arthritic condition that will eventually make her permanently lame. She might well manage to hunt for several years so long as I give her plenty of bute but in the meantime I must stop riding her immediately and get a second opinion on her condition.

I felt hungrier but happier with every detail of the movement-restricting bony lumps gradually forming in her back legs. It's such a relief that she's staying. Ari will hunt again. I'm sure of it. And it won't be at the back, missing out the big jumps with a tremulous pensioner on her back.

WEDNESDAY 26 FEBRUARY
CLOUD NINE CAFÉ, COLWALL

Shylock is sitting opposite me eating pancakes and dripping lemonade down his school jersey. Facing a stack of unpaid feed bills and unable to buy fresh sawdust I've turned to Archie as lender of last resort to see me through the remaining weeks of the hunting season.

Unlike the rest of his family, the Clog is a pillar of financial rectitude. He has been known to travel to the cashpoint machine in Brecon purely in order to check that the compound interest on his savings account is being calculated correctly. Being only twelve years old keeps his outgoings to a minimum and aside from lucrative birthday donations he has a tidy income from what he calls his Egg Money. He earns this by fluffing up his blond curls so that he looks like an adorable baby chick himself and hawking the free-range eggs from my father's hens to the foreign students and holiday cottagers at Cathedine at prices so inflated they make Fortnum and Mason look cheap. His record earner was getting £5 for a dozen eggs that he'd packaged with authentic wisps of straw and smears of mud but Nell claims had suspicious red smudges on their sides where he'd wiped the supermarket date stamps off them.

By the time I dropped him back at school for rugby practice bloated with tuck he'd agreed to lend me £500 at 12% interest per annum but with the proviso that he had an option to claim Ari and/or Norm as his tetrathlon competition horse once he grew a bit taller.

THURSDAY 27 FEBRUARY
THE ROSE AND CROWN, REDMARLEY

It looks as though I've turned to the wrong usurer. Mark Bennet has summoned me to an emergency drink in order to take back all the unkind jokes he made about Alec at the Colwall meet. Far from being a trumped-up laughing stock, he has decided, Alec is just the kind of person the Ledbury Hunt wants to attract. Would he be back for another day this season? Might he appreciate a day out on one of Mark's own horses? Was there any chance he would accept a role on the hunt committee?

I eventually got to the bottom of this volte-face when Mark

produced a badly discoloured and foul-smelling section of newspaper that he admitted had been lining the cage of his sister's hamsters for the last few weeks. There in the financial pages, smiling out from behind a mosaic of dirty hamster footprints in a crisp striped shirt, quiet tie and charcoal flannel suit, stood Alec. He was shaking hands on a rostrum with some uber-beancounter from the CBI underneath a caption praising his success in combining a healthy share price with an aggressive policy of trans-Atlantic expansion. Cripes.

12

March

SATURDAY 1 MARCH
RIPPLE, NEAR WORCESTER

My luck has finally run out. Norm and I were out for precisely seventeen minutes yesterday morning before another horse trod on his heel and brought our hunting season to a close. There are three more meets left on the Ledbury's calendar but Christy is shipping a semi-paralysed Smartie back to his owners tomorrow and with my glamorous sidekick and both our horses lost to injury I'm the last girl standing.

Norm is back in the hands of the vet who first inspected him at Barry Joyce's yard, swaying goonishly from a dose of tranquillisers and having stitches sewn across the over-tread lacerating the soft bulb of his heel. Ari has had her legs X-rayed, her spavin condition confirmed and the beginnings of tendonitis diagnosed in one of her forelegs. I've been told that although she'd cost well over £4,000 to replace, her arthritis means her approximate value is somewhere around the £1,000 mark. That, said the vet jadedly, is horses for me. It's not all bad news though. They won't be fit to dazzle Leicestershire this year but Norm should be better within a week or two and with a summer of rest Ari will be sound for next season.

SUNDAY 2 MARCH
THE COT

Being grounded is infinitely tougher than I expected. I've been inundated with concerned phone calls asking after Norm's condition – far more than Bee's broken collarbone ever inspired. But once we've commiserated briefly over my horseless state the sympathy runs dry as each caller tells me about the epic run I missed on Friday. A roving dog fox had shot out of a ragwort-circled fly-tip behind the coffin factory near Eastington Heath at such speed that even Anthony the Whip and Mark Bennet were left behind on the dramatic eight-mile chase that followed. Again and again I was talked through jumping a steep six-bar wooden gate that was the only way to keep up with the hounds when they turned uphill towards Malvern. Each account was more wildly embroidered than the last until at length I took the phone off the hook and sat, lost in reverie, imagining and re-imagining each footfall of my approach to the gate had I been out there with them on Norm.

MONDAY 3 MARCH
THE COT

The sight of Queenie being hosed down tired and elated from today's hunting has sent the invalids into a decline. Norm and Ari spent the late afternoon scraping out a hollow in the sand pit. When they heard me coming to catch them they then urinated into it lengthily and took turns rolling in the gritty, ammonia-infused mixture. I think it must be a cry for help. Confined to their stables and the sand pit for four whole days, they've developed the numb, listless stares of polar bears brought from the ice cap to live in a zoo.

WEDNESDAY 5 MARCH
THE COT

After a long dormant spell my social life has suddenly lurched into overdrive thanks to a sudden rush of invitations from people who can't believe Bee has left for London already and I'm going at the end of the month. In an area where the natives classify immigrants of fifteen years' standing as newcomers, our seven-month sojourn at the Cot is on a par with the life span of a fruit fly.

Tonight's was my third supper in almost as many days with people who say they've been meaning to invite Bee and me over for ages. Whether I'm visiting a newly married young bloodstock agent or a pair of thick-middled farmers these evenings are remarkably similar. The man of the house and his guests knock back a few drinks and bedtime stories in a drably decorated sitting room warmed primarily by a roaring television until his domestic goddess of a wife appears to shoo the children into bed and tell us that the pot roast is ready. Despite being produced in a scullery where terriers lie on the Aga acting as muddy tea-cosies and tendon liniment takes up half the ancient fridge, the food is delicious.

On each occasion a succulent mouthful of beef and perfectly browned roast potato weakens my defences so that when the interrogation starts in earnest across the table I am not ready for it. A typical opening salvo is the stating of the apparently open secret that Bee and I have been having an ongoing threesome with a married member of the hunt. The facts stand for themselves so all my hosts want to know is if he is any good in bed. When denying every racy rumour about our exploits begins to make me feel boringly virtuous I shrug and give Mona Lisa-style quarter smiles – normally on Bee's behalf. This works for a bit, but without the juice of confessional gossip to sustain them, a long day devoid of nannies or any kind of domestic help takes its toll on my hosts and by ten o'clock one or both of them will have fallen asleep at the table. At this point I tiptoe out to the Renault 5 knowing I've been a serious disappointment.

THURSDAY 6 MARCH
THE COT

I've joined the ranks of the agricultural cyclists. Freed from their miserable incarceration of sand pit and stable, Ari and Norm have been strapped into their warmest waterproof overcoats and turned out to graze in the relative wild of a paddock at Pigeon House Farm surrounded by the hedges they so valiantly jumped out hunting. Each day I don my astrosuit, strap their feed buckets to my handlebars and pedal off to Eldersfield feeling a bit like Velvet Brown and her paper horses as I freewheel past Gadbury cross-country course fantasising about winning the open class at the upcoming spring hunter trial if only I had Norman to ride.

It's a fun journey. The budding blackthorn lanes are a favourite promenading place for the cock pheasants that survived the shooting season to swagger about in and I sometimes stop off to chat with the gypsies beginning to fill up the local lay-bys with their super-deluxe caravans.

FRIDAY 7 MARCH
BUSHLEY PARK, NEAR TEWKESBURY

I'm standing at Bushley, straddling the border between Worcester-shire and Gloucestershire at the cleft of a buttock-shaped bend in the River Severn in what could be the canvas of a sweeping land-scape painting of the Ledbury's Friday country. It's a perfect picture of all that I'll be leaving behind when my lease on the Cot runs out in a few weeks' time. Turbulent grey skies have been brushed in over my head, the air is clear and the ground dabbed with only a light crisp of frost. Behind me is the weir, the squelchy island of Severn Ham and a faint profile of the elegant old stone hall and market buildings of Tewkesbury. The enchanting pale hues of the river meadows swinging left past Forthampton, Chaceley and on to the ripples of higher ground at Tirley have been done in water-colours, a silvery haze of denuded ash, birch and willow trees shim-mering across sheets of undrained floodwater.

Facing me are the homely woods of Sarn Hill and the gentle roll of fields lapping up in the distance to Windmill Tump and

Cornyburrow beyond. Across the foreground runs a touch of oil paint for the ribbon of road winding to Hereford and the first tracts of heavy clay plough and winter plantings that draw my eye towards Cold Elm and Longdon. The marsh, the commons and all the farms beyond the buzzing trim of the M50 are hidden from the scene but I could talk you through a dozen different ways to make the gradual climb to the Malvern Hills through them.

I still haven't got the neat name tags and accurate scale of an official hunting report off pat. I think the thickly applied coniferous burst of verdure far over to the north-west could be Coneyburrow, yet given my sense of distance it might just as easily be The Stanks or even Holdfast covert. But I have crisscrossed the view at my feet many times this past winter, in prickling hail and in sunshine so unseasonal that I've sweated and itched against the thick woollen sleeves of my hunting coat. I've galloped, I've limped, I've swanked at the front and waited ashamed at the back. This landscape will never again be to me just the pretty backdrop to walk off a pub lunch that it was when I first arrived in the green flush of September. At nearly every gateway or scrub of trees there is now a memory waiting for me.

Today all eyes are on Billy Chadburn leading the crowd of dark-coated riders as the hounds run up the hill at full cry. A retired cider brewer for Bulmers who shared his chicken paste sandwiches with me says Billy has been charged with scattering the ashes of a recently deceased farmer over the scenery before us as he gallops across its springy turf. The old man had made special provision in his will to have his ashes sprinkled over the country on a clear day when a fox took the hunt on 'a quick thing'. Without binoculars I can't tell whether the billows of dust following Billy's horse over a double set of hedges and up the sandy farm track beyond are coming from the ground or his saddlebags.

But I do remember that at the end of the track there's a gatepost Bee whacked her knee on before Christmas when she lost her grip on her reins and Ari plunged into it. Further on is a quagmire near a silage rack where I once unwisely squatted for a pee only to roll bare-bottomed into the slurry when Norm spooked suddenly and tugged me off balance. There was no option but to scoop the cowshit out of my jodhpurs with a broken slate, drag them back up around my waist and not let the others see the expression on my face when I had to sit down in the saddle again.

I've come to know this place better than I know the back of my hand. The bland, elegant paw that has dangled from my arm for the last twenty-seven years is unrecognisable. My middle knuckles are so distended with bruising that I can't make my palm lie flat any more and all trace of the smattering of freckles that used to run up to my wrist has been lost under a muddy glove of brown skin that covers my entire hand. Cold has thickened my once slender finger joints and given them a purple gangrenous hue that makes me worry that, despite the veins that bulge like al dente spaghetti across the reverse of my hand, blood is either finding it hard to reach or else leave them. My forefinger has a grubby plaster where the nail I tore off loosening the bolts on the lorry ramp used to grow and the other nails are flecked with the telltale white marks of calcium deficiency. Fox-hunting has endowed the Ledbury with a landscape worthy of Gainsborough and Constable but it's given me the kind of knotted flesh and squeam-inducing skin tone Lucian Freud would have a field day with.

MONDAY 10 MARCH
THE COT

My country mouse status has been properly confirmed at last and by the internet of all things. After receiving an urgent e-mail from Sally Evans last week warning everyone in the hunt about a virulent computer virus, I quickly sent a precautionary message to everyone in my online address book. Days later my inbox is still stacking up with abuse from urban technoheads asking where the hell I've been for the last year not to know the virus is a notorious hoax and urging me to get back in the loop or die. Bee has joined in the electronic stone-throwing, writing from a new, ominously corporate e-mail address to tell me that she's embarrassed for me.

TUESDAY 11 MARCH
THE COT

I thought Tony McCoy was supposed to be a champion jockey. The wretch has fallen off twice in his first two races of the Cheltenham Festival taking £60 of mine with him.

THURSDAY 13 MARCH
PIGEON HOUSE FARM, ELDERSFIELD

What a difference a week of living barefoot in the park makes. Norm and Ari are unrecognisable as the smart hunters I deposited in the field last Wednesday. With the weather uncommonly dry for this time of year I've taken off their shoes and overcoats, let their manes begin to grow long and their chins cover with bristles to keep out the cold on frosty nights. The horses have the washed-out look of celebrities snapped by the paparazzi while out shopping for junk food without their make-up on.

Norm has bloated up Marlon Brando style and become similarly shy and reclusive. I normally arrive to find him out of sight, mooching around behind a clump of thorn bushes method-acting his way into being Colonel Kurtz. Already looking flabbier and hairier than I ever thought possible, Ari reminds me of a once A-list starlet who has been resting too long between jobs. Conscious of her diminished box office power she no longer kicks up a fuss if room service delivers her breakfast late and seems to be considering filling the lull in her career by having a child. Unfortunately for her she'll have to go over to Eastnor and do the dirty with Debbie Jarvis's stallion rather than follow the vogue amongst Hollywood's leading ladies for skipping the birthing scene and adopting a ready-to-go baby.

On the topic of flab, I'm encountering some problems in that area myself. Even a couple of miles of bicycling each day can't sustain the exquisitely firm but rounded bottom that I acquired on the hunting field. With every passing day my buttocks are gradually softening and subsiding down the back of my legs like a pair of melting jellies. After all those weeks of bedridden one-armed banditry Bee's bum must be a horror story beneath the Dry Clean Only power suit that I suspect cloaks it these days.

FRIDAY 14 MARCH
THE COT

An awful day. It's lucky worry has killed my appetite because my larder only runs to water and spearmint gum these days. As if punting the last of the Egg Loan on McCoy yesterday and then watching in horror as he broke his collarbone wasn't bad enough, now I really am in a fix. I still haven't paid last month's rent, I can't get any cash from anywhere, Archie has withdrawn his lines of credit and I've had several phone calls from debt collection agencies hounding me to make a minimum payment on my various credit cards. It's not a matter of scrimping to keep the horses on the road any more. I owe thousands of pounds in debts that I can't service.

TUESDAY 18 MARCH
MALVERN THEATRE

Mark Bennet and I have been to a matinée performance of the local am-dram group's version of *Fiddler on the Roof* to celebrate the delay of the second reading of the Hunting Bill. Every day of procrastinating about what to do about Saddam Hussein is a day gained for fox-hunting. At this rate the Bill won't return to Parliament until the autumn and the sport should continue for at least another winter.

I'm far less sure of my own chances of survival. I was welcomed home by a pair of bailiffs who had come to seize the lorry. Their plan to auction it off in order to pay the outstanding balance on one of my loan agreements foundered when its starter motor failed and the brakes jammed on but the experience was still sufficiently frightening to concentrate my mind. Unfailingly polite though they were, the money-collecting lads with the haulage truck weren't interested in hearing that I was writing a book that might get published some day. They just wanted the dosh I owe and sharpish. They aren't alone. Norm and Ari still need their feet trimming and a bucket of muesli each day and it's embarrassing to be in arrears with Matt Heller and the lady who lets out her grass at Pigeon House.

THURSDAY 20 MARCH
THE COT

The bailiffs are back. They failed to find this laptop but they've taken the Renault 5, my video recorder, the stereo, both saddles and my riding boots – all of which I've been warned will be sold for a fraction of their value. Judging by the heaps of warning letters that arrive each day now that the landline and my mobile have been disconnected, today's haul is not going to raise nearly enough money.

If the phones were working I'd call Bee and Christy pleading for cash and sympathy but the truth is that I've run out of friends to ask. There's nothing else for it. I need a quick sale of my most precious asset to raise a decent lump sum. Tomorrow I must bicycle halfway to Tewkesbury to see a man about facing the unavoidable.

March

BLACK FRIDAY
21 MARCH
PIGEON HOUSE FARM, ELDERSFIELD

Ari and I are standing under the copper beech tree at the topmost corner of her paddock, straining our eyes for a last glimpse of Barry Joyce's blue lorry winding its way along the oak-edged lane to Corse village. Ari's being very noisy, neighing at such a pitch that her outraged, inconsolable screeches ring out across the wet green fields, perhaps even reaching the bend in the lane where Norm is now being driven out of sight. I'm keeping very quiet. Barry is taking Norm back to his yard. There he'll be shod and schooled and given a haircut before being advertised for sale in next week's *Horse & Hound* and I can't think of a single word of reassurance to offer Ari.

How on earth is Barry going to cram Norm of all characters into a little box of platitudes, stencilled one inch high by two inches long, in the Horses for Sale section? He's got forty words in which to count the ways that Norm is worth £7,000 o.n.o. I love Norm for his fleshy, muscled bottom and because he jumps coffins and picnic tables and the Stanks rasper without any help from me. I love him for his comfortable long-striding trot. I love the way he shows off and tucks his nose in like a proper dressage horse when he thinks people are watching and lies down and sunbathes if he thinks they're not. I love him for being crotchety in the mornings and always bucking the first time I ask him to canter. I love him for his greediness. I love him for interrupting his cold showers after hunting to drink the icy spray from the hosepipe in through his nostrils. I love the way he makes everything fun and doesn't like getting into the lorry if he doesn't think Ari's getting in too. I even

305

love him for his white socks, his appalling behaviour at the opening
meet and the way he refuses to conform to the usual owner/animal,
master/servant relationship. That's 160 words for a kick-off and I
haven't yet got on to how the very idea of him always cheers me
up or how he nibbled my collar this afternoon before stoically
climbing up the ramp of Barry's lorry, let alone all the jargon about
his breeding and competition experience.

Barry's been sweet about the sale. He won't put up with requests
for getting first refusal if Norm comes on the market again but he
does say comforting things about how good horses like him rarely
get mistreated. It's no use though. Where horses are concerned
instead of loving and losing like this I'd far rather have stayed put
in my Earls Court basement and never loved at all. The Plan was
meant to take my mind off Mr Smith, not have my heart broken
by an overgrown pony.

SUNDAY 23 MARCH
THE COT

Broken it is though. I've been to church for the first time since
Christmas to pray that Norm goes to a good home and entreat
God for some last-minute money-generating ideas.

I thought I was in a pretty bad way as I lay awake grieving all
last night but Ari is the really distraught one. She won't eat, not
even the special mixture of oats and molasses I offered her today,
and she has spent every minute since Norm was taken away
whinnying for him and relentlessly pacing a muddy track along
the hedges at the edge of her field.

There's also something cruel about the return of the balmy

sunny weather of last September. Staunton and the Leadon Valley are as idyllic as ever but for me there's a bloody great hole in it all where Norm should be.

BRIGHT WHITE WEDNESDAY
26 MARCH
HIGH ELM END, NEAR TEWKESBURY

Barry dropped past last night to say he's had an offer on Norm before he'd even been advertised. Apparently the lad who wants him can't ride for toffee but he's a cracking chap who wants to take up hunting. Moreover he's good for the money and isn't bothering with a vetting. If I want to say goodbye he's due to fetch Norm at three o'clock this afternoon.

Seeing Barry made me compose myself for the inevitable. If he thought I could be reduced to tears over a horse he'd have had me sectioned on the spot. However, after deciding not to torture myself with seeing Norm again, at 2.30 p.m. I suddenly got a desperate urge for one last look at him and pedalled over to Barry's place panicking that he would have gone before I got there. I arrived an hour later so sweaty and scarlet in the face that when I saw Norm looking out over his stable door I dunked my head into the water trough to cool down. When I took it out Barry was standing by my side with a horse blanket to dry myself on. Clearly anxious that nothing blew the sale at this late stage he insisted that I drag a mane comb through my hair and wait for my puce cheeks to subside a little before we went to see Norm and his new owner.

Opening the shabby stable door I was initially blinded by the beautiful sight of Norm restored to his best. Still amply covered but firm from a few days' education in Barry's expert hands, his mane had been neatened and his coat had been given some kind of wax polish. Deprived of a hay net he was calmly gnawing at the knot in the twine rope tying him to the wall. When he saw me he blinked, whickered in recognition and moved forward to inspect my pockets for mints. It was only when I'd fed him some Polos and rested my cheek against his as I stroked the golden downy hair behind his ears that I noticed Alec standing in a dark corner of the stable. Without saying a word he moved forward and, planting one of his hideous tasselled loafers heavily into a fresh pile of horseshit, kissed me. He didn't stop kissing me until Norm, after many minutes of sighing and bored groaning, lost patience with his new owner and headbutted us into the wall.

It was a great kiss. Delivered slowly and with complete confidence, it was initially softly exploratory, but backed up by Alec's lovely broad shoulders and hands that held my face steady between them, it soon became knee-weakeningly forceful. In terms of heart-stopping, then pulse-racing elation, kissing Alec makes jumping the Stanks rasper seem like hopping over a punnet of parsley.

FRIDAY 28 MARCH
THE COT

The cynics among you may want to look away now. Today is my third straight day of bliss. I've discovered there's only so much kissing you can do. In the recuperative intervals between siestas Alec and I take picnics across the farm to the remotest stretches of the Leadon. We lie in the shade of the willows playing cards while the sausages fry or tear off our clothes and leap over the watercress beds where the wine bottles cool to swim in the deep cold trout pools. Best of all, we make plans. There must be something faulty with Alec's wiring. Whereas most boys are nervy about their girlfriends leaving a spare tooth-brush at their flats, he has already suggested that I might like to keep a pair of horses in the orchard at the end of the garden of his house in Somerset.

It's not roses every last step of the way though; colonies of stinging red ants sometimes gatecrash our picnics and Alec complains that my hands are so roughened by the outdoor life that each caress feels as though he's being sandpapered. For his part he needs to learn that however affectionately such comments are intended, I don't regard having my breasts described as 'text-book' or my character traits likened to a cross between Huckleberry Finn and Penelope Keith as particularly high praise. That said, we're in the glorious position of having the reciprocated hots for one another. I can't get over my surprise and soaring happiness at the idea that Alec can detect some kind of point to me and I know that I'll want to ring him up even when I've got absolutely nothing to say.

SUNDAY 30 MARCH
MAISEMORE PARK, NEAR GLOUCESTER

No story of a fox-hunting season in the Leadon valley would be complete without the scene that I am witnessing now.

A couple of thousand people are standing stock still in a crook of the low hills rising from the Severn floodplain. Racecards are fluttering in the breeze, dogs have taken shelter from the blazing sun under cars, even the noisy drinkers in the beer tent have spilled out to join the hushed crowds scanning the clear skies to the east. The Ledbury point-to-point is drawing to a close. I am down on the course by the steeplechase jump Alec and I have been stewarding all day, standing as close to it as we dared in order to pick up the electrifying tremors of the horses as they sped towards us and flew over five abreast in a fluid mass of muscle and hooves. Somewhere on the slope above us all the activities of the day, from Eddie Backhouse and Matt Heller fighting off the girls at the entrance to the weighing-in tent to Jack Nightingale and Anthony the Whip parading the winner's enclosure with Hef's white charger and the hounds, have come to a standstill. The masters have stopped rushing about organising the overspill car park, the secretary and her minions have paused from their fretting, Mark Bennet has left the table of trophies and prizes unguarded and Bee's lord has paused in his weary trudge up the hill shouldering an uneaten champagne picnic and the news that she's ducked out of today to spend the weekend with Daniel and his parents. Even the commentator has broken off his patter.

From down here it seems as though nearly all the friends and enemies I have made over the winter are lining up to take a curtain call. Through my binoculars I can see Mr Yarwood and his lovely wife, the people who more than anyone else made our time here so special, peering up from the trade stands. Just along the ridge Mr Jevtic is talking to Peter and Sally Evans with his green wellies tilted forward in a snowplough position. Over in the collecting ring Mary Clarke the milkmaid and Barry Joyce have been interrupted as they cut a deal over a sluggish chestnut filly that pulled up in the maiden chase and Jane the talent scout is clustered with the Queens, the Duchess and Hump the terrier man.

But it's not me they're waiting for. Flying into view over the blossom-covered hedgerows of Spring Hill like a great rotor-powered ladybird is the scarlet-painted personage that over the years has provided the swansong to so many of the Ledbury Hunt's best adventures – the air ambulance helicopter. Some poor jockey is being scraped out of the open ditch and flown to the specialist spinal unit in Swindon. If anything were going to succeed in crushing the hunting bug out of me where a winter of rats, chilblains, tepid baths and near-constant penury has failed, it would be the sight of the paramedics erecting a screen around the fallen body while the crowds wait for the last race.

A young man in the prime of life is lying gravely injured, perhaps paralysed, behind those green sheets of canvas but all I can think of is who I can persuade to coach me up so that Norm and I are ready to have a go at the members' race next year.

13

April

TUESDAY 1 APRIL
WESTBOURNE PARK, LONDON

I am probably the only person in London reading the weather forecast. I mean really reading it – properly, the way you do a novel, anxious to find out how the story turns out and hoping for a happy ending.

Bee, whose floor I'm sleeping on, set out for her office with an umbrella after a quick look at the breakfast bulletin's prediction of wintry cloud cover over London, but I've been hunched over the morning papers for more than an hour. I can't read about the cold, blustery day anticipated for western England without shivering in sympathy for Norman and Ari huddling for shelter in the lee of the wide Somerset hedges surrounding Alec's garden as the rain lashes through their sparse clipped coats and they wait in vain for me to appear with the supper buckets. Imagining them cold and wet runs fluidly into picturing them gravely ill with grass sickness, bleeding from a hidden stake of old iron fencing or having their spring break ruined by joyriding village kids galloping them bareback round their orchard when Norm should be resting his tired legs and Ari watching her blood pressure for the sake of her unborn child.

When hail started splattering across the canal and pounding on the panes of the kitchen window a few minutes ago I removed my thumbnail from its uneasy resting place beneath a sleet-laden cloud plonked on the weather map just north of Bath and rang Bee for reassurance. She has picked up some very weird ideas since her return to the rat race. Annoyed at being distracted from scanning the Square Mile for a chief analyst scalp, she refused to speculate on how long a heavy sleet shower with a wind speed of fifteen miles an hour would take to reach Castle Cary from Bristol and tried to make out that Norman and Ari are 'only farmyard animals'.

Happily repatriated with Daniel and her head-hunting salary, she now considers The Plan to be entirely defunct. She has returned to her old London life with a new head of ash-blonde highlights and hardly a backward glance. I, on the other hand, can't wait to put myself back out to pasture. I still have occasional daywear cravings when I pass a gorgeous sundress hanging in a shop window, but while Bee's out buying white suede sofas and joining gyms I am already dreaming of September and the start of a new fox-hunting season that once again the government threatens will be this country's last. The fresh generation of fox cubs that have already been born this spring are luring me back to the Leadon valley. I've just spent the best winter of my life in his shadow and I haven't got the measure of Charlie yet.

Yet to my enduring astonishment I do seem to have made

headway on the Peppermore operation. Alec has some way to go on the reckless insolence front but his clothes aren't ironed and colour coordinated any more and he's let the inside of his beloved BMW get choked up with headcollars and its paintwork stay smeared with stale horse feed. Nor did he stop calling me Molly Long Legs for more than a couple of hours when hoof oil spilt all over some crucial company reports in his favourite briefcase.

Now, for the second week running, he's rashly leaving the world's pavements to accrue chewing gum unchecked and deserting his office while he launches his hunting career in a bid to become my own tame 'desperately fine specimen of a genuine English traditional type which has become innocuous since the abolition of duelling'. We're going to have a look at an Irish mare stabled in Sussex that he likes the sound of. According to the blurb it's a former master's horse that jumps like a dream but is quiet enough for a novice to manage. Built like a heavyweight wrestler and taller than Norm, it's also a far cry from feeble Hector.

But before that we're stopping off to meet Christy for lunch and tell her we're in love. Alec thinks this will be a perfectly straightforward procedure but I have my doubts. My guess is that when she sees her normally squeaky-clean brother wearing a knackered old bobbly sweater set off by three days' growth of stubble and clutching this week's *Horse & Hound*, she'll howl with laughter and insist we've staged the best April Fool since Bee came up with that artfully stuffed cat.